Praise for

Wendy Markham's

books

"[A]n undeniably fun journey for the reader."
—*Booklist* on *Slightly Single*

"Markham successfully weaves together colorful characters.... Readers will delight in the main character's triumphs, share in her pain and overall enjoy the ride."
—*Romantic Times BOOKreviews* on *Slightly Married*

"Wendy Markham writes some of the funniest chick lit books out there...laugh out loud funny."
—*Bookloons* on *Slightly Engaged*

"This is a delightfully humorous read, full of belly laughs and groans... It is almost scary how honest and true to life this book is."
—*The Best Reviews* on *Slightly Single*

"The inventive premise of Markham's winning novel involves a love triangle in both the past and the present. Markham's latest is an appealing, wholly original yarn."
—*Booklist* on *Mike, Mike & Me*

Also by

Wendy Markham

SLIGHTLY MARRIED
SLIGHTLY ENGAGED
SLIGHTLY SETTLED
SLIGHTLY SINGLE
MIKE, MIKE & ME

Slightly Suburban

Wendy Markham

SLIGHTLY SUBURBAN

A Red Dress Ink novel

ISBN-13: 978-0-373-89561-8
ISBN-10: 0-373-89561-5

www.RedDressInk.com

Printed in U.S.A.

For my slightly suburban friends,
Kyle Cadley, Kathy Kohler and Maureen Martin,
who know how to hug,
make birthdays special,
mix fun and fancy cocktails
and throw tiara parties fit for a queen!

1

It's all about the timing.

And I keep getting it wrong.

Take tonight: Friday night. Well past nine o'clock.

I'm *finally* ready to leave my eighth-floor office (with a partial if-you-stand-on-the-sill-and-stretch view of the Empire State Building) at Blaire Barnett Advertising.

All day, I told anyone who would listen—which, as it turns out, was apparently only myself, Inner Tracey—that when six o'clock rolled around, I was outta here.

(Yes, six. Leaving at five is about as acceptable in the industry-that-never-sleeps as wearing tan nylon Leggs with reinforced toes.)

So when 5:55 rolled around, there I was, about to bolt from my just-cleaned-off desk.

But I decided to hold off a minute so that I could pull out a compact and put on some of the new lipstick I dashed into Sephora to buy en route from a Client meeting this morning.

Yes, Client meeting. As opposed to client meeting. At Blair Barnett, Client always starts with a capital C. Given that logic, my business cards should read *tracey spadolini candell.*

Anyway, my timing was off. I took too long with the lipstick. As I was loafing around putting it on and thinking happy TGIF thoughts, Crosby Courts—whose personal theme song should be "Tubular Bells"—stuck her sleek dark haircut into my doorway.

"Hot date?" she asked.

"Yup. With my husband." Jack—who also works at Blaire Barnett, down in the Media Department—was taking me to see *Black and White,* that controversial indie drama that caused the big splash at Sundance in January.

Was being the key word here.

No, it didn't happen.

Yes, we'd already bought the tickets at the big Regal Multiplex off Union Square and had managed to snag dinner reservations afterward at Mesob, the buzzy new Ethiopian place on Lafayette. We were planning to head over to Bleeker for drinks and music after that. Big night out on the town.

But here in the cutthroat world of New York City advertising, personal plans are insignificant. You can be getting married in five minutes and your boss will hang up from an urgent Client phone call, turn to you standing there all white lace and promises, and say, "I hate to tell you this, but…"

Which is exactly what Crosby, copywriter on the Abate Laxatives account and my supervisor since I became junior copywriter last year, said as she watched me slick on a gorgeous layer of raspberry-hued lusciousness. "I hate to tell you this, but…"

What I wouldn't give to have a dollar for every time I've heard that exact phrase from her. If I'd had any idea that this coveted Creative Department position was going to be way more demanding and far less fun than the lowly one I left behind in the stuffy Account Management Department, I wouldn't have lobbied so hard for a copywriting position in the first place.

So now, three-plus hours after I was supposed to meet Jack for our hot date, he's presumably enjoying *injera, tibs* and *wat* at Mesob with his friend Mitch, who willingly ditched plans with his latest girlfriend to go in my place.

No surprise there. These days, Mitch is a fixture in our lives. Much ado about that later. For now, suffice to say that one of my favorite vintage SNL skits—"The Thing That Wouldn't Leave"—is now playing itself out almost nightly in my living room, starring Mitch in the title role. And it's not the least bit amusing in real life.

Anyway, when I spoke to Jack between the movie and the restaurant reservation, he told me to meet him and Mitch downtown for drinks whenever I finish resolving the Client crisis here. I don't really feel like going now, though—especially with the perennial third wheel on board for the duration of the evening. I'd just as soon head home, take a long, hot shower and fall asleep in front of a good bad movie.

But Jack is counting on me so off I go, this time *sans* lipstick. The luscious raspberry wore off hours ago, along with that TGIF glow.

Before the elevator, I make a pit stop in the ladies' room, where I find Lane Washburn, who works in the bullpen, emerging from a stall. She's just changed out of her size zero business suit, and it drapes about the same from its wire hanger as the sparkly, clingy black size zero cocktail dress does from her protruding collarbones. Really, I mean that in the most loving way.

How do I know she's a size zero?

Because the last time I checked, Saks wasn't selling negative sizes. If they were, I'd peg her for a –2.

"Ooh, you're all fancy! Where are you going, Lane?"

"Out for drinks with my boyfriend." She leans into the mirror to put on bright red lipstick. "How about you? No plans for tonight?"

"Going out for drinks with my husband," I return, and see her give me the once-over.

In that? she's thinking, not in the most loving way.

I am thus obligated to lie, "I was going to run home and change first, but I got hung up on some Client stuff. Now I'm three hours late."

Instant sympathetic understanding in her big blue eyes. "That stinks. So now you have to go like that?"

Um, I really was always going to go like this. Is it that bad?

I look down at my brown heeled pumps, topaz Ann Taylor pencil skirt that's rumpled across my thighs, white blouse and the chestnut cashmere cardigan sweater that I used to love because Jack gave it to me for Christmas and said it's the exact shade of my hair and eyes.

I'm sure I'll probably love it again when I pull it out of my closet wrapped in dry cleaner's plastic next fall. But by March, I'm always sick of my heavy winter clothes—even cashmere—and anxious to start shedding them for pastel sleeveless silk and cotton pieces. Which is still a long way off.

Anyway, I look fine for drinks with Jack and Mitch.

Still, I open another button on my blouse to make the outfit less prim. Which exposes most of my right boob. Oops.

Buttoning up again, I tell Lane, "That's the thing about living in the city. It's not like you can just run home before you go someplace after work."

"Where do you live?"

"Upper East Side. How about you?"

"East Fifty-fourth at Second Avenue."

Ah, practically around the corner. If I lived that close, I'd run home to change.

I watch Lane put her lipstick into a black cosmetics bag, then zip that, along with her clothes, into a matching black garment bag hanging on a stall door. Wow, she's organized.

I guess I could have had the foresight to bring a nice dressy outfit to work, like she did.

However, I was too bleary-eyed and stressed this morning from getting less than five hours' sleep after being stuck at the office till midnight last night.

You know, since I moved into the Creative Department, my life is not my own. It's really starting to make me wonder…

Okay, it's not *starting* to make me wonder.

It's *continuing* to make me wonder:

Is this how I really want to spend my life? (Or at least, the career portion of my life, which lately seems to encompass everything else anyway.)

At which point, I wonder, do I finish *wondering* and start *deciding*…and *doing?*

Something else to wonder: if I did bring makeup and a change of clothes to work, would I have to carry them in a quart-size Ziploc and a Handle-Tie Hefty?

The answer to that, at least, is clear: absolutely. The beautiful matching luggage set Jack and I bought for our Tahitian honeymoon was lost a few months ago by the airline somewhere between New York and Buffalo when we flew up to spend Christmas with my family.

Lane, who probably spent Christmas skiing in Switzerland, tosses her auburn hair. “Well, have fun tonight, Tracey! See you Monday!”

She swings out of the ladies’ room in her fabulous, sexy little number.

The number being 0, you’ll recall. In lieu of –2.

I look at myself in the full-length mirror next to the hand dryer.

I’m usually a 6 or 8, though I’m a 4 at Ann Taylor, which is my favorite place to shop. Did I mention I’m a size 4 there?

If there’s anything I’ve learned these last few years, it’s that everything is relative.

Because, you know, back in my size 12–14 days, I would have been envious of someone like size 6–8 me.

You know, this is utterly exhausting. Am I ever going to be satisfied with who I am?

I keep thinking maybe I would be…if I lived somewhere else. But here in *If You Can Make It There, You’ll Make It Anywhere,* the competition is fierce. Everywhere you turn, someone is more attractive, more successful, more respected, thinner, happier, just plain old *better.* And everyone is richer.

Here in Manhattan, Status Quo is a curse. There is tremendous pressure to achieve greatness—on a personal, professional, spiritual and, yes, global level.

I'm telling you, all this striving can really exhaust a girl.

Lifting the sweater, I tuck the blouse in more tightly and twist the waistband of the skirt, which has shifted slightly so that the side seams aren't lined up with my hips. It's a little big on me, even without my trusty Spanx, which I opted not to put on this morning.

The silver lining in having to work these long hours is that I rarely have time to overeat anymore—and sometimes, to eat at all. Not only have I managed to keep off the fifty pounds I lost over six years ago, but I actually weigh a few pounds less than I did on my wedding day.

So why am I not satisfied?

With my weight?

With my job?

With my life?

With my outfit?

I make a face at the mirror. I might be pleasantly unplump these days, but I'm unpleasantly uncomfortable.

In general, yes. And mostly, right now, in these clothes. Too much bulk caused by too many layers. I wish I could change into something more fun and sexy. I wish I could *be* someone more fun and sexy.

But you're not, grouses Inner Tracey. *You're an overworked married woman who's closing in on thirty.*

Does that mean I have to look frumpy on a Friday night?

Yes, because changing would mean going all the way uptown, then all the way down, which, depending on the time of day and various acts of man, God, Mother Nature or the Metropolitan Transit Authority, could take hours.

Forget it.

See what I mean about living here? You can strive all you want, but even the most mundane things are extra challenging.

You know, I haven't felt this bummed about life since *The O.C.* was canceled.

My long camel-colored coat—also cashmere, a steal at Saks last April—feels cumbersome as I plod down the corridor toward the elevator. Ho-hum. I look like every other corporate drone in the city.

Plus, my leather shoulder bag, bulging with work I need to go over this weekend, weighs a ton. Lugging it back and forth to the office, I've accumulated all kinds of extra junk in there—loose change, wrappers, magazines, papers—the kind of stuff you'd toss into the ashtray or backseat of your car if you had one. But a car is a liability here in New York, so I wind up carrying all of this around town on my back, which—no surprise—has been killing me lately.

Here's a brainstorm: Maybe I should start wheeling a little wire cart, like those wizened old widows who live in the boroughs. Instead of groceries or laundry, mine will be filled with PowerPoint presentations and endless notes from endless meetings.

For a split second, it sounds like a great idea. Maybe I'll start a new trend! Maybe I can design a sleek little black cart, patent it, quit my job—key point—and become a rich and successful entrepreneur, marketing chic carts to Manhattan's upwardly mobile young women.

Mental Note: or maybe you're just losing your mind.

Yeah. That's probably it.

"Night, Tracey," Ryan Cunningham, an assistant art director, says as I pass him in the hallway.

"Night. Have a good weekend."

"I'll be spending it here," he says, striding on past. "Same as usual."

Having endured my own share of seven-day workweeks, I shake my head in empathy, glad it isn't me this time.

You know, lately I really miss the good old days in account management. Not that I knew that they *were* good old days at the time—or that I'd even want to go back there, because it's not the same.

There used to be four of us who shared a big cubicle space on the account floor—along with countless margarita happy hours, office dirt, diet tips, recipes, advice—you name it.

But Brenda quit two years ago when her husband, Paulie, got promoted to sergeant on the NYPD. Now she's a stay-at-home mom in Staten Island with two kids and a third on the way.

Not long after that, Yvonne retired to Florida with her husband, Thor. I still can't quite picture Yvonne, with her tall raspberry-colored hair and tall kick-ass kick-line body (she was a Radio City Rockette back in the fifties), and Thor (her much younger Scandinavian not-just-a-green-card-marriage-after-all husband) hanging around some retirement community.

But Yvonne has reclaimed her showgirl past and is entertaining the "geri's," as she calls them, with a torch-song act at the residents' club.

Of our original foursome, only my friend Latisha still works at Blaire Barnett. She's an executive secretary for one of the management reps. We try to get together as often as we can, but when we do manage, it's kind of lonely with just the two of us.

Anyway, I'm usually too busy with Client demands to go for drinks or lunch, and Latisha's got her hands full with a husband, Derek, and two kids. Her son, Bernie, is in preschool—and wait-listed at every decent grammar school, so it's nail-biting time. Her oldest, Keera, has a learning disability and Latisha's trying to get her through junior year with stellar grades so she'll have a prayer for an Ivy League college, which she has her heart set on.

See what I mean?

Back in my hometown, Brookside, New York, no one ever worried about getting into an Ivy League school. You were lucky if you got a higher education at all. I went to a state college. A lot of my classmates went to community college, joined the military or just started working.

Now they all think I'm this huge success merely because

I moved to Manhattan, have a business card and once rode an elevator with Donald Trump, who was at Blair Barnett for a meeting. Do I have to mention I wasn't even at the meeting?

That didn't matter to anyone back home.

Seriously, when my mother introduced me to the new church organist at midnight mass at Most Precious Mother, the organist exclaimed, "You're the one who rode the elevator with Donald Trump! It's so, *so* nice to meet you!"

See what I mean?

Here at Blaire Barnett, the eighth-floor reception area is dimly lit and buttoned up, as you would expect at this hour, and as I wait for the down elevator, there's no sign of The Donald.

I can see fellow Creatives bustling up and down the halls.

A handful of others scurry out of an up elevator that, frustratingly, doesn't change direction on my floor. They're clutching cups of coffee and take-out bags, obviously here for the duration.

They all work on the agency's new spacetrippin.com account, which is just what it sounds like: a company that arranges dream vacations into outer space. Laugh if you want—we in the Creative Department have certainly gotten some good mileage out of it—but it's a legitimate new business, started by a venture capitalist who has millions to spend on start-up advertising.

"I really hope you've got an umbrella, Tracey," one of the

spacetrippin.com guys tells me as they head back to their offices. “It’s nasty out there.”

Uh-oh. I really hope I’ve got an umbrella, too. On a good hair day, my straight brown hair doesn’t exactly incite photoshoot offers from the agency’s Lavish Locks Shampoo account group.

This isn’t a good hair day. Douse me with rain and mist, and a bad hair day goes catastrophic.

I dig through my bag and come across everything else one can possibly need in the course of daily urban travels: Band-Aids, gum, tampons, car-service vouchers, low-fat granola bars, a book, sunglasses and a Metrocard—which I shove into my coat pocket for easier access, along with my iPod.

There are also plenty of things no one could possibly ever need, anywhere: a dried-out pink Sharpie, a limp Splenda packet spattered with coffee stains, an expired 20%-off Borders coupon and a couple of loose, bleached-out Tic Tacs.

But no umbrella. The little fold-up one I usually carry is in the pocket of my jacket at home, I remember. I took it along when I ran out in the rain to get milk the other night, and I never put it back.

Well, maybe the rain will let up by the time I get downstairs. It’s taking long enough.

I wait impatiently, thinking about my father and brother who work at a steel plant back in Brookside, near Buffalo. When they’re done with work, they punch out, walk out the door, get into their cars and drive maybe three-tenths of a mile at most to their houses. I bet they could do their commute door to door in sixty seconds or less, no exaggeration. Who says there are no perks to being a steelworker in a fading, blue-collar, Great Lakes town?

Come on, Tracey. You don't want to be a steelworker. And you don't want to move back to Brookside.

No, but I wonder if I really want to be a junior copywriter at Blaire Barnett Advertising in Manhattan, either.

Maybe I want…

Maybe I don't know what I want.

Other than to get the hell out of this building before Crosby Courts reappears and summons me back to her lair.

I stick my iPod earbuds into my ears and turn it on. Some good, loud music will be an appropriate way to kick off the weekend, right?

Right—except the charge is depleted.

And let me tell you, there is nothing worse than riding the subway without an iPod. It's the only way to tune out the chaos of the city.

I'm contemplating taking the stairs when at last a down elevator arrives. Naturally, it's already filled to overflowing with office workers impatient to launch their own overdue weekends.

I wedge myself in and ignore the grumbles from behind me as the doors slide shut two inches from the tip of my nose. Something—it had damn well better be someone's umbrella—is poking into my butt.

Outside, Lexington Avenue is still engulfed in an icy March downpour. Getting a cab would be akin to landing that Lavish Locks print ad: It ain't gonna happen.

Blaire Barnett offers a car service to employees who work past ten. Do I dare go back upstairs to wait it out?

I check my watch. It would be about twenty minutes...

But no, I do not dare. On any night at 10:00 p.m., there's a car-service backup. Friday nights are worse. Plus, it's raining. That's at least another hour delay.

Anyway, Crosby is still up there. If she sees me, she'll need me to tweak a line on the copy I just rewrote for the hundredth time, and twenty minutes will turn into tomorrow morning.

So off I splash to the number six subway a few blocks away. I duck under scaffolding and awnings at every opportunity, but there's no way around it: I'm drenched.

As I hover in the doorway of a bank on the corner waiting for the light to change, I call Jack from my cell.

"Hey, where are you?" he asks, and has the nerve to sound boozy and jovial.

"I was headed for the subway, but now I'm thinking I might just go home. By the time I get down there—"

"No, don't go home. I miss you. It's Friday night."

Aw...he's so sweet. He misses me.

And it *is* Friday night...

"Come on, Tracey!" I hear a voice saying in the background. "We're having fun! Get your keister down here."

Oh, yeah. I momentarily forgot about Mitch, aka pain in said keister.

"I don't know," I tell Jack, "I'm really wiped out, and it's pouring, and I'd have to take the subway—"

"It'll take ten minutes, Trace."

So will going home.

But it's Friday night and I miss my husband. I sigh and tell Jack I'll be there.

As I head toward the subway entrance, I reach into my pocket for my Metrocard.

It's gone. Seriously. I pull out the linings of both pockets to make sure it isn't crumpled in with a dry used tissue or something. Nope.

I must have dropped it. Or maybe someone pickpocketed me in the elevator.

It wouldn't be the first time that's happened—although never in my office building. A few months ago, when I was caught up in a herd of commuters at Grand Central Station, some kid stole a twenty I had tucked into my pocket. I felt myself being jostled, realized what was happening, and shouted, "Thief! Thief!" as the kid took off.

A National Guardsman was right nearby—post 9-11, they patrol all the major transportation hubs wearing camouflage, which always strikes me as slightly ridiculous. The camouflage, I mean. Are they trying to blend into the background? They'd be better off wearing cashmere overcoats with plaid Burberry scarves and polished wingtips.

The National Guard did not come to my rescue when I was robbed. Apparently, Homeland Security is only interested in apprehending potential terrorists, not pickpockets. Understandable, I guess.

I haven't run into any yet—terrorists, I mean—but that doesn't mean I'm not always on the lookout. Don't think the prospect of suicide bombers doesn't cross my mind every single time I walk down the steps into the subway.

Like right now.

As always, I warily scan the crowd to make sure no one appears to be packing an explosive vest. You can never be sure.

If you see something, say something—that's my motto.

Well, not just *my* motto. It's actually the Metropolitan Transit Authority's motto, but I'm down with it.

I spot a couple of candidates who look as if they might be up to something, but they're probably just your garden-variety street thugs. There's a woman who's acting furtive and seems to have something strapped across her front, but then she turns around and I see that it's a baby. Close call.

At the automated ticket machine, I feed a couple of soggy dollar bills into a slot that keeps spitting them back out again. After many frustrating tries, I wind up waiting on a seemingly endless line at the booth.

Finally, new Metrocard in hand, I'm through the turnstile, where I almost head to the uptown stairs out of habit. Home is a mere forty-three blocks and five stops up the line,

I think wistfully. Jack is about the same distance in the opposite direction.

Should I just forget about meeting him? I so wish Mitch weren't there. I so wish Mitch weren't everywhere. Lately, he's camped out on our new (custom-upholstered, a Christmas present to each other) couch night after night, watching sports with Jack.

Hey, if I go home now, I'll have the couch—and remote—all to myself. I have to admit, *E! True Hollywood Story* sounds better than anything else right now.

But Jack is counting on me. And who knows? Maybe Mitch will take a hint and leave when I get there.

No, he won't. He loves us. Even me. Jack is always telling me that. "He loves you, Tracey. He thinks you're great."

I'm so great and he loves me so much that a few months ago, Mitch decided to move into a studio apartment right around the corner from us. Thank God there were no openings in our building. He checked.

Don't get me wrong—he's a terrific guy. He and Jack have been friends since college and he was best man at our wedding. It's just that my weekdays (and nights) have become so challenging that when I'm not at work, I want my husband—and our apartment, and our couch, and our remote—to myself.

I guess I should probably stop being so nice to Mitch whenever he's over, so he won't want to hang around. Or I should get Jack to tell him we need more time to ourselves. Or I should tell him myself.

Yeah. Or we could just move far, far away.

I trudge down the stairs leading to the southbound number six track, where I sense something is amiss.

My first clue: the platform is a squirming sea of humanity wearing a collective pissed-off expression, and the loud-speaker is squawking. The announcement is unintelligible, but it's not as if they can possibly be saying, "Attention, subway riders, everything is running like clockwork tonight and we'll have you where you're going in no time. Have a great weekend!"

Hopefully it's just a temporary delay.

I wearily force my way into the crowd, steering clear of the edge of the platform because really, the last thing I need right now is to fall onto the tracks and get hit by a train. Although, I wouldn't really be surprised. If I lived to be surprised.

"Excuse me, what's going on?" I ask the nearest bystander, who, if she were any nearer, would be huddled inside my coat with me.

She explains the situation, either in a language I don't understand—meaning, something other than English or Italian—or with a major speech impediment, poor thing.

I smile and nod, pretending to get it.

Meanwhile, I eavesdrop on the guy whose elbow is pressed into my rib cage mere inches from my right breast. He's saying something into his cell phone about a derailment down near Fourteenth Street.

Derailment?

Forget it. There's no way in hell—which is pretty much where I am right now—that I'll ever make it down to the Village.

I have no other choice but to squirm my way back to the stairs as—wouldn't you know it—an uptown train comes and goes without me on the opposite track.

When at last I make it up the stairs and am heading toward the other side, I hear another train roaring into the northbound track below. Already? They usually don't come this close together.

I break into a run, shouting, "Someone hold the doors!"

Nobody does, dammit.

I reach the platform just as they're dinging closed, and this guy standing on the other side of the glass—some lame guy in a wet trench coat who could have held the doors, because I can tell by his expression that he heard me—offers a helpless shrug.

I dare to glare, hoping belatedly that he doesn't have a gun, and watch the train trundle off toward my distant neighborhood without me.

Oh, well. Another one will be along in a few minutes, right?

Wrong. So, so wrong.

Twenty minutes later, this platform is nearly as crowded as the other side, and someone near me has terrible gas. I keep trying to move away, but the stink keeps moving, too.

By process of elimination I've isolated it to three possible people: a guy with a goatee and backpack, an old lady, or an attractive businesswoman who's about my age and may be trying too hard to appear nonchalant.

I've also just been treated to an a cappella rendition of Billy Squiers's "Stroke Me," sung by some dirty old man whose fly is down—making it less serenade than suggestion. When I refuse to throw some change into the hat he passes, he tells me to %@#$ Off, with an accompanying hand gesture.

By the time the next train comes hurtling into the station—so packed that the only way to get on is to literally shove past people crammed by the doors, who shove right back—I am wondering, once again, why I live in New York City.

I mean, seriously…what am I doing here?

Yes, my husband is here. And my job. And my friends. And all my stuff.

But…why?

These days, unless one is supremely wealthy—and we're not—the quality of life in the city seems pretty dismal. Traffic, poverty, crowds, the smell…I can't imagine it's that much worse in Calcutta.

Okay, maybe that's an exaggeration. They have monsoon season in Calcutta, right? And a lot of curry. I'm not crazy about curry.

But there's a lot of curry in New York, too. And this might not be a monsoon, but as I splash back out into the deluge, I decide it's worse. Whatever's falling out of the sky has now frozen into sleet, or hail, and it's pelting my face and head.

Remembering that there's probably nothing to eat at home, I detour two blocks to the deli. I pick up a loaf of whole-grain bread, a half pound of turkey breast, lettuce, an apple, a diet raspberry Snapple and a couple of rolls of toilet paper because we're almost out.

"Twenty-seven fifty-eight," says the clerk.

I blink, look down at the counter and shove aside a big fruit basket that's sitting there in shrink-wrap. "Oh, this isn't mine," I tell her.

"I know."

Then why did you add it to my bill? And would it kill you to crack a smile?

Wait a minute. The fruit basket alone would have to be at least fifty bucks.

"*How* much was it?" I ask again, gesturing at my stuff, because I thought she said—

"Twenty-seven fifty-eight."

Jeez. Can this measly little pile of groceries possibly cost that much?

Yes, it can, and Unsmiling Cashier is waiting for her money.

I open my wallet again, wondering why I'm surprised. I mean, after all these years of living in Manhattan, I know things are superexpensive. Yet every so often, I still find myself caught off guard at cash registers.

All that's left in my wallet are two ones and a wad of receipts.

With a sigh, I pull out my American Express card. As Unsmiling Cashier runs it through the machine, a quick mental calculation tells me that in my hometown, this would run me ten bucks, maybe twelve. Tops.

Back out in the monsoon, I make my way to the doorman building that seemed like such a luxury when I first moved here from my dumpy little studio in the East Village.

As luck would have it, Jimmy, my favorite doorman—who actually flew up to Brookside for our wedding a few years ago—isn't on duty tonight. He always cheers me up.

Unlike Gecko. He's on duty tonight and always has the opposite effect. He's the ultimate pessimist. I swear, you could win the lottery and he'd immediately list every past lottery winner who ever went on to get divorced, go bankrupt or commit suicide. He's just that kind of guy.

"What a crappy night, huh?" he comments as he opens the door and I blow in on a gust of frozen precipitation.

"Yes," I say.

"I mean literally."

Uh-oh.

I know what he means by that.

"The M.C. has struck again," Gecko informs me.

"Where?" I hold my breath.

"Third floor."

I sign in relief. That's six floors away from ours.

The Mad Crapper has been terrorizing our building for over a month now. He never strikes in the same place at the same time, so he's been impossible to catch. Some tenants want to band together and organize a twenty-four-hour surveillance team with mandatory participation.

I really hope it doesn't come to that. Because really, the last thing I want to do after a long, exhausting day at work is lurk in a shadowy corridor waiting for some stealthy figure to come along, squat and deposit a steaming pile of fresh crap before my very eyes.

Anyway, who's to say the Mad Crapper isn't living right here among us?

Sharing much T.M.I. about the latest strike, Gecko follows me to the mailroom, where I retrieve a stack of bills and catalogs from our box, along with an envelope addressed to Resident.

Uh-oh. Is this from the Citizens Vigilante Group?

No, thank God.

Even better.

"Building's being fumigated again on Monday," Gecko informs me as I open the envelope and skim the super's note telling me just that.

"Again? Why?"

"Roaches," says the perennial bearer of bad news. "Seventh floor's infested."

Infested. Now there's a word that can't possibly have a positive connotation under any circumstances.

"Uh-oh," I say, making a face.

"Uh-oh is right. They're probably crawling around in your place, too. Keep an eye out when you turn on the light."

"Believe me, I will."

It's not like I've never seen a roach. Just about every apartment in New York has them at some point or another. But I freak out every time one scuttles past.

Going back to the Crapper's latest M.O.—the culprit apparently signed his most recent offering with a fecal flourish—Gecko follows me toward the elevator.

"Have a good night," he calls after me as I step in.

"You, too."

"I doubt that," he replies dourly as the doors slide closed.

For once, I'm right there with him.

On our floor, I make my way to apartment 9K, the tiny Ikea-furnished one-bedroom where we've been living for—is it almost five years now?

Five years. No wonder.

After unlocking three dead bolts, I step inside and promptly crash into a chair.

Not because somebody left it practically in front of the door, but because that's where it belongs. There's just no other place to put it.

I drop my barbell—I mean, bag—on it.

Ah, relief.

Rubbing my aching shoulder with one hand I turn on a lamp with the other, and check to see if roaches are scurrying into the corners.

No. But they're probably there, tucked away into the cracks, watching me.

Just to be sure none has invaded our space, I give the apartment a good once-over. That takes all of four or five seconds, because there's not much to it. Two boxy rooms—living room and bedroom—plus a galley kitchenette and bathroom.

Maybe the place would seem more spacious if we got rid of some of this clutter, I think, trying to be optimistic.

Like what, though? Our toothbrushes? The television set?

A booming sound overhead makes me jump, until I remember that a family of circus freaks moved in upstairs last month.

Seeing them in the elevator, you'd think they were a perfectly respectable Upper East Side family of four: Dad in suit with briefcase, Mom in yoga pants pushing designer stroller, one older kid who's invariably plugged into something handheld with earphones, one younger kid placidly rolling along in said designer stroller.

The second they get home sweet home, though? Sideshow, full swing. Our ceiling shakes so violently you'd swear there are elephants, giants and fat ladies stomping around up there. Jo-Jo-the-dog-faced-boy scampers to and fro in an endless game of fetch, and there must be at least a couple of klutzy Wallendas who regularly fall off their trapeze onto the uncarpeted floor.

I'm betting a full-time live-in decorator is there as well, because furniture is rearranged as regularly as most of us pee. And I think there's a resident carpenter, too—that, or a serial killer, because I hear what sounds like a hammer and a buzz saw at all hours. (Jack claims it's just high heels and a blow-dryer, but he has a high noise tolerance. I could be standing right over him, talking to him, and he doesn't hear me. I swear, it happens all the time.)

Oh, and I don't know what happens to Older Kids' ubiquitous earphones when he crosses the threshold of his bedroom—which has to be right above ours—but he's not using them there. Our room vibrates day and night with the audio from his television and iPod speakers and arcadelike video-game system.

Valentine's Day was a nightmare. To celebrate the third anniversary of Jack's popping the question—yes, I'm big on commemorating relationship milestones—I staged this whole cozy scene for when he got home from work. There I was, waiting in our bed with lingerie, candles, champagne, chocolate fondue and Norah Jones (her new CD, I mean, not Norah herself—we're not into threesomes).

About five minutes into our romantic evening, our room filled with deafening screams—not mine, and not pleasure. Then came the squealing car-chase tires, cursing and gunfire. Talk about a mood wrecker. Obviously, the kid was tuning in to some cable movie or a PlayStation game that wasn't rated E for Everyone.

If you ask me, our upstairs neighbors should be censoring their kid's audio-video habits.

That, or we should get the hell out of Dodge.

You know what? I really think it's time.

Because, suddenly, I can't take it anymore.

The circus freaks, the cramped quarters, roaches and pesticides, Mitch, the prices, the subway, Gecko, the Mad Crapper, my job, Crosby, the elevators, the lugging and hauling, the bodily contact with strangers.

When Jack and I first got engaged, I remember, I wanted to move.

But he said—and I quote: "one major life change per year is my quota."

Ever since, there's been at least one major life change per year. First we were newlyweds, then he got promoted at work, then I got promoted at work…

Worst of all, in the midst of the job shuffling, my father-in-law died suddenly.

Jack's had a somewhat contentious relationship with his father for most of his life, and his parents' divorce after more than thirty years of marriage didn't help matters. As the only son, with two older sisters and two younger, Jack has always been his mother's favorite—and his father's least favorite.

Jack Candell Senior was a high-powered ad exec on Madison Avenue for years, and he pretty much pushed his son into the industry when what Jack really wanted to do was go to culinary school.

I think—no, I know—Jack Senior was hoping his son would become a wealthy, high-profile account-management guy, like he was. Instead, Jack found his way into the Media Department, where he's great at what he does, but hasn't become the big shot Jack Senior wanted him to become, and probably never will.

Over the years, Jack and I maintained regular contact with his father—mostly at my urging. My family is tight-knit and it just doesn't feel right to me to shut out a parent. I'm the one who made sure we stopped to see Jack's dad when we were up in Westchester, and I'm the one who invited him—and the woman who was his fiancée at the time, soon to become his wife—to the surprise thirtieth birthday dinner I threw for Jack.

Did they come?

No. But his father did write out a big check and stick it into a card with his apologies for being busy elsewhere that night. The card was one of those generic ones you get in a box of cards, not even a "special son" or "thirtieth birthday" one.

Jack was hurt when he found out I had extended an invite and his father turned it down, and his mother, Wilma, was livid.

"He's a bastard," she told me privately. "I don't like to bad-mouth him to my kids. But he always has been a bastard, and he will be to his dying day."

Which, sadly, wasn't all that far off.

Not long after the party, we got one of those chilling early-morning phone calls: Jack's sister Jeannie, with the news that their father had suffered a fatal heart attack.

Jack's since had a hard time dealing with all that was left unreconciled—or at least, in his perception—between him and his dad.

He's thanked me, many times, for trying to bridge the gap, for what it was worth.

Anyway, time is helping to heal.

And I think a fresh start is in order.

We're a couple of months into this calendar year, and so far, there's been nary a major life change in the Candell household.

Yet.

2

The next morning:

"Happy anniversary!"

That's me, to Jack, all kiss, kiss.

"Er...anniversary?"

That's Jack, to me, all deer in headlights.

I know what you're thinking: typical male, forgot his wedding anniversary already. This honeymoon is more over than cargo capris. From here, it's all downhill, like that old Carly Simon song where married couples are fated to cling and claw and drown in love's debris.

Well, I, Tracey Spadolini Candell, am here to say: *Wrong!*

Of course Jack and I are still happily married.

And it isn't our wedding anniversary.

Jack just thinks it is.

But not for long.

"Wait...we got married in October, Tracey. This is March..." Jack's eyes dart to his watch calendar, just to be sure. "Right. March."

He looks relieved.

"I know." I perch on the arm of his favorite chair, which he sat in, fresh from his morning shower, newspaper poised and stereo playing, right before I kiss-kissed him. "But it's the eighth. We met on the eighth, remember?"

"Of December," he says, after another brief mental calculation. "We met on the eighth of December."

"Right. But this is kind of like our diamond anniversary, if you think about it."

Apparently, Jack really is thinking about it, wearing the same expression he had the other day when I asked him what inning it was in the Knicks game he was watching.

Look, I'm no ditz. I'm not a big sports fan either, but I've been married to this one long enough to know basketball games have quarters and baseball games have innings. When I said *inning* it was a slip of the tongue because I was weak from hunger at the time, and we were supposed to be going out to dinner after the game was over.

He hasn't let me live it down. *"Hey, guess what, Mitch? Guess what, Jimmy the Doorman? My wife thinks basketball has innings. Har dee har har."*

Good stuff. I'm surprised Conan hasn't called.

"Diamond anniversary?" he echoes now, wearing that same *my wife is slightly crazy* look.

It doesn't bother me nearly as much as it did back when we were newlyweds and I was much more emotional and touchy. Probably because I, too, have a look: the one I flash at him whenever he stands cluelessly in front of the open fridge telling me we're out of butter, or mustard, or milk.

Um, no, hello, it's right here in this gi-normous-can't-miss-it plastic jug, see? All you have to do is look beyond the week-old container of moo goo gai pan you insisted you'd eat for a snack, and the wee jar of quince jam that came in a gift basket from some Client back in December, which you also claimed you'd eat for a snack, and, voila! Milk.

Like my friend Brenda once told me, love might be blind, but marriage is no eye-opener.

"I sway-uh, Tracey, no married guy I've ever met can find anything around the house," she said in her thick Jersey accent, "not even when it's right in front of his face. Scientists should do some kind of study and find out why that is."

I figure scientists are still pretty wrapped up in global warming and cancer, but as soon as there's an opening, I'm sure they'll get to it. Because it really is strange.

You know what, though? I don't really mind Jack's masculine faults. In fact, I find most of them endearing. Except for the one where he farts under the covers and seals the blankets over my head, laughing hysterically. He calls it the Dutch Oven.

I figured all guys also do that. But when I asked my friend Kate about it, she reacted like I'd just told her Jack was into golden showers.

"What? That's disgusting," she drawled in her Alabama accent. "Billy would never do that to me!"

As if Billy—who is a total douche bag—isn't capable of flatulence, or, for that matter, far worse behavior where Kate is concerned.

But I won't get into that at the moment. So far, I haven't dared get into it with Kate, either. I'm waiting until the time is right to mention that I saw her husband walking down Horatio Street in the Meatpacking District late one night with a woman who wasn't Kate.

Granted, I was walking down the same street at the same hour with a guy who wasn't Jack.

However, I had just come from my friends Raphael and Donatello's place, and the guy, Blake, was a friend of theirs and while infinitely gorgeous and masculine, not the least bit threatening to my marriage, if you catch my drift.

Blake and I were both a little loopy from Bombay Sapphire and tonics and were singing a medley of sitcom theme songs when I spotted Billy and the Brunette.

They weren't kissing, or groping, or even holding hands, but there was definitely something intimate about the way they were walking and talking. As in, she might have been a colleague but she definitely wasn't *just* a colleague, and they might have been coming from a restaurant but they definitely weren't coming from a dinner meeting.

And she definitely, *definitely,* wasn't his sister. For one thing, I know—and strongly dislike, but that's neither here nor there—his sister, Amanda.

For another, if that woman turned out to be some other unlikable Billy sister I haven't met, then there's something distinctly *Flowers in the Attic* about their relationship.

How do I know Billy and the woman aren't platonic? Sometimes I just get a feeling about things for reasons I can quite put my finger on, and that was one of those times.

Blake—who must have met Billy at Raphael and Donatello's wedding three years ago but probably wouldn't know him if he fell over him, which was not unlikely in his Bombay Sapphire-fueled condition—was oblivious to the situation.

He launched us into the theme song from *One Day at a Time* as I saw the rest of Kate's life—as a divorcée—flash before my very eyes.

Maybe I was jumping the gun. Maybe they really were just colleagues.

Blake elbowed me as I stopped singing and turned to watch Billy and the woman get into a cab together.

"Tracey, you're supposed to back me up. Let's try it again," Blake said, and sang, "Thiiiis is it…"

"Thiiis is it," I obediently echoed in tune, watching the cab make a right turn onto Hudson, heading downtown, instead of continuing on the next short block, making a right onto West Fourth and heading uptown.

Billy and Kate, of course, live uptown. Shouldn't he have been heading home at that hour on a weeknight?

And even if she lived downtown, if they were going their separate ways, shouldn't they have gotten separate cabs? There were plenty around. Believe me, I checked.

I know, I know, I said I wouldn't get into this whole Billy thing at the moment, but I can't help it. It's been weighing me down for weeks now and even though I know it could have been perfectly innocent, I also know that it wasn't.

Getting back to Jack—who doesn't know about Billy on Horatio Street and who, I'm absolutely certain, would never be heading downtown in a cab with a strange woman at that hour of the night—he's still waiting for my explanation about our diamond anniversary.

"Twenty-five is the silver anniversary," I explain to Jack as patiently now as I do when he's being Ray Charles in front of the fridge, "and fifty is gold, and seventy-five is diamond."

"We haven't even been alive seventy-five years," he says just as patiently in his reasonable Jack way, and looks longingly at the section of newspaper he was about to unfold.

"Not years—months. We met at the office Christmas party seventy-five months ago today."

"Really?"

He actually looks moved by this news. The fact that he tends to find me endearing is part of the reason I love him so much—and find him endearing in return. Except when he's Dutch Ovening my head. But I guess there's a little leftover frat boy in most grown men, Billy aside.

(Or maybe not, because Billy's recent behavior—all right, suspected behavior—strikes me as pretty damn immature and reckless. Not to mention immoral.)

"So it's our seventy-five-month anniversary?" asks my endearing Jack. "I can't believe you actually keep track of these things, Tracey."

I'll admit—but not to him—that I actually don't. Not until this morning at around 6:00 a.m. when, unable to sleep, I glanced at the kitchen calendar and happened to realize what day it was—right around the time the circus freaks kicked into high gear up in 10J.

"Well...happy anniversary," Jack tells me. Then, having concluded being endeared by my observation of our milestone, he goes back to reading the sports section of the *New York Times*.

"Wait...Jack?"

"Mmm." He turns a page.

"So it's been seventy-five months since we met. Wow!" I say brightly. "And almost two and a half years since our wedding."

"Yup." He's reading the paper.

"Remember when we didn't want to come back from our honeymoon?"

He snorts a little and looks up. "Who *does?*"

True. But we really, really, really, *so* didn't want to.

Maybe because we had the most amazing honeymoon ever: we went to Tahiti and stayed in one of those huts on stilts above the perfect, crystalline aqua sea. I had been dreaming of doing that but didn't think we could afford it. Jack surprised me.

Naturally, we spent much of that week lolling around that lush paradise scheming ways to escape our dreary workaday life. Anything seemed possible there, thousands of miles from this claustrophobic Upper East Side apartment with its water stains and dismal, concrete view.

The honeymoon flew by and the next thing we knew, we—and our luggage—were careening home from J.F.K. through cold November rain in an airless Yellow Cab that smelled overpoweringly of wet wool, mildew, chemical vanilla air freshener and exotic B.O.

"Remember how we both wanted to quit our jobs and move away from the city," I go on, "but you said one life change per year was your quota?"

"Yee-eess…"

I have his full attention now, but he's not letting on. He's pretending to be captivated by a story about Yankees spring training. Which, ordinarily, really would captivate him. Except, I know he's suspicious. He must realize where I'm going with this.

"Then remember how on our first anniversary I asked you about it again—" (I'd have bugged him sooner but I'd gotten over my initial impulse to flee when spring came early and our building was sold and the new owner nicely renovated everything) "—and you didn't want to talk about it because you had just gotten promoted?"

This time, he doesn't bother to answer.

"You know, I haven't even brought this up in ages," I say, "because I've been feeling like things are going great and why rock the boat…"

Renovated apartment, Jack's promotion to assistant media director at Blaire Barnett, my move to junior copywriter…

Yeah, aside from what happened with Jack's father, things have been relatively even-keeled lately. Much more even-keeled than ever before in my life.

Except…

The circus freaks moved in overhead, and someone's shitting all over the building, and we can't afford to live here, and I don't think I can take another day of riding the subway or lugging stuff around or brainstorming clever taglines for Abate Laxatives—although I just had a sudden brainstorm. Hmm…

Mental Note: explore working the Mad Crapper into the Abate campaign.

"I feel like it's time, Jack," I tell my husband, getting back to my other, more palatable brainstorm. "Seriously, we've been together seventy-five months and I really feel like we need a major change."

"Tracey, we can't move to Tahiti."

"That's not what I meant."

He sighs and folds the paper, putting it aside. "You want to have a baby?"

Huh?

"A baby?" I echo. "No. I don't want to have a baby—yet," I add, because presumably I will one day soon wake up with the urge to reproduce.

At least, that's what my friends keep telling me. Including Raphael, who is about to become a father at last. Not via the original old-fashioned means, since his significant other—Donatello, his husband—is also ovarian challenged.

Not via a surrogate, either, which was one of their earliest plans. When I (and every other female they've ever met, plus a good many they haven't) refused to lend them a womb—not that I don't adore and wholeheartedly support their efforts—Raphael and Donatello decided to go the more recent old-fashioned route: foreign adoption.

Sadly, that didn't work, either. You'd be surprised how many countries forbid a monogamous, healthy, well-off gay couple to adopt from their overflowing orphanages.

Or maybe you wouldn't be. Maybe you don't approve, either. But let me tell you, Raphael and Donatello deserve a chance as much as any stable, loving couple, and they are going to make terrific daddies. I know this for a fact, because they've had plenty of practice on the parade of foster kids they've been caring for over the past few years. Now one of those kids, Georgie, is going to become their son.

As for me…

"My biological clock isn't ticking yet," I inform my husband. Then I add cautiously, "Is yours?"

"Nah. I just figured you'd start thinking about it sooner or later. Or now."

You may be wondering why this is only coming up after two-plus years of marriage.

Well, it's not. It's been brought up (by me) and shot down (by Jack) before.

I actually thought I might be pregnant when I skipped a period right around the time we got married. My ob-gyn said it was probably due to wedding stress. Still, I took a pregnancy test on our honeymoon. Of course it was negative.

Even then, I wasn't entirely convinced. When I did get my period, I was actually disappointed, and went through a brief period during our newlywed year when I was gung ho to start a family. After all, hadn't I always wanted children? Hadn't I been told enough times by my evil ex-boyfriend, Will, that I have birthing hips? Hadn't I once even won a Babysitter of the Year award from my hometown Kiwanis Club? (I was seventeen. Which pretty much tells you everything you need to know about my high-school social life.)

So, yeah, I've always wanted to start a family for legitimate reasons.

Mostly, though, I just hated my job as account executive and I was desperate for a way out.

At that point, anything—and I mean *anything*—round-the-clock morning sickness, childbirth without pain meds, endless sleepless nights, death by firing squad—would have been better than taking the subway to midtown every morning and dealing with my anal-retentive boss, account group director Adrian Smedly and an array of bitchy Clients.

Luckily for me, Jack didn't think an eight-week maternity leave was sufficient incentive for motherhood. At the time, I was a little miffed. But since it takes two to make a baby the original old-fashioned way, and I couldn't find a willing sperm donor (just kidding), I reluctantly set aside the baby dream—halfhearted and short-lived as it was.

Not so long after, I found my salvation—or so I thought, pre-Crosby Courts—when I was at last moved into the Creative Department.

Meanwhile, Jack and I pretty much dropped the baby-making subject. I figured it would come up again, though, when one of us found a burning desire to procreate—or play hooky from work for a few months.

Or forever.

Which is how I feel right about now.

Seriously. I need to get out at some point. I've been at Blaire Barnett, aside from a brief foray as a catering waitress at Eat, Drink and Be Married, for my entire adult life. I'm so over agency life. And city life.

Things have to change.

So last night when I was eating overpriced turkey on overpriced bread with overpriced lettuce and drinking an overpriced Snapple, while keeping one eye out for cockroaches, trying to ignore the deafening crashes from 10J and watching the ten o'clock news with its usual urban murder and mayhem, I came up with a plan. A good one.

Nope, pregnancy isn't my proposed ticket out this time. This new plan doesn't involve nearly as much physical pain. Or sex.

Unless, of course, I need to use my wiles to bribe Jack.

Just kidding. I don't really do that.

Much.

"So, look, I think we should start thinking about moving," I tell my husband, officially launching Operation Fresh Start. "We said we were going to do it someday, and we've got the down payment."

Thanks to his dad, who surprised us with a pretty big chunk of change for our wedding gift. I say surprised because even though he was filthy rich, he also was never the most generous guy in the world, and like I said before, he and Jack weren't on the best terms.

But he had mellowed a little over the years, and he did give us money to use toward a house. Jack—who, as a media planner, is proficient with handling large sums, though it's usually the Client's tens of millions and not our own tens of thousands—decided to invest it in a CD until we need it. That sounded like a good idea to me, and Jack and I have always been on the same page about our household finances.

Unlike my parents, who have always argued over money—not that they've ever had any.

Also unlike Kate and Billy, who have also always argued over money—not that they've ever had any shortage of it, as bona fide blue bloods.

Anyway, Jack might be getting an inheritance, too, once his father's will is sorted out. Jack Candell Senior had remarried a few months before he died, and his new wife is contesting his will, which left everything to his kids. She says he made a new one leaving—surprise!—everything to her. Only there seems to be some discrepancy about that.

Even without a cut of his father's fortune, though, Jack and I can probably afford a decent house in the suburbs.

"So," I say to Jack, "we've got the down payment, and I think we should start thinking about a move. Out of the city."

Jack looks at me, shifts his weight in his chair. "I don't know."

Okay, the thing is...I didn't ask him a question, so why is he answering one?

"You don't know...what?" I ask. "What don't you know?"

"Just...why do you want to leave the city?"

"I'm sick of it. It's crowded and noisy and expensive and stressful and dangerous and it smells and we're surrounded by strangers, some of whom are circus freaks and pickpockets and perverts. I can't take it anymore. I want to live in a small town."

"You grew up in a small town."

"I know, but—"

"You left your small town the second you were out of college and moved five hundred miles to New York because you didn't *want* to live in a small town. Remember?"

Of course I do, but he doesn't. I didn't even meet him until I'd been in New York a few years. I hate when he uses my past against me like this.

Okay, he's never really done it before. But he's doing it now, and I think I hate it.

"So are you saying you want to go back?" he asks.

"To Brookside? God, no!"

"Good. Because I don't think I can live there. Nothing against your family."

"I *know* I can't live there. Everything against my family."

Don't get me wrong—I love my family. Do the Spadolinis have their little quirks and oddities? Absolutely. Like, as much as they resent stereotypes about Sicilians and organized crime, they do have a hush-hush sausage connection (my family pronounces it zau-zage, and I've never been sure why).

What the heck is a sausage connection, you may ask? Or you may know already, though unless you're Spadolini *compare,* I doubt it.

See, my brother Danny knows this guy, Lou, who furtively sells homemade zau-zage out of the trunk of his car and let me tell you, it's the best damn zau-zage you'll ever taste, see?

It's even better than Uncle Cosmo's homemade zau-zage, which has too much fennel in it, see. When one of my nephews once told him that, he inadvertently started what is now referred to in Spadolini lore as the Great Zau-Zage Wars of Aught-Six.

So, yeah. We have our quirks and oddities, just like any other family.

Well, Jack's family doesn't exactly have quirks and oddities, per se. The Candells may have an organic-produce connection, but their (probably organic) family tree is barren of colorful relatives like Snooky and Fat Naso and Uncle Cosmo of the Homemade Zau-zage and Spastic Colon—who will tell you, usually over a nice zau-zage sandwich, that one has nothing to do with the other, but I'm not so sure.

Oh, and the Candells don't discuss bowel function—or malfunction—around the Sunday-dinner table, either. In fact, they rarely even gather around the dinner table on Sundays or any other non holidays in the first place. When they do, it's usually for takeout. Usually chicken. Not KFC, though. The Candells don't go for battered, deep-fried food.

My family would batter and fry lettuce—iceburg, of course. They privately refer to the Candells as a bunch of health nuts, and they don't mean that as a compliment. When my brother Frankie Junior found out at our wedding that Jack's sister Rachel is a vegan, he practically shook her by the shoulders and screamed, "What the hell's the matter with you? For the love of God, eat a cheeseburger, woman!"

So, while I do love my family, I do not want to live anywhere near them or, for that matter, in the bleak and notorious blizzard belt of southwestern New York State.

You've probably heard about the prairie blizzards of yore, and the historic Buffalo blizzards fifty miles north of my hometown. Let me tell you, that doesn't compare to what we get in Brookside every year once the Lake-effect snow machine kicks into gear—and it lasts for months on end. Our Columbus Day and Memorial Day family picnics have both been snowed out more than once.

A few Christmases ago, my brother Joey parked his van on my parents' side yard and when Lake-effect snow started falling, it quickly became mired. He had to leave it there overnight. Well, the snow kept falling, foot after foot after foot, and by the next afternoon, the van was completely buried. I'm talking *buried*—no one knew the exact spot where he had parked it, so it couldn't even be dug out. Joey had to rent a car until well after Martin Luther King Day, when the roof emerged after a fleeting thaw.

So, long story that could go on and on—no, I don't want to live in Brookside.

But I don't want to live in Manhattan, either.

"I want to live someplace where the sun shines and we can have a house, and a garden—" I see Jack cast a dubious glance at the barely alive philodendron on the windowsill "—and trees," I go on, "and a driveway—"

"We don't have a car."

"We'll get one. Wouldn't it be great to have a car, Jack? We'd be so free." It's funny how basic things you took for granted most of your life—like cars, or greenery, or walls, ceilings, and floors without strangers lurking on the other side—can seem luxurious when you haven't had them for a while.

"I don't know," Jack says again.

"Come on, Jack."

"But...*I get allergic smelling hay!*" he quips in his best Zsa Zsa Gabor as Lisa Douglas imitation, which, I have to say, isn't all that great.

"There's no hay. I'm not talking about the country. Just the suburbs. It's time for a change."

"I'm not crazy about change."

"Change is good, Jack."

"Not all change."

"Well, whatever, change is inevitable. We might as well embrace it, right?"

Jack doesn't seem particularly eager to embrace it—or me, for that matter. He's starting to look pissed off. He aims the remote at the CD player and raises the volume a little.

"I just feel like we're stagnating here," I tell him, above Alicia Keys's soulful singing. "We can't go on like this. We need a change. I desperately need a change, Jack."

I should probably drop the subject.

But I've never been very good at that—not one of my more lovable qualities, but I can't seem to help myself.

"I really think we're missing out on a lot, living here," I tell Jack.

"Missing out? How can you say that? This is the greatest city in the world. It's filled with great restaurants and museums, and there's Broadway, and—"

"When was the last time we took advantage of any of it?"

"I took advantage of it just last night," he points out, and immediately has the grace to look apologetic and add, "It wasn't that much fun without you."

"Well, I feel like all we ever do is go to work and come home, and on the weekends, we scrounge around for quarters and hope we can find an empty washer in the laundry room. Wouldn't it be great to have our own washer? We could leave stuff in it if we didn't feel like taking it out the second it stops. We wouldn't have to worry about strangers coming along and touching our wet underwear."

"I don't worry about that."

"Well, I do," I say, shuddering at the memory of walking in on the creepy guy from 9C fondling my Hanes Her Way. "Seriously, Jack. I want a washer. In a laundry room. In a house…"

"That Jack built."

"No! You don't have to build it," I assure him, and he laughs.

"No, it's Mother Goose," he says, and I'm relieved that he seems a lot less pissed off. "Didn't you ever hear that nursery rhyme? This is the cat that killed the rat that lived in the house that Jack built. Or something like that."

"There are rats," I say darkly. "They're living in the alley behind this building. I saw one the other day when I took stuff down to the Dumpster."

"There are rats all over the city."

"Exactly! And now there's a bad roach problem in the building."

"How do you know that?"

"Gecko told me. He also told me the Mad Crapper has struck again." I fill him in.

"Nice." Jack rolls his eyes.

"Why do we live here, Jack? Let's move."

Oh my God! He's tilting his head! He only does that when he's seriously contemplating something!

Then he straightens his head and says, "This isn't the greatest time to invest in real estate."

"Sure it is!" I don't care, the initial head-tilt gave me hope, and I'm clinging to it. "This is a great time! We've paid down our credit cards, we don't have kids yet, we're both making good money in stable jobs…"

Mental Note: save part II of Operation Fresh Start—in which we quit our jobs, or at least I do—for a later discussion.

"I don't mean it's not a great time in our personal lives," he clarifies. "I mean it's not a great time in the country's general economical climate."

"Oh, come on, Jack. It's not like there are soup-kitchen lines around the block. The economical climate is fine," I assure him, while wondering, *um, is it?*

"Anyway," I add quickly, lest Jack point out that lately my current-events reading has mostly been limited to page-six blind items, "real estate is the most solid investment you can make."

"Not necessarily."

"So you're saying you don't think we should buy a house somewhere?"

"No, I'm not saying that."

"Then what are you saying?" I ask in a bordering-on-shrill voice I hate.

But I swear, sometimes Jack's utter calm makes my voice just go there in response. I can't help it. It's like the lower-key he is, the shriller I become.

He shrugs. "I don't think we should jump into anything."

"We've waited over two years!" Shrill, shrill. Yikes. I try to tone it down a little as I ask, "How is that jumping in? The least we can do is start looking at real-estate ads."

"That's fine," he says with a shrug. "Go ahead and start looking."

I promptly reach into the catchall basket on the floor by the chair, which is overflowing with magazines I never have time to read anymore.

Pulling out the *New York Times* real-estate section—which I pored over while he was still in bed earlier—I thrust it at him.

"What's this?"

"The listings. For Westchester."

"Westchester?" He frowns. "We never said we were moving to Westchester."

"Back when we got married, we said we'd look in Westchester."

"Did we? I don't remember."

I frown.

"What? It was a long time ago," he says with a shrug.

"Well, then, to refresh your memory...we decided Manhattan is too expensive, the boroughs are also expensive and if we're going to pay that much we might as well live in Manhattan—"

"Which we can't afford," Jack observes.

"Right. And Long Island is too inconvenient because we'd have to go through the city to get anywhere else, and the commute from Jersey can be a pain, Rockland is too far away, Connecticut is Red Sox territory..."

Kiss of death for Jack, the die-hard Yankees fan. I am nothing if not thorough and strategic.

"So," I wind down, "by process of elimination, it's Westchester if we're going to live in the New York suburbs at all."

"You've got it all figured out, don't you?"

"Yup." Pleased with myself, I watch him scan the page of listings.

Westchester County, directly north of the city, is an upscale, leafy suburban wonderland. It just so happens that Jack grew up there. His mother still lives there, as do two of his four sisters.

"Won't it be nice to live near your mom?" I ask Jack. "This way, you wouldn't have to run up there every time she needs something. You'll be close enough to go running over there all the time."

To some sons, that might sound like a threat. But Jack adores his mother. They're really close. And as mothers-in-law go, Wilma Candell is the best.

"And when we have kids," I add for good measure as he scans the newspaper page without comment, "your mom can spend a lot of time with them."

"I thought we weren't talking about starting a family yet."

"We aren't. We're talking about finding the house where we're going to eventually raise our family when we start one."

Jack barely gives the paper another cursory glance before handing it back to me. "Okay, well…good."

"Good…what?"

"This is good. There are houses in our price range, so if we decide to look up there at some point, at least we'll have something to look at."

We have a price range? And these houses are in it?

Hallelujah.

"But we have to strike while the iron is hot," I tell him, and add for good measure, "You know, we can't let the grass grow under our feet."

"Slow and steady wins the race," Jack returns with a grin.

"Maybe," I say, slipping from the arm of his chair onto his lap, "but a rolling stone gathers no moss."

What does that even mean? I don't know. But it sounds motivational.

I guess not to Jack, though.

"We'll look someday," he says, pushing a clump of my hair out of my eyes, "when we're ready."

"I'm ready."

"For family starting?" he asks, and I laugh and shake my head.

"No family starting yet," I tell him.

Jack reaches for the remote, aims it at the CD player and presses a couple of buttons. Alicia Keys gives way to U2's "With or Without You."

Which happens to be a major aphrodisiac—at least for me.

Go ahead, try it—listen to that song and see if it doesn't instantly put you in the mood.

The opening bass is enough to do it for me, every time—and Jack knows it.

"How about a dry run on the family-starting thing, so to speak?"

I loop my arms around his neck. "I'm game...if you're game for a dry run on the house-hunting circuit next weekend."

Jack tilts his head.

I kiss his neck.

Bono sings.

We are so there.

3

"Let's take a drive through the village first, shall we?" asks Verna Treeby, slipping behind the wheel of her silver Mercedes.

Yes, we shall, because Verna Treeby of Houlihan Lawrence Real Estate is calling all the shots today here in suburbia on this cold, gray Sunday.

Jack settles himself into the backseat, and I climb into the front. I was thinking maybe he'd be the one to sit up here, but he made such an immediate beeline for the back that I'd swear someone must have said they're giving away cold Heinekens and Fritos back there.

Alas, the air has that leathery new-car smell mingling with Verna's designer perfume; nary a hint of Fritos.

"And we're off," Verna says cheerfully, pulling out of the

real-estate office parking lot and onto Main Street in Glenhaven Park.

I cast a quick glance over my shoulder to make sure Jack is paying attention.

He's looking out the window, as he should be. So far, so good. Unless he's staring off into space, wondering why he's here.

Frankly, there might be a teensy chance of that.

Because even though we agreed last Sunday to spend this Sunday looking at houses, I'm thinking he's either been in weeklong denial, or had no intention of honoring his promise to me.

The biggest indicator: when Mitch asked us last night—while the three of us were walking home from a late movie—if we wanted to hang out today and watch the basketball playoffs, and Jack said yes.

"We can't, we have other plans," I said to both of them, and wound up feeling like the mean mommy who doesn't allow Super Soakers or sweetened cereal.

"What kind of plans?" Mitch asked nosily.

All right, maybe not nosily. Maybe just curiously.

Maybe I'm just pretty damn sick of Mitch and his questions and his hanging out.

Of course Jack hedged, so I was the one who had to break it to Mitch that we're probably moving to the suburbs.

Mitch didn't say much in response. Mostly he just gave

Jack a reproachful look, and me the silent treatment as we covered the remaining half block to his building.

After we left him off, I said to Jack, "I guess he's going to miss us when we move, huh? Or you, anyway."

"Not just me. He loves you, Tracey."

Yeah, yeah, yeah. Mitch loves me. If he loves me, he'll set me free.

"Anyway, it's not like we're moving tomorrow," Jack says, "so…"

That pause seemed ominous to me.

I found myself wondering how he was going to complete that thought.

So Mitch will have plenty of time to get used to the idea?

Or…

So Mitch will have plenty of time to convince our future suburban next-door neighbors to sell their place to him?

I probably should have asked Jack to finish the sentence, but I couldn't bring myself to do it.

Anyway, here we are, embarking on a new adventure as future home owners, and I don't want anything to put a damper on this day because so far, it's going well.

I was pleasantly surprised by Verna, the listing agent on a bunch of houses whose ads caught my eye. Not surprised by the fact that she's sporting a Palm Beach tan in mid-March and has a fresh-from-the-country-club preppy pink sweater, gold jewelry, blond pageboy caught back in a black headband. I was more surprised that she's treating us so well when most of the listing pages taped in the window of Houlihan Lawrence run upward of a million dollars.

But when I called Verna earlier in the week and answered a few questions—including the dreaded "What price range are you looking in?"—she didn't tell me to try the outer reaches of New Jersey. She said, "Sure, come on up!"

The thing is, anywhere else, our price range—half a million bucks, give or take a hundred grand—would buy a mansion. In my hometown on the opposite end of New York State, I don't think houses that expensive even exist. But here in the tristate area, that's the lower end of the housing market, and I'm thinking Jack and I will be lucky if we find something.

Glenhaven Park is the first town we're visiting as we launch our official house hunt here in Westchester County. We chose it—well, I chose it—because Jack and I have driven through it a few times while we were up here visiting his mother, and I think it's charming.

It has always struck me as one of those old-fashioned small-town movie sets. You know: leafy streets lined with sidewalks that attract strolling pedestrians and kids on bikes; flag-flying Victorian houses with blooming gardens; red-brick schools and white church steeples. In the business district, turn-of-the-century storefronts line the brick sidewalks. Running through the center of it all is a grassy commons where cobblestone paths meander among ancient shade trees, lampposts, benches and statues.

Beyond the village proper, some of the surrounding roads are unpaved and lined with crumbling old stone walls. That's where the horse farms and country estates are.

Here in the heart of town, there are plenty of expensive homes, too—as in a million dollars and well on up. But I circled ads for a bunch of houses in our price range, so I'm excited to see what our money can buy.

We could definitely afford a two- or even three-bedroom condo in the complex perched on a hill above the town, but I'm tired of sharing walls, a ceiling or a floor with strangers. I want a regular house, with a basement and an attic. I want a garage and a driveway and a car to park there. I want a dome-topped mailbox on a pole, the kind where you put the red flag up for outgoing mail, and I want a yard with trees and a swing set (eventually) and yes, a septic tank. I want to step out my back door on a hot August afternoon to pick fresh tomatoes and basil for a salad, and cut an armload of bright-colored zinnias to put in a vase on the dinner table, just the way my mother always did on hot August afternoons back in Brookside.

I want my future children to grow up the way I did, and the way Jack did.

Although, my parents' cozy, well-worn house in Brookside is a far cry from the stately six-thousand-square-foot Bedford colonial where Jack was raised. His parents sold it after the divorce.

And while Brookside is a bona fide small town, it's seen

better days, unlike this one. Here, you get the feeling that better and better days just keep on coming.

At least, I get that feeling judging by the lineup of cars parked in the diagonal spots along Main Street: BMWs, Lexuses—even a Ferrari. Every other car is an SUV, with a few Hummers thrown in for good measure.

"I'm sure I don't have to tell you both that Glenhaven Park is very commutable. You took the train up from Manhattan this morning, right?" Verna points at the Metro-North rail station as we pass.

"Actually, we took the train up to my mother-in-law's—she lives nearby—and borrowed her car to drive over here," I tell Verna.

"Oh! So you're familiar with Westchester already, then." She brakes at an intersection, glances into the rearview mirror, maybe at Jack. "Where does your mom live?"

I can't tell whether she's talking to me, or to Jack. Wilma isn't my mom, she's my mother-in-law, as I just mentioned. But maybe Verna misunderstood. Or maybe she's trying to engage Jack in the conversation.

Good luck, Verna.

Jack's been pretty quiet from the moment we woke up this morning, back home in Manhattan.

True, I had set the alarm for an ungodly early hour for a Sunday, and Jack is never exactly chatty before he has his coffee. But he wasn't chatty afterward, either, or during the hour-long ride up the Harlem line on Metro-

North, or at his mother's condo during our short visit with Wilma.

It could be that he's changed his mind about ever moving to the suburbs after all. Or maybe he's just upset that he has to miss watching the March Madness game today.

Knowing Jack, that's probably it. He grumbled about it the whole time he was setting the TiVo this morning to record it.

"My mother-in-law lives in Bedford," I tell Verna when Jack neglects to answer the question, probably too busy wondering how on earth he'll carry on if there's a massive blackout in Manhattan and TiVo fails him.

"Really? So you grew up there? Then for you, this is coming home again." This time, Verna is definitely looking into the backseat via the rearview mirror, talking to Jack.

And this time, Jack replies. "Well, I didn't grow up here in Glenhaven Park, so…not exactly."

"She means Westchester in general," I tell him, wishing he could be more agreeable. "And since Bedford's practically next door to Glenhaven Park—ooh, how cute!" I interrupt myself to say, gazing at a children's boutique called Bug in a Rug.

It's housed in a Victorian building painted in shades of pink and cranberry, with striped awnings. Totally charming. If you have kids.

Or charming even if you don't, because I, for one, am totally charmed.

"Jack, look at that amazing rag doll in the window! Wouldn't Hayley love that for her birthday?"

"It's bigger than she is," he observes.

True. Still…

"I think she'll love it." Hayley is my niece—my brother Danny and his wife Michaela's daughter, back in Brookside. She's turning three in June and is obsessed with dolls.

I turn my head to keep an eye on the shop as we drive past, noting its location. Very cute. Very charming.

Speaking of charming—which is not a word I use often, but I've found myself speaking it, or thinking it, pretty constantly since we arrived in Glenhaven Park: "Ooh! Look at that—is that a bakery?"

"Yes, isn't it charming?" Verna asks, equally well versed in the local vernacular.

"*So* charming. Look, Jack, it's called Pie in the Sky." Perched up on the second floor of a skinny building, the exterior is painted sky blue and the sign is hand-lettered on a fat, white cloud in the plate-glass window. "I love it. Isn't that a great name? It's so fitting!"

"It's almost as fitting—and charming—as Bug in a Rug," he fake rhapsodizes. "Although, unless they're selling bugs or rugs, I really don't see why that—"

"So I take it they make good pie at that bakery?" I ask Verna, cutting off Jack. Usually, I find it amusing when he mock gushes. Not today. I don't want Verna to pick up on it and decide not to sell us a house here.

Okay, okay, maybe I'm being paranoid, but I really want things to go well. I really feel like Glenhaven Park can be my new hometown.

"Oh, absolutely! They make great pie."

"I love pie!"

Not that I ever allow myself to eat much of it these days. But back when I was fat, and depressed, I could have eaten a whole pie by myself in one sitting. It's one of my favorite things in the world.

"If you have time while you're here in town, you really should stop in and pick one up to take back to the city with you," Verna advises. "The prices are so reasonable and the key lime, especially, is scrumptious. They make it only once a year, for Saint Patrick's Day, so they have it this weekend."

Scrumptious, charming and reasonable prices?

What's not to love about Pie in the Sky?

Or Glenhaven Park, for that matter.

Yes, I can so see us living here—Jack and me. Without Dupree. Er, I mean Mitch.

I feel like celebrating. I might even allow myself a piece of pie.

"The first house we're going to look at is right back this way," Verna informs us, turning right around a corner, and then right again.

I'm half expecting the scrumptious and charming streetscape to give way to a pocket of seediness, but so far, so good.

The houses are set a little closer to the street and to each other here, but that's no biggie. Not a derelict or a rat in sight.

"Here we are." Verna glides the Mercedes along the curb.

For a second, I think she's referring to the two-story stucco Tudor with the white wooden trellis arching over the front walk.

Whoa—I love it! I absolutely love it! I can just see—

Oh. Oops. We're still gliding.

When we do come to a stop, it's in front of the house next door to the Tudor.

A house that…isn't half-bad. Seriously. I don't absolutely love it on sight, but…

"It's nice," I tell Verna, mustering some enthusiasm.

"Isn't it?"

Sure it is. Especially if you like small, low ranch houses circa 1971, with vinyl siding in a deep yellowy gold precisely the shade of First Morning Pee.

So this is our price range. It could be worse.

It could also be a whole lot better.

I don't dare look at Jack as Verna leads the way up the walk, maneuvering her shiny black patent-leather loafers carefully around the puddles left over from last night's rain.

"That azalea will be scrumptious in a couple of weeks." She points at the overgrown shrub that obscures most of the living-room picture window.

I nod and murmur something appropriately passionate

about the soon-to-be-scrumptious azalea, while scanning the listing sheet she just handed me.

Built in 1972—what'd I tell you?

It's billed as the Perfect Starter Home, which right off the bat tells you—at least it tells me—that you're probably not going to want to stay long. The nine-hundred-square-foot house has a front entryway, plus an LR, Updated EIK, 2 Brs, 1B, At Gar, FP.

This I have learned by doing my homework this past week, translates to Living Room, Updated Eat-In Kitchen, Two Bedrooms, One Bathroom, an Attached Garage and a Fireplace.

There is also a Level Lot with Mature Plantings, catchphrases I noticed in quite a few ads as I was perusing the papers. I'll admit, I've never given much thought to Level Lots and Mature Plantings, but some people must be into them. And you have to admit, there's not much appeal to a Steep, Rock-strewn Lot or Immature Plantings, which would be…what? Saplings?

I don't know.

I just hope the inside of this place is more promising than the outside, because I'm already not loving it, Perfect Starter Home or not.

Verna unlocks the front door—which is made of yellow-orange wood and has an arched window in the top—and we step inside. There, we find ourselves standing on a rectangular patch of tile patterned to look like flagstone.

This, I assume, would be the front entryway, separated from the carpeted LR by a flat gold metal strip of flooring. It's like we're standing on this ugly little fake stone pier jutting into a turquoise shag sea that smells strongly of cat.

On the upside, there probably aren't any rats in this house.

On the downside: in addition to a strong cat aroma, there are warping sheets of wood paneling, fake brick veneer on the fireplace and those small slatted windows you have to crank open.

The Updated EIK is no better. Avocado-green appliances, green—a different shade of green, like emerald—indoor-outdoor carpeting, sagging dark brown cupboards with black metal pulls. Okay, so…updated when? 1973? And the tiny eat-in alcove, which lacks a table and chairs, is mostly occupied by a plastic step-pedal garbage can and a litter box. I'm not sure which smells worse.

Onward we trudge, encountering a highly pissed-off-looking black cat who doesn't look the least bit pleased to see us.

Bathroom: blue tub, blue sink, blue tile and an even smaller, narrower, crank-open window, which is located just at boobs level in the wall above the tub. No curtains, shade or blinds. The lovely Tudor next door has a prime peep-show view. Nice.

Bedrooms: small rectangles, pretty much the same size, though the master is distinguished by a shallow double closet with pressboard slider doors that aren't quite operating on the track. In fact, one is swinging free from the top track and nearly knocks me unconscious when I go to open it.

Garage: oil stains on the only patch of floor visible amid heaps of things like broken-down lawn furniture and rusted yard tools. It smells of spilled gasoline. Heavy scampering overhead alerts us that something—maybe another cat, maybe God-only-knows-what, a raccoon? A bear cub?—is living in the rafters.

As we go back through the house, Verna keeps pointing out all the potential. I honestly do keep trying to see the place without the home-owner clutter, the god-awful furniture, the cheap, shiny drapes, the litter box, and oh, yes, not one but two pissed-off black cats who watch us warily and stealthily follow us from room to room.

Finally, as we return to the living room, I look over my shoulder at Jack and raise my eyebrows, as if to ask, *Well? What do you think?*

Jack shakes his head slightly at me, as if to say, *I'd rather endure all eternity amid the rats and roaches, beneath the circus-freak family, with the Mad Crapper creeping ever nearer to our doorstep.*

I nod in complete agreement as Verna leads us out the front door, pointing out the additional potential in the concrete slab, which she generously refers to as a "porch."

The whole experience is somewhat depressing, and the fact that it's starting to drizzle outside doesn't help. I give the house one last glance as we drive away. I mean, I'm sure there could be potential here somewhere.

Maybe some savvy buyer could knock the place down and start fresh amid the Mature Plantings. But that savvy buyer is not going to be us.

"It's not quite what we're looking for," is how I phrase it to Verna, who wants to know what we thought.

"Mmm, hmm. Well, it *was* on the small side," she says.

I nod vigorously, as if small is the deal breaker.

What I want to say is, "Got anything that doesn't reek of cat pee?"

But who knows? Maybe cat pee is all we can afford in Glenhaven Park.

Nope.

We learned on our next stop that we can also afford a partially gutted wreck whose owner started a massive renovation and then either ran out of money, or was run out of town on a rail—something like that. Verna kind of mumbled the details, which involved running. Maybe from the cops, or a gun-toting ex-wife.

Anyway...the gutted wreck is out of the question, affordable or not.

We then find out that we can also afford a flooded basement. The two-story Victorian on a nice block is actually promising until we start to descend the subterranean stairs. There must be at least two feet of standing water there.

Verna, ever the optimist, begins, "You can always pump it out..." Then she catches sight of our expressions. "You're right. You don't want this place. Let's move on."

House number four, another seventies ranch, is empty, so we don't have to try to envision it without furniture or home-owner clutter. But there's a definite pall hanging over it from the moment we cross the threshold.

"The seller is very motivated. The owner passed away suddenly last summer..." Verna pauses to close the door behind us and fumble for the light switch.

Jack and I exchange a glance, wondering just how motivated a dead guy can possibly be.

"Anyway," Verna goes on, "his nephew, who inherited the house—" Aha, lightbulb moment. So the seller is the nephew, who is apparently very much alive, living on the West Coast and hoping to unload it. According to Verna, "I'm sure he'll entertain any offer you might want to make."

The house is your basic seventies ranch, no frills, but no cat smell or piss-yellow siding, either. White paint inside and out, hardwood floors, rectangular rooms. There are three bedrooms and two baths, as well as a nice screened-in patio off the back, and a deep lot with trees, which I guess don't qualify as Mature Plantings? Or do they? I'm still not entirely down with this real-estate jargon.

"What do you think?" Verna asks as usual, when we finish our tour.

It's all very basic, very okay, very affordable.

But like I said, there's just this...pall. That's the best way to describe it.

I'd be willing to bet the dead guy died right here in the house. Who knows? Maybe he's still hanging around.

"I don't know…it's a little dark," I tell Verna.

"Picture it on a sunny day, without the vinyl blinds. It would be so much more—"

"No, Tracey's talking about the way it feels, not the way it looks," Jack cuts in. "Dark as in sad and depressing."

So he gets it, too. I shoot him a surprised and grateful look. Good to know we're in sync—and that houses really do have personalities.

Heaven only knows house number five does. Meet the plain girl who's nice enough but just tries too hard to be liked.

Architecturally, it's what you draw with crayons on manila paper when you're in first grade: a simple rectangle with a triangle sitting on top of it. First floor: door centered between two windows, second floor: three windows, each placed directly above a window or door on the first floor.

Most people would drive by and never give it a second glance if it didn't self-consciously scream, *Hey, look at me! Here I am!*

The outside is painted in an elaborate scheme of greens with tan trim—on what little trim there is, anyway. There's a wooden shingle by the door—the kind you see on old sea captains' homes in New England. You know: **Josiah Whalen House, Circa 1691**.

This one reads—in that same antiquated font: **Bob and Bev Stubiniak House, Built 1986**.

"What do you think?" asks Verna as we walk through the living room, dining room, kitchen, three bedrooms and one and a half baths. "Can you see yourselves living here?"

Frankly, I can't even see Bob and Bev Stubiniak living here. Not only are they not home at the moment, but judging by their shelves, wall calendar and closets, they appear to be people who don't read, don't have a social life, and don't have clothing, and are passionate about neutral shades.

Curiously, however, the house smells like someone just finished baking cookies. Potpourri is bubbling away on the stove and scented candles flicker on the tables. The stereo is on and tuned to a classical-music station.

Clearly, Bob and Bev read every book in print on selling your house and staged their home accordingly.

"It's just not for us," I tell Verna as Jack looks at his watch and wonders about the basketball tournament and what's for supper. Trust me, I can read his mind.

"Can we see the last house?" I ask Verna. "And then I think we'll call it a day."

"Absolutely." She too looks at her watch, wondering whether she can squeeze another pair of house-hunting young marrieds—with a higher price range and a more enthusiastic husband—into her day.

No, I can't read her mind, but her agenda is obvious, and can you blame her?

As she drives us toward house number six, I look over the listing sheet.

Four bedrooms, two full baths, rocking-chair porch, half-acre lot. Built in the 1920s, a Sears Catalog House.

"What's that?" I ask Verna. "Sears Catalog House?"

"Just what it sounds like."

I haven't got a clue what it sounds like, other than…

"Uh…it came from a Sears catalog?" I ask dubiously.

To my astonishment, she nods.

Granted, I haven't spent much time with a Sears catalog since I wrote my last Christmas letter to Santa when I was eight. Back then, I pretty much circled everything Barbie, tore the pages from the catalog and stuffed them into an envelope addressed to the North Pole.

In my adult life, the only thing I have ever personally bought from a Sears catalog—which I borrowed from my grandmother—is a Crock-Pot. Never a house.

I suppose I might have missed something, but I don't remember seeing four-bedroom homes for sale between the Craftsman tools and the Kenmore vacuums.

Must have been a Roaring Twenties thing: get your coonskin coat, flapper dress, gramophone and four-bedroom house all in the same place.

"Back in the day," Verna says, "you could mail-order a kit to build a house."

Back in the day—not the Jazz Age, but a while back—you could also order a Barbie Dream House from Sears. I remember my father cursing and putting mine together on a snowy December morn.

Picturing a plastic grid with pop-out pieces and pages of inscrutable instructions, I have to ask, "Are you sure we should bother looking at this one?"

I'm talking to Jack, but it's Verna who answers, "It's a little outdated, but I really think it has potential."

Which is the equivalent of saying the wallflower has a nice personality.

I'm about to tell her to forget it when Jack says, "I'd like to see it. My grandma Candell lived in a Sears house in Mamaroneck when I was a kid."

Grandma Candell was not a huge presence in my husband's life, as she got along with her grown son, Jack Senior, about as well as Jack Senior got along with Jack Junior. Yet in a way, she's responsible for our dream wedding: we were able to afford the Shorewood reception only because Jack sold the shares of Disney stock his grandmother had given him for his birthday as a little kid.

I remember feeling sorry for him when I heard that, thinking it would be a blazing hot, sunny January day in Brookside before my grandmothers ever gave me stock certificates for my birthday. They believed in candy and toys and hand-crocheted capes that you were embarrassed to wear to school because when was the last time a cape was in fashion, for God's sake, but your mother made you wear it anyway because of course Grandma made the cape out of love and you didn't want to hurt her feelings.

Anyway, if it weren't for Grandma Candell and her cold

hard stock-certificate birthday gift, Jack and I would have danced our first dance as a married couple at the church hall's basketball-court-slash-dance-floor where I once threw up after too much zau-zage and birch beer at a CYO mixer, instead of in a beautiful ballroom with a view of the shimmering October sunset on the lake.

And if it weren't for Grandma Candell and her Sears Catalog House in Mamaroneck, Jack and I wouldn't have come to see this Sears Catalog House in Glenhaven Park.

This is it.

This is the house for us.

I know it, from the moment we pull up in front.

For the first time ever, I wonder what Jack's grandma Candell's first name was.

I really hope that it's something quaint and sweetly old-fashioned like Daisy or Lily, because we most certainly will be naming our daughter after her someday.

But that's a different story.

Let's get on with this one, shall we?

4

First of all, the house has definite curb appeal.

White with black shutters, window boxes, a redbrick chimney. There's a porch on the side with a low forward-sloping roof held up by fat square pillars. No rocking chairs, but I can easily picture them there.

I can easily picture *us* there.

I can easily picture us lounging in the living room with the Sunday papers, or entertaining our family in the dining room with its built-in corner china cupboard, or tucking in our children in the two upstairs bedrooms beneath the gabled roofline.

You know how the dead guy's house had a pall?

This place has the opposite aura. There's a well-loved, happy feeling about it, and no wonder.

Verna tells us, "The current owners, Hank and Marge—" Hank and Marge. Don't you love it? Talk about sweetly old-fashioned! "—have lived here since they were married in 1950."

"Nineteen-fifty?" I echo as I open and close the doors of the shallow cupboards on either side of the brick fireplace in the living room. The shelves are lined with dozens and dozens of paperback romance novels.

"Yes, and they raised their six sons here. Now Hank is sick with emphysema, and they just can't take care of the house anymore. So they're moving to a condo to be near their daughter and son-in-law up in Duchess County."

For a moment, I'm struck with a bittersweet pang as I imagine Jack and me, married almost sixty years, him with emphysema, unable to care for our house, me plowing through stacks of romance novels, and us having to move to a condo in Duchess County with our as-yet-unborn daughter Daisy or Lily and our son-in-law.

Or maybe I'll be the one with emphysema. I used to be a smoker. The older I get, the more difficult it is to believe that I went all those years puffing away without worrying the least bit about the deadly damage I was doing to my body.

Or maybe I did worry, somewhere in the back of my mind, but not enough to quit. What an idiot.

Now all I want, desperately, is to live to a ripe old age with my husband.

Oh, and the other thing I want, just as desperately? This Sears Catalog House.

Don't get me wrong—there are some drawbacks.

The house reeks of stale cigarette smoke, and is filled with wallpaper, brown paneling and wall-to-wall carpeting in shades of brown and green.

The kitchen is tiny and outdated—yet I can see past the ancient appliances, worn orange-brown linoleum, harvest-gold laminate countertops, and tan and brown-flecked wall-paper that's bubbling a little behind the sink and grease stained above the stove.

There's no master bedroom—the two downstairs are tiny, and the two upstairs, while bigger, have such low slanted ceilings that Jack bumps his head twice. But who's to say we can't knock down a wall or two and/or raise the roof?

Well, okay, Jack's to say.

Because when I mention doing just that, he says, "What? We can't go around knocking down walls and raising roofs!"

First of all, there's only one roof, and second of all, I'm not suggesting that we go around knocking down walls, as in door-to-door with a sledgehammer. Just one or two walls, right here in our own home.

I mean, future home.

"Sure we can," I tell Jack. "We can reconfigure the first-floor bedrooms, or put cathedral ceilings in upstairs so that you won't give yourself a concussion every time you get out of bed in the morning."

"How are we going to do this work?" he asks succinctly.

"You're pretty handy," I say.

He raises an eyebrow, undoubtedly noting he's not the least bit handy.

Which is exactly what I'm thinking.

But there are times when flattery can get you everywhere. Or at least, to Glenhaven Park.

Then again, Jack doesn't look flattered. He looks confused. And a little annoyed.

"I think the downstairs bedrooms could be opened up to make a scrumptious master suite," opines Verna. "And with this spacious backyard, there's plenty of room for a nice deck off the kitchen."

Ooh, great idea. A nice deck off the kitchen to go with the rocking-chair porch off the living room. I gaze out the window and envision myself lounging there with the romance novels I'm going to be reading when I move here.

And there in the spacious backyard, nibbling the low-hanging budding branch of a Mature Planting, are a graceful doe and her spindly-legged fawn.

"Jack, look!" I spaz out, clutching his arm. "Deer! There are deer out there!"

Wow. This is so perfect. Too perfect. Next thing you know, a whistling cartoon bluebird will land on a bough.

If I didn't know better, I'd think Verna had hired the woodland creatures and staged the whole bucolic scene.

Wait, did she? Because she's following my gaze out the window wearing an iffy expression. For all I know, there's a guy out there crouching in the azaleas with a clipboard and a headset saying, "All right, Ed, cue the fairies and sprites."

"There are a lot of deer in Westchester," Verna says almost apologetically.

"This is so amazing. I mean, to be surrounded by nature instead of concrete…it's just so incredible."

"Yes, we love our deer here in Westchester!" she gushes right back at me, so I must have been imagining the apologetic tone. Of course I was, because why would she be apologetic over Bambi and friends?

"We have to live here," I say, partly to Jack, but mostly to Verna, who is, after all, the fairy godrealtor who can make it happen.

"So you're interested, then?"

"We're interested." Belatedly, I add, "Right, Jack?"

"What was the asking price again?"

Verna tells him.

He nods thoughtfully, rubbing the spot where his beard would be if he were able to grow one. "Well, we've just started looking, so we're not going to jump on anything, but when the time comes, I think this is what we have in mind."

"When the time comes? Jack, the time is *now*."

"Tracey—" he sounds kind of stressed and casts an eye

toward Verna, as if to say *let's not talk about this in front of her* "—we don't even know that we can afford—"

"Yes, we do. I preauthorized us for a mortgage, and—"

"What? Where? When?"

"Who? How?" I quip.

Jack is not amused.

"At the bank," I tell him, sticking with the original questions, "the other day during my lunch hour. And believe me, it wasn't easy getting out of the office to do it."

"Why didn't you tell me?"

Why *didn't* I tell him?

The truth is, I'm not sure.

Maybe I was afraid I'd be forced to admit to Jack that we wouldn't qualify for as much house as we need.

Maybe I was afraid that talking to the bank would make it seem too real to Jack, and he'd be scared away.

Or maybe I'm a control freak and like to handle the details on my own, because if I wait for Jack, things tend not to get done.

But I don't want to say any of that.

So I shrug and tell him, "Because I've barely seen you all week, between your work schedule and mine. I didn't think it was worth waking you in the middle of the night to tell you, and I was going to tell you yesterday, but Mitch was around." To Verna, who can't help but listen in, I add, "Mitch is Jack's best friend."

"Best friend?" Jack rolls his eyes. "That makes us sound like eleven-year-old girls."

"Sorry," I say, and amend it to, "Mitch is Jack's sidekick."

To which Jack mutters, "What are we, superheroes?"

"No, but he's definitely your sidekick."

"I thought you were my sidekick."

"I'm your *wife.*"

"Oh! So *that's* why you keep turning up," he says teasingly, "day after day, night after night, in good times and in bad..."

"No, that would be Mitch," I shoot back. "I'm the one who's rarely home. He's the one who's always there. But I guess he won't be if we move up here, will he?"

"We're moving up here to get away from Mitch?"

"No!" Not just Mitch. The rats and the roaches and the circus freaks and the Mad Crapper, too.

Especially the Mad Crapper.

And Mitch.

"We're not moving up here to run away from anything, really," I tell Jack. "It's not that. It's more that we're running to something. The next phase of life. A home, neighbors, parenthood..."

"You want to have a baby?"

"Not now!" I tell him, exasperated. "Someday. Yes. When we're settled. When it's right. I think we'll just wake up someday and know it's time for that. Just like we realized it's time right now for this."

Verna—who remains silent—removes her cell phone from the pocket of her cute Kelly-green kilt-type skirt, which I can't help but think might look slightly ridiculous on anyone other than Verna, a bagpiper or a JV cheerleader.

She flips her cell phone open and checks it—or at least pretends to. Then, looking up at me and Jack, she says, "I have to return a call. I'll step outside for a few minutes if you don't mind."

We assure her that we don't mind, but I personally doubt there's a call to return. My guess is that Verna smells a commission and wants to leave us to discuss delicate financial matters in private.

The minute the door has closed behind her and we're alone, I say to Jack, "We have to get this house. I love it. Don't you?"

"It's a nice house," he admits. "But I wasn't thinking we were going to come up here today and snatch up the first house we look at."

"This isn't the first house we looked at."

"All right, the fourth."

"It's the sixth."

"Who buys the sixth house they look at?"

"Who walks away from the sixth house they look at even though it's perfect just because they feel like they should look at a hundred more?"

"I didn't say we should look at a hundred more, and it's not all that perfect, Tracey."

"No, I know. It needs work..."

"And being pretty handy, I guess I'm the one who's going to do this work?" he asks dryly.

"Look, I know you stink at handyman stuff, but—"

"I stink?" he interjects, looking wounded.

"Only when you Dutch Oven my head," I crack.

Jack is not amused.

"Come on, Jack, you know I was talking about handyman stuff."

"I wouldn't say I *stink* at it. I just haven't had much practice."

Pssst. Trust me. El Stinko. Do you know how long it took him to put together a cardboard CD cabinet he bought at Wal-Mart?

"Well," I tell him brightly, "just think—if we buy this house you'll get plenty of practice."

"I don't think I should practice on an actual house, Tracey. Shouldn't I start small? Like maybe a birdhouse?"

"Stop kidding around, Jack. I'm dead serious here."

"I'm serious, too. I have no idea how to knock down a wall. Or build a bookshelf, for that matter."

"How hard can it be to knock down a wall?" I mean, seriously, don't you just get a sledgehammer and start swinging? "Anyway, we can hire someone."

"What, did you preauthorize us for a handyman, too?"

"Jack, stop fooling around."

"I'm sorry. It's just that I don't want you to set your heart on this place and get your hopes up, and then be disappointed."

"Why do I have to be disappointed? It's not like the house isn't for sale…it's listed. And it's not like we can't afford it, because we can. All we have to do is pay the asking price, and it's ours!"

"You make it sound so simple."

"It *is* simple. You make it sound like I'm trying to sprout fairy wings and fly."

"That, I'd love to see." He pauses to smile, then the smile fades and he says, "I've barely had time to get used to the idea of moving, and all of a sudden here we are, looking at houses."

"If I waited for you to want to move, some other couple will already have celebrated their golden anniversary in this house."

Note that he doesn't argue with me there.

"Jack, the thing is, I know how you are. You *hate* change."

Note that he doesn't argue with me there, either.

"And you know how I am. I love change. I thrive on it. I *crave* it, Jack."

He sighs.

"I think we should make an offer for the house," I say firmly. "We'll just offer the asking price and see what happens."

"Nobody offers the asking price."

"Sure they do."

"Who does?"

"People who want to make sure they get the house," I explain with exaggerated patience. "Which we do. Don't we?"

"Regardless of whether we want it, Tracey, the owner sets

the price higher than he expects to get so that there's room for bargaining. Trust me. I deal with this on a daily basis."

"What are you talking about? You've never bought a house in your life."

"No, but I'm in media, remember? I decide how clients should spend millions of dollars."

Oh. True. Too bad we don't have millions of those dollars at our own disposal. Then we could write out a check on the spot and hire someone else to knock down walls to our heart's content.

Or even buy some other house, one that's in perfect condition, so that knocking down walls isn't even necessary.

But you know what?

Even if we had more money, I don't think I'd want another house.

This one has character, and it's a happy house. You can't put a price on that.

"Let's go through the house again," I tell Jack. "One more time. Okay?"

"Okay."

So we do. And this time, I fall even more in love with the place, quirks and all. I love the uneven floorboards in the hall outside the downstairs bathroom, the painted bedroom doors with china knobs, the high ceilings, the baseboards and crown moldings.

Back in the kitchen, I lace my fingers through Jack's and lean my head on his shoulder. "Well?"

"It is a pretty great old house. It reminds me a lot of my grandmother's house."

"Then let's make an offer, Jack. Please? You decide how much…as long as you don't lowball it."

"I don't know…"

"Jack, someday we can be old and gray here together, watching the deer frolic outside the window. Don't you want that?"

"Old and gray?" he asks dubiously. "Not particularly. And the deer aren't exactly frolicking, and anyway, about the deer—"

In the next room, the door opens again. Verna's back.

Jack whispers to me, "Listen, we'll talk about this later. Don't let on to her that we're interested."

"She already knows," I whisper back. "So shouldn't we just—"

"No, we shouldn't."

"Sorry about that." Verna appears in the doorway, tucking her phone back into her pocket. "So, what do you think?"

"Thanks so much for your time," Jack says smoothly. "We definitely got a good sense of what's available here in our price range."

Is it just me, or is he making it sound as if our work here is done?

Verna doesn't seem surprised, or all that disappointed as she says, "Okay, then, let's head back to the office. Or can I show you something else?"

"No, I think we're all set," Jack says, like a restaurant patron turning down a dessert menu.

I give the house one last longing look from the front seat of Verna's car as we drive away.

I really hope Jack knows what he's doing.

Back at the office, Verna gives us her business card and tells us to be in touch. We tell her that we will, and go our separate ways.

I wait until we're back in Jack's mother's car and pulling out onto the street to ask, "So are we going to make an offer, or aren't we?"

"We have to talk about it."

"I know. So let's talk. Oh, but," I add, remembering, "first we have to stop off and get the pie, so look for a parking spot down there."

"The pie?"

How can he be so clueless?

"The key lime pie from that bakery. Remember?"

"Oh, right." He still sounds clueless. "Okay."

We drive along looking for a parking space.

There aren't any, but we do pass quite a few cars with turn signals flashing, pulled alongside occupied spots that have drivers loading in bags or just getting behind the wheel.

I wonder if one of the stores is having a big sale today, or something, because it seems pretty busy.

"No spots," Jack says as we arrive at the end of the main drag.

"There have to be spots."

"Did you see any?"

"No. Go around the block and try again," I tell him.

He does. More of the same.

"There must be something going on down here today," I tell him.

"Like what?"

"I don't know…some kind of festival, or something."

"A festival?" he echoes dubiously, and looks around. "I don't see a festival."

"Maybe it's an indoor festival. Go around one more time."

"You like key lime pie that much?"

"Yes."

No. But for some reason, I really want that pie.

"Why don't we get it next time we're here?" he asks, checking the dashboard clock.

"You mean, when we come back up tomorrow to make our offer? Because they only make key lime at this time of year, for Saint Patrick's Day. If we're not coming back tomorrow, we should get a pie now."

He just sighs and shakes his head. "Trace, by the time we find a place to park, get the pie, get back to my mother's and then catch a train to Manhattan, it's going to be late enough as it is."

"Fine. We'll just miss out on the pie. Kind of like the house."

He sighs again.

"Come on, Jack. If we can't buy the house, can we at least buy the pie?"

"I didn't say we couldn't buy the house."

"We're going to make an offer?" I ask him.

"We really qualified for that much mortgage?" he asks me in return.

"We really did, between our two salaries and our savings, without even taking your future inheritance into consideration."

"Possible future inheritance," he cautions. "Let's talk about this back at home, where we can concentrate. Okay?"

"Okay. Forget the pie then. Let's just get home."

"Are you sure?"

"Positive."

Jack nods thoughtfully, eyes focused on the street beyond the rain-spattered windshield as we drive on.

"You know what?" he says.

"What?"

"It would be nice to live this close to my mother. Was it just me, or did she seem kind of frail this morning?"

"It was just you," I tell him. Wilma seemed the same as always to me—beautiful and capable and utterly put together, even if she was just wearing a bathrobe. Which she called a "dressing gown," in her elegant Wilma way. Just like she calls a couch a sofa and a porch a veranda. Speaking of which…

"Maybe we shouldn't jump into anything," I tell Jack, deciding to use a little reverse psychology on him. It's worked in the past.

Jack's head snaps toward me. "You changed your mind?"

"No! I just don't want to push you into anything you're not ready to do."

"If you didn't push me into anything, we wouldn't be married."

"Jack! That's so..."

Okay, it's so true. Yet unromantic.

"I don't mean it in a bad way, Trace," he says. "Sometimes I just need a little nudge. Let's go drive by the house again, one last time, okay?"

"Sure," I say, not sure how I feel about that. Or anything.

Until, of course, I see the damn house and fall madly in love with it all over again.

"We have to get this house," I tell Jack. "And you know what's going to be the first thing we do when we get it?"

Not that I said when, and not if. I've always been a strong believer in making things happen through positive thinking and brainwashing Jack.

"I don't know," he says. "Let me guess...knock down a wall?"

"No, get some rocking chairs!"

"First thing?" he asks, heading back to the main road again. "I know you said we'd be old and gray there, but don't you think the rocking chairs can wait awhile?"

"They're for the porch. The rocking-chair porch. Remember?"

"Remember what?" he asks. "Seriously. You lost me."

"Did you not read the listing sheet?"

"Sure I did."

"Did you not notice the rocking-chair-porch part?"

"I did not notice that part. Should I have?"

"Yes. Want to see it?" I fish in my purse for the listing sheet.

"That's okay, I'll take your word for it. I can't read and drive at the same time."

As we head down the street, I notice a bunch of blue Mylar balloons tied to a mailbox in front of a small Victorian-looking house. "Look," I tell Jack. "One of our neighbors just had a baby."

He just shakes his head. "Do I turn at the end of this block or the next one to get back to Bedford?"

"The next one."

"Are you sure?"

I look up, check the intersection. A sign at the side of the road reads Bedford 4.

"Yup, this is it," I tell him, thinking again how great it will be to live four miles from my mother-in-law.

No, I'm not off my front-porch rocker; I totally mean it. Wilma is not your average meddling mother-in-law. I adore her, and I'm sure it's mutual. We've always gotten along great, aside from one minor little blip when I was afraid she was trying to commandeer our wedding plans.

But I'm sure I was being overly sensitive, and anyway, that's ancient history.

As we leave Glenhaven Park behind, I tell it, *We'll be back. I promise.*

5

Walking up the path toward Wilma's condo, I'm eager to tell her all about the house.

"Don't tell my mother about the house," says Jack, who can be quite the annoying little mind reader when he wants to.

"Why not?"

"What if we don't get the house? Hey—is that a For Sale sign?" he asks, pointing at the unit two doors down from his mother's.

"It is, but no way are we moving to Harvest Haven Estates. It's a retirement community."

"Not officially. They can't officially keep young people from living here," he says defiantly.

I'm not sure that they can't, and anyway, I can't imagine

that legions of hipsters are barnstorming the sales office, eager to partake in the daily canasta tournaments and power Bunco games. Then again, there's a pool, tennis courts and golf course…

That gives me momentary pause.

Then I spot the front draperies parting in Wilma's next-door neighbor's picture window, and something that looks like an oversize Q-tip wearing glasses peers out through the crack. Ah, that would be Wilma's nosy neighbor, Bonnie.

Judge Judy must have gone to a commercial.

Harvest Haven Estates is chock-full of Bonnies.

"Jack, we so cannot live here," I tell him firmly.

"Why not?"

"Because we're not Hume Cronyn and Jessica Tandy, that's why not."

"Aren't they dead?"

Oops. Are they?

They must be. "Yes, and that's my point. Listen, if it'll make you feel better, I'll host a weekly bingo game at our new place."

He grins. "With prizes?"

"You bet your sweet bifocals."

"You're the best, Trace."

"I just really want us to get that house in Glenhaven Park."

"I know you do."

"And you want it, too, right?"

"Yeah. I do. If we can get it."

I wish he sounded more confident.

"Look, I promise that after I watch the game we'll sit down at home and figure out if we can afford the house and how much to offer. Okay?"

"Okay. And we can afford it. Remember? I pre—"

"Qualified. I know. But the bank doesn't know everything about us."

I hate to break it to him, but they pretty much do. Now, anyway.

We let ourselves into Wilma's condo, which is very nice, but always makes me feel a little sad. The place is crammed with her take in the divorce settlement: elegant furniture, art and antiques that once graced their Bedford mansion. It all looks slightly out of place here. Kind of like my friend Kate looked out of place in Target when I once dragged her there, clad in head-to-toe Chanel, on a day trip to Jersey.

Per unspoken house rules, Jack and I take off our shoes by the door and leave them on the mat alongside a pair of adorable pink sneakers and a pair of crummy mud-encrusted loafers that can only mean one thing: our nieces Ashley (adorable pink shoes to match her adorable pink name and adorable face) and Beatrice (crummy…you get the idea) are around here somewhere.

Quelle surprise.

The twins belong to Jack's ridiculously fragile sister Kathleen, a stay-at-home-mom with a full-time live-in nanny who takes to her bed at the slightest hint of a hangnail or PMS. I mean Kathleen, not the nanny, who has never suffered a minute of PMS as he's actually a manny. Mannies are all the rage in Kathleen's monkey-see-monkey-(well-to-)do pocket of suburbia.

When she hired the manny—whose name is Sam—Kathleen kept talking about how enriched the girls will be, having a male role model.

Which begs the question, *Hey, Kathleen, what's your husband, Bob—chopped liver?*

And begs a second question, *Kathleen, is it true that you fired your last nanny, Lupe, because she was drop-dead gorgeous and liked to iron in the nude?*

(Don't ask me how I know this. I just do, okay?)

The good news is that for all his ho-humness, my brother-in-law, Bob St. James, is a loving, loyal husband who would never, ever, in a gazillion years have a steamy fling with a sizzling nude-ironing *señorita* under his own recently replaced slate roof that cost upwards of fifty dollars per square foot.

(I'll tell you how I know this. Bob told me. In mind-numbing, minute detail.)

Anyway, anyone can see that Bob is still crazy about Kathleen after all these years, and they're meant to be together. Anyone other than Kathleen, anyway. Not only is she insecure, but she's convinced that she's married to a hot studmuffin no woman can resist.

Kathleen is the anti-Connie Spadolini. My mother is the ultimate housewife.

Kathleen is...well, not. Despite not working and employing a live-in manny, she's always dumping the seven-year-old twins off on her mother's doorstep.

To be fair, Wilma doesn't seem to mind. She dotes on the girls, whom she likes to parade around the condo complex and introduce as her "two sweet peas in a pod." Never mind that they're sweet as lemongrass and look nothing alike.

To be even more fair, the girls never had a chance.

Well, Ashley may have had a chance. She was actually named after one of the Olsen sisters (I always thought Jack was kidding about that—but, sadly, he was not) and could have popped out of a *Full House* rerun: a blue-eyed blonde, pretty, and with that same freakishly large head. Thanks to her overbearing, indulgent parents, Ashley is vain, bossy and spoiled rotten.

Beatrice is dour, demanding and equally spoiled, and not only has to deal with limp hair and a cruel overbite (soon to be corrected by expensive orthodonture), but was not named after the other Olsen twin—but after a childhood paper-route customer of Kathleen's husband, Bob. The first Beatrice, a reclusive and bitter old spinster, somehow amassed and hoarded a small fortune, which she left to be equally divided among Bob the Former Paperboy and her seven cats.

No, by "equally," I don't mean Bob got half and the cats got the other half. Bob was bequeathed exactly one eighth of Dead Beatrice's estate, with the remaining seven shares divided among Fluffy, Fifi and the gang who are presumably living out their golden years in some upscale feline version of Harvest Haven Estates.

In any case, the windfall was obviously significant enough for Bob and Kathleen to not only buy and perpetually remodel a house in Westchester—*sans* mortgage—but to saddle not-Mary-Kate with a name that, sadly, really does suit her.

Lately I've been trying to call her Bea, which if you think about it can be a cute and sporty kind of name for the right kind of girl. Say, a redheaded English princess.

But it hasn't stuck.

Maybe Beezus would be better, à la Beverly Cleary. But somehow, I doubt Kathleen will go for that. She's very particular about what people call her girls. Particularly when they call them "guys," as in, *"Come on, guys, stop licking that candy and putting it back into the bowl,"* for which I have been scolded in the past.

"Looks like the girls are here," Jack tells me as we venture across the plush white carpeting in our socks.

"Well, we aren't staying long, right?"

This stinks. Not only am I forbidden to gush to Wilma about our future house, but I'll probably be sucked into another game of Operation, which the little cheaters have rigged so that they control the red-nose buzzer.

"No, we'll say a quick hello and hit the road, so I can catch the game. Mom?" Jack calls. "Where are you?"

"We're in here," Wilma calls from the den. "Come see what my sweet peas are up to now! Hurry!"

Uh-oh. For all we know, she's roped to a chair and the sweet peas are holding lit matches to a heap of dry kindling beneath her feet.

No, it's worse.

"We're putting on a show!" Ashley announces.

God, no. Please, no.

Their last show—an impromptu Valentine's Day pageant featuring Ashley's off-key rendition of every love song she'd ever heard and Beatrice as the ticket-taker-slash-stagehand-slash-onstage-love-interest—was interminable.

But it seemed as though I was the only one who thought so. Jack vegged out, Wilma beamed, Kathleen was your worst stage-mother nightmare, and Bob filmed the whole thing and insisted on immediately playing it back so we could all see it again—with a lot of freeze-framing and instant replaying at Ashley's request.

The stakes are higher than ever now that Kathleen's set her sights on showbiz and enrolled the girls in some kind of local after-school acting academy for rich kids. She and Wilma—who once upon a time dreamed of a stage career herself—are convinced Ashley and Beatrice are the next Olsen twins or Doublemint twins. I kid you not. Lately Kathleen's been gunning for a chewing-gum commercial gig and has been writing and sending their photos to Wrigley's. I guess she's thinking the chewing-gum people will be so bedazzled they won't notice that Ashley and Beatrice couldn't be less identical if one had a penis.

All I have to say is thank God almighty that Blaire Barnett doesn't run the Wrigley's account because Kathleen would make my and Jack's lives a living hell.

Although her daughters seem bent on doing just that right here, right now.

"You're just in time." Wilma pats the cushion beside her. "Come sit on the sofa with me. We'll be the audience."

No, Wilma, you be the audience. We be outta here.

"I don't know," Jack hedges, looking at his watch. "Tracey really wants to hustle it back to the city."

Oh, sure, pin it all on me. As if he's not itching for the couch, a beer and the TiVo remote.

But I don't even protest, because if the twins are putting on a show, I really want to hustle it back to the city. Right freaking now.

"You can't go!" Ashley whines. "Grandma, tell them they can't go! It's our Best Show Ever!"

Oh, well, in that case, break out the *Playbills* and up with the curtain!

"What *is* the show?" I ask the girls as Jack and I reluctantly take our seats in the audience.

"West Side Story."

"Really." I look around, in case I missed a troupe of Jets and Sharks on my way into the room.

Twirling back and forth in a skirt made from a couple of Wilma's lace napkins tucked into the waistband of her jeans, and feeling oh-so-pretty, Ashley announces, "I'm Maria."

But of course.

"Congratulations." I force a smile. "How about you, Bea? Are you in the show, too, this time?"

"She's Anita. And everyone else. And the ticket taker."

Is your name Bea? I want to snap at Ashley.

But of course her name isn't Bea, or even Beatrice, and she's the longtime spokesmodel for the pair, so I don't snap.

Instead, I turn back to her sister. "Wow, Bea, you're Anita?"

"Yeah."

Mental Note to Bea—Dear Bea: Sullen doesn't suit you. Your best bet in life is to develop a sparkling personality, or a sterling academic record, or some kind of talent—other than musical theater. Macramé would be good. Smooches, Aunt Tracey

"So you're Anita and...who else? Tony? Officer Krupke?" I'm trying hard to remember my *West Side Story* lore as well as root for the underdog here, as usual.

"Yeah," says Bea.

"She's everyone else, too."

Thank you, Maria.

Part of the problem is that Bea is just not a lovable-loser-with-a-heart-of-gold. She's basically a miserable kid, and bratty, to boot. She's also—

"Beatrice is the next Rita Moreno." That's Wilma, all proud and delusional.

Hmm. I can't say that I look at Beatrice St. James and think: next Rita Moreno.

"Wait until you see her do that 'I Want to Live in America' number. She's really something."

I smile, nod and look at Jack. *Make it stop.*

He looks at his watch, opens his mouth.

"Hey, Beatrice," commands our budding diva, before Jack can speak. "I have to go run my lines, warm up my voice and get into character. Announce that the show will go on in five minutes."

"Ashley, say please when you talk to your sister," Wilma chides.

"Please," Ashley says. Then, gesturing at a pair of card-table chairs that sit facing each other, she adds, "And hurry up and finish building the balcony, too."

Imagine, the next Rita Moreno and a budding set designer, all rolled into one.

"The show will go on in five minutes," Bea drones.

"Thank you, Beatrice," Ashley says demurely, channeling Maria.

"You know what?" Jack looks at his watch again. "I don't think we can stay, guys."

"YOU HAVE TO STAY!"

You know those movies where the serial killer, who until now has been acting like the meek, mild-mannered milkman, suddenly snaps and goes all diabolic and guttural? That's pretty much what Ashley sounds like.

We stay.

Not because we're afraid of a seven-year-old with crazy eyes, but because we're a loving aunt and uncle.

And all right, maybe a little afraid.

As the twins launch into the opening number, I decide to pretend I'm anywhere but here. Tahiti, or our future new house, or in a Client meeting at seven o'clock on a Saturday night…anything is preferable to watching Beatrice rumble with herself.

It isn't until later, when the show is in full swing and we sit listening to the tone-deaf duet sing "Tonight" that I'm struck by something.

What if we move to Westchester and Kathleen starts dropping the twins on our doorstep the way she does Wilma's?

Even if she doesn't do that, Wilma has the girls all the time. She'll probably pop in and out to visit us with them in tow.

Not that I don't love my nieces—

"Todaaaaaaay, the minutes feel like hours," Ashley sings in a glass-shattering off-key soprano, *"the hours go so slowly…"*

Isn't *that* the truth.

Merciful God in heaven, get me *out* of here.

Maybe it wasn't such a great idea for me and Jack to look for houses up here near his family after all.

"So," Jack says as we settle into our seats on the train home to Manhattan, "I'm thinking you were right."

"About…?"

"About living near my family."

Oops, did I say something aloud? I hope I didn't also share my fiendish fantasy about having the twins' voice boxes surgically removed.

"It'll be great to see my mother and everyone all the time," Jack says.

Oh.

I nod vigorously. Jack's family all the time. What could be better?

"And if we have a car," he goes on, "we can drive up to Brookside to see your family all the time, too. We won't have to deal with plane tickets, and it'll probably take less time than it does to deal with all the hassles and delays at the airport."

Jack's family *and* my family! All family, all the time!

Dear God, what have I done?

I have to tell him we'd be making a big mistake.

"And the house was pretty great," he adds, which gives me pause.

"The house *was* pretty great."

"And the train ride really isn't bad, either. It's kind of nice."

"It is," I agree, imagining all those hours of uninterrupted time we'll have on the commuter train, sipping coffee and sharing the paper.

"So are we going to make an offer, or what?" Jack asks, like it's suddenly up to me.

"Do you want to?"

"Yeah. I do. Do *you?*"

A couple of hours ago, I was certain we'd found our dream house.

Have I really let the devilmint twins change my mind? I mean, in the grand scheme of things, I'm sure they won't be invading our space the way, say, Mitch and the circus freaks and the Mad Crapper have.

"Yeah," I tell Jack. "I do. I think we should go for it. And if Hank and Marge refuse our offer, then it just wasn't meant to be and we'll start looking somewhere else."

Like, say, Jersey. Or Tahiti.

Later that night, of course, with the hall outside our apartment reeking of the Mad Crapper's latest offering, I'm back to wanting that house in Glenhaven Park more than I've ever wanted anything else in my life.

Except, of course, for when I wanted to marry Jack.

Which had a happy ending, of course.

I guess there was a time when I wanted Will, my ex-boyfriend, just as badly as I want this house...and look how that turned out.

No happy ending there.

Wait a minute. Of course there was a happy ending. Not getting Will was meant to be, because not getting Will led me to Jack.

Either this house is meant to be, or it isn't.

So after the game, and pizza, and a close look at our finances—Jack and I officially launch Operation Fresh Start. We call Verna and put in an offer on the house.

We come within thirty thousand dollars of the asking price.

Verna promises to get the offer right in to Hank and Marge's agent.

We hang up the phone and look at each other.

"Well," I say. "We did it."

"Yeah."

"How do you feel?" I ask, because as always, it's impossible to tell.

"Pretty good," he says with Jack aplomb. "Why? How do you feel?"

"Like a nervous wreck. I hate that our entire fate is in somebody else's hands."

"That's because you're a control freak," he says affectionately. "And anyway, if you think about it, your fate is never truly in your own hands."

"I know, but I like to think that it is."

"I know you do. You just go on believing that. It keeps us both going."

"Really?"

He smiles, hugs me and goes off to the bathroom with *Entertainment Weekly* magazine.

Wouldn't it be great to be a guy?

Or at least, a girl who didn't always second-guess her every move and flip-flop between wanting something desperately one minute, and hoping fate will whisk it out of reach the next.

I know it sounds crazy. Why would I want us to not get the house?

Who the hell knows? At the moment, I'm hoping we get it, so I can't remember why I was hoping, in an earlier moment, that we didn't. I guess it might have had something to do with it being a whole lot easier not to worry about goodbyes, and packing, and spending all that money, and commuting, and Jack's family…

Wow.

All I have to do is remember the twins' butchered rendition of *West Side Story,* and I really hope we don't get the house. What was I thinking?

I mean, they'll probably show up to serenade us on our anniversary, and Christmas caroling at our door in December, and there will be school plays and community theater and God help us all.

But we put in an offer.

Like I said, it's completely out of our hands—pure torture for a control freak like me.

But there's nothing more to do now but wait.

6

Saint Patrick's Day might just be my favorite holiday, after Christmas. And Thanksgiving. Oh, and New Year's Eve, and my birthday, if I don't have to work. July Fourth is fun, too; I never have to work then, and Jack and I can see the fireworks from the roof of our building.

But after those other holidays, Saint Patrick's Day is definitely my favorite.

The past few years, Jack and I have spent it with a bunch of our friends at this great Irish pub down the block from our apartment.

Everyone eats corned beef and cabbage, gets really hammered on green beer and sings along to U2, the Pogues and Sinéad O'Connor tunes on the jukebox.

The crowd at our usual table near the back of the bar changes slightly every year, but we can count on the core group: Kate and Billy, Raphael and Donatello, Latisha and Derek, Buckley O'Hanlon and, of course, Mitch. Both of the latter usually bring whatever random girl they happen to be currently dating. This year, however, they're both solo.

Right now, the night is still young: the waitress has just set down our mugs and bowls of beer nuts, which I know are disgusting but I happen to love. Everyone at our table is still stone sober, and it's probably not the best time for me to say, "Hey, guys, Jack and I have an announcement to make."

But not being known for my exquisite timing, I, of course, say it anyway.

"Oh, Tracey! You're pregnant!" That's Raphael, who, it should be noted, doesn't have an ounce of Irish in his Latin blood. Yet in honor of the occasion, he's dressed like a leprechaun, which involves a green, sequined top hat, tunic and tights—a little something he said he threw together at the last minute, courtesy of an extensive wardrobe closet at *She* magazine, where he's the fashion director.

Pregnant? He thinks I'm pregnant?

"Do I *look* pregnant?" I glance down at the clingy top I'm wearing. I knew it wasn't entirely flattering when I put it on, but it's green so I didn't care.

And anyway, I didn't think it was all *that* bad.

"Let's put it this way…if you were a celeb, I would have you on a serious Bump Watch on my blog."

Terrific. I push away the beer nuts immediately.

"Raphael! She looks great. You look great, Tracey," Donatello assures me after giving his boyfriend a little swat on the arm. "You're glowing! So when are you due? Oh, and congratulations, guys!"

"I'm not pregnant!" I say, really hating this bump-inducing green top. "Would I be drinking this beer if I were pregnant?"

They look dubiously at the beer, at my non-baby-related bump, and at each other.

"No! I would not," I answer the question for them.

"Of course you wouldn't, Tracey," says Latisha, patting my hand. "Although, if it gives you any peace of mind, my ob-gyn did tell me it was okay to have a beer every now and then when I was pregnant with Bernie. I just didn't want to tempt fate, though, so—"

I cut in, "I don't need peace of mind, because I'm not pregnant."

I'm drowned out by Kate, who announces in her loud Alabama accent, "Ah had a glass of wine or two when Ah was pregnant. Hay-ell, Ah even had a martini one night, and everything turned out just fahn for me. So you just go ahead and drink that beer, Tracey."

"I am not pregnant!" I pretty much shout.

Sheesh!

Meanwhile, I'm thinking "everything turned out just fine" for Kate? Hello?

I mean, I guess that depends on how you look at it, and

it probably has nothing to do with that prenatal martini, but I wouldn't call the situation fine.

Not that I don't have a soft spot in my heart for Kate and Billy's two-year-old daughter, who's an absolute clone of her mother, after whom she was named. She's absolutely adorable, with her honey-blond hair and aquamarine eyes which are, as fate would have it, exactly the shade of Kate's fake blond hair and colored contacts.

Then again, maybe it isn't fate. Raphael is convinced Kate is dyeing her daughter's hair and has bought her tiny aquamarine contact lenses. I wouldn't put a kiddie spray tan past her, but dye and contacts for her two-year-old are pretty over the top, even for Kate.

She's absolutely obsessed by her daughter and treats her like a little dress-up doll. For a while, she was into matching mother-daughter outfits, then baby designer stuff. Her latest thing is hats: little Katie can frequently be seen sporting a newsboy cap or fedora.

Anyway, getting back to the more pressing problem: lately, our little sweetheart has morphed into...how can I put this delicately?

I can't.

Suffice to say, Screaming Jesus is not an overstatement.

Kate indulgently blames her offspring's outrageous behavior on the terrible twos, and Billy ignores it altogether. But they've been through four nannies in as many months, so I'm thinking they're seriously deluding themselves.

"So guys, what's your news?" Buckley speaks up from the far end of the table. He's got on a green sweater and one of those soft leather jackets that cost an absolute fortune, and he's looking amazingly hot tonight if I do say so myself.

I'm allowed to say so myself, because I'm a married woman and anyway, it's been several years now since Buckley declared his love for me.

The love was unrequited, of course, because I was engaged to Jack at the time.

True, it was definitely requited at one time in my life, when I had a secret crush on my best straight-guy friend. But back then, I was on the unrequited end because Buckley had an irritating girlfriend, Sonja. They have since been engaged and broken up, and the last anyone heard from Sonja, she had moved back to Boston and was involved with the Red Sox—either professionally or sexually, depending on whom you talked to.

Anyway, the timing was never right for me and Buckley, and these days, I know he's as over me as I am over him.

Still, one can't help but be a little wistful when one's former secret crush and current best straight-guy friend becomes an overnight literary success, with his name at the top of the *New York Times* Trade Fiction list and his picture in *Entertainment Weekly* magazine.

Yes, Buckley's first novel, which was published a few months ago, was a breakout bestseller, much to everyone's surprise—most of all, his own. I think he thought he was destined to spend the rest of his life toiling away writing freelance book-jacket copy in a dinky studio apartment.

He's just moved to a one-bedroom with a view and landed a lucrative contract for a second and third novel.

All of this has left Buckley a little dazed, but as down-to-earth as ever, which is what I love best about him. In a platonic way, of course.

"Yeah, what's your news?" prods Derek, Latisha's husband, his arm draped along the back of her chair with the ease of a longtime husband. Everyone else is looking impatient as well, and I can't wait to share our joy and excitement with them.

Well, everyone but Mitch, who already knows our news and sits sulking on the other side of Jack, and Billy, who couldn't be less interested.

Oh, wait, yes he could. I watch him pull his BlackBerry from his pocket and hold it on his lap, scrolling with his thumb.

Kate sees him do it. She gives him a scowl, then a hard elbow. Billy winces, but goes on scrolling.

Who cares if Billy doesn't care and Mitch is disturbed by our news? Everyone else will be happy for us.

"Okay, so the news is..." I glance at Jack, who is sitting next to me with a mug of green beer.

He's shaking his head at me. Not a sympathetic *Don't worry, honey, I still love you even if that hideous top does give you a frontal pooch* nod. Rather, it's a warning nod, the kind that says, *Don't share our news until we really have some news to share.*

Too late, though. You can't announce that you have news

and then not say what it is, or worse yet, go on letting people think you're pregnant just because you made an unfortunate wardrobe choice.

"The news is, Jack and I put in an offer on a house!"

"A carriage house in the Village?" Raphael claps his hands together. "That's fabulous, Tracey!"

"A carriage house in the Village?" I echo, bewildered. "Huh? Where did that come from?"

"Didn't you tell me you wanted one, Tracey?" he asks, looking equally bewildered beneath his shiny green hat.

"That was you," Donatello informs him. "Telling me. And everyone else who will listen."

"Oh! Right. That *was* me. I'm dying for a carriage house in the Village."

"Which we couldn't afford before we became fathers, and definitely will never be able to afford now."

"Donatello, we need to maintain a certain stylish, sophisticated quality of life or it's not worth living."

Donatello rolls his eyes. "Who are we, Posh and Becks?"

Raphael flashes his husband a beatific smile. "Oh, I'm nothing if not Posh, darling."

"You're also full of...blarney," Donatello mutters, shaking his head.

"Getting back to that carriage house, I think that if we can just—"

"Here, have some beer nuts, Raphael," Latisha cuts in strategically, and slides the bowl his way.

Raphael makes a face. "Beer nuts are disgusting, Latisha."

"Really? I think they're magically delicious." Latisha helps herself to another handful.

Kate asks quickly—before Raphael can turn the subject back to his nonexistent carriage house or, God forbid, his ongoing David Beckham fantasy—"Okay, so what's the deal with your house, Tracey and Jack?"

"It isn't even *our* house yet," Jack cautions.

"But I'm sure it will be, because the owners are considering our offer." That's me, determined not to let anyone rain on this parade.

"Where is it?" Derek asks.

"Westchester."

"Wait…Westchester?" Latisha echoes. "That's way the hell up in the suburbs."

"It's just north of the Bronx," I point out. Which, P.S., is where she lives.

"The Bronx is part of the *city.*"

"That's a technicality," Buckley tells Latisha. "Anyway, maybe their house is just over the border between the Bronx and Westchester."

Yeah. It isn't.

You know…I have to wonder, where's the joy? Where's the excitement? This isn't what I expected. I probably should have waited till everyone was drunk as skunks.

I gulp some beer, thinking it might help somehow if I,

personally, am drunk as a skunk. Latisha asks, "What town is this house in?"

"Glenhaven Park," Jack tells her.

"Whoa. That's *way* the hell up in Westchester."

"Why don't y'all just look in the city?" Kate drawls. "There are plenty of places for sale."

"Because we don't want to live in the city," I explain patiently. "We want to live in the suburbs."

"But why?" Donatello asks. "Everything you need is right here. And *everyone,*" he adds pointedly.

"You guys, it's not like we're moving cross-country. It's just a short train ride away, and we'll have plenty of room for visitors, so you guys can come up whenever you want."

Leave it to Mitch to respond to that. "It won't be the same. Still…how long is the train ride, anyway?"

"Did I say short? Okay, it's not *that* short," I say quickly.

"It's an hour," Jack informs his sidekick, and I can see the wheels turning already.

"But isn't it going to cost you guys a fortune to commute from there?" Derek asks.

"No, we'd get monthly passes from Metro-North," Jack says. "They're discounted that way."

Mitch perks up at that. I can read his mind. He's planning to get a monthly pass, too, God help us.

"Well, they're not *that* discounted," I say quickly.

Jack levels a look at me.

"What?" I ask innocently.

Jack just shakes his head.

Realizing our little Raphael O'Shenanigan has been awfully quiet, I sneak a peek at him.

Aw.

He looks like a forlorn leprechaun who's just learned that the pot at the end of the rainbow is filled with beer nuts.

"Raphael?" I ask tentatively. "What do you think?"

"I think you should wait until an apartment opens up in our building, Tracey. That way we can be like Lucy and Ricky and Fred and Ethel, just like I always pictured."

Touched, I say, "You don't look a thing like Ethel, sweetheart."

"Tracey! I'm Ricky."

Well, he does look a little like Ricky Ricardo. Ricky Martin, too.

"So you're saying Tracey and I are the Mertzes?" Jack asks dubiously.

"Well, you can't be now that you're moving away, can you?" he asks irritably.

"Raphael, stop that," Donatello scolds as Jack and I exchange a glance.

"You know," I say gently, "Lucy and Ricky eventually moved to the suburbs. Maybe you and Donatello could—"

"No, thank you," Raphael cuts in darkly. "That was the kiss of death for the show, and Lucy and Ricky got divorced. The whole thing went to hell in a handcart when they moved to the suburbs."

"Actually, Lucy and *Desi* got divorced," Buckley points out. "Lucy and Ricky aren't real."

"They are to me, Buckley," Raphael replies, and adds reproachfully, "Tracey, I thought we were going to grow old together right here in the city."

"Um, I thought you were going to grow old in the city with me," Donatello pipes up.

"And I thought Tracey was planning to grow old with me in the suburbs, but if you really want her, I'm sure we can work something out, Raphael," Jack puts in good-naturedly.

"Tracey and I have been together for years," Raphael says sadly. "We're a team, like Lucy and Ethel."

"I thought you were Ricky and Ethel," Mitch says under his breath, and I kick him under the table.

"It's the end of an era," Raphael declares.

"God, I hate when eras end." Latisha shakes her head. "First Yvonne retires to Florida, then Brenda becomes a stay-at-home mom, and now you, Tracey."

"But I'll still see you at work every day."

"Mmm, hmm."

I really hate it when she goes all soul-sistah attitude on me.

"Mmm, hmm? What do you mean by that?"

"I mean, all you talk about lately is how you wish you could quit your job. How long do you think you're going to last if you have to ride a train for an hour to get to it?"

"Tracey has to last forever at Blaire Barnett if we're going to buy this house," Jack tells her, "because we can't afford it without her salary."

"Right," I say, feigning great enthusiasm for working and commuting…forever.

"So when do you find out whether you get the house?" Kate wants to know.

"Any day now," Jack answers. Our Realtor put in our offer yesterday, and we're waiting to hear back."

"You guys really would love this house," I say optimistically. "I keep picturing us all there some fall weekend, playing touch football on the lawn, cooking and drinking wine and listening to music…"

"Is the music 'Heard It through the Grapevine' and 'Whiter Shade of Pale'?" Latisha wants to know. "Because I don't think that's us. I think it's the cast of *The Big Chill*."

Everyone laughs. Even me. Even though this hasn't quite gone the way I had hoped.

"Come on, guys—let's toast Tracey and Jack." Buckley lifts his green mug. "We're all really happy for you two."

I wish I believed that, and looking around the table as they clink glasses, I can't help but wonder if we're about to gain a house, but lose our friends.

When I get home from work the next night—exhausted, cranky, starving and still way hungover from too much green beer—Jack is already there.

"There's a message from Verna," he announces the second I set my aching feet over the threshold.

"Ooh! What did she say?" I brace myself for the news.

"I don't know. I didn't call her back yet. I wanted to wait for you."

"How did she sound?" I ask, hurriedly tossing my coat and bag onto the chair and kicking off my painful pumps. Ouch. My big toes have both poked through the stocking seams and that drives me crazy.

"What do you mean, how did she sound?" Jack asks.

Here's another thing that drives me crazy: sometimes my husband just doesn't get what I'm talking about.

"I mean, did she sound happy? Frustrated? Upset?"

"Why would she sound frustrated or upset?" Jack asks cluelessly.

Grr.

"She might be," I say, trying hard not to sound pissy, "if Hank and Marge turned down our offer. Never mind, let's just call back. Where's the phone?"

He hands it over, along with Verna's business card.

"Are you nervous?" I ask him as I dial the number.

"I didn't think I would be, but yeah," he confesses, "I am, a little."

I didn't think he would be, either. Somehow, the fact that he is (which should probably make me feel worse) makes me feel better.

"What if we didn't get the house?" I ask him, crossing my fingers.

"Then we keep looking."

"But this was it. This was our house." The phone is trembling in my hand as it rings on the other end and I reach my other hand out to Jack, who squeezes it.

"Verna Treeby."

"Verna? It's Tracey and Jack Candell. You called us?"

"Yes, I did. I gave your offer to the owners' agent, and she said they got two other offers on the same day…"

My heart is starting to sink.

"One was the same as yours and the other was higher…"

My heart lands in the vicinity of my torn stocking toes.

"…but when she checked with Hank and Marge, they said that since yours came in first—by only about twenty minutes—the house is yours if you're willing to meet them halfway on the difference between your offer and the asking price."

I gasp. "We will! Tell them yes!"

Belatedly remembering Jack, I look at him and whisper, "Okay?"

He nods, grinning. "Definitely."

"Terrific. Congratulations. I'll get back to the owners' agent right away, and call you back with the details."

"Thanks, Verna."

I hang up and look at Jack.

"We did it."

"Hey," he says, hugging me close, "you're crying."

"Yeah." I sniffle. "I'm so happy. I feel like this is a dream come true for us. I just have this gut feeling that from here on in, everything's going to be—"

I break off, stricken, remembering something.

It happened back when we were engaged, planning our wedding. Up until a certain point, I thought the planning had been a nightmare because I had my heart set on an October wedding at Shorewood Country Club and the fates seemed to be conspiring against me.

When my dream unexpectedly came true and we landed Shorewood, I decided it would be smooth sailing from there on in.

A few weeks later, as the plans for everything other than the reception location were crashing down around me, I said, and I quote, *The next time I have a gut feeling about anything, do me a favor and slap me.*

If Jack wasn't standing right here, I'd definitely slap myself now.

"Everything's going to be what?" he's asking.

"Never mind."

"No, what?"

"Never mind!" I snap at him. "Sorry. I'm tired and hungry and cranky. Just forget I said anything."

He shrugs. "Done. Want to order Chinese to celebrate?"

"Shouldn't we go out to dinner to celebrate?"

"If we're going to have a mortgage from now on, we're going to be eating in a lot."

"Oh. Good thinking."

I can't help but think it's a little depressing, though. I mean, are we going to be on an austerity budget from here on in?

I try telling myself it'll be worth it if we just get to live in that house, but...

Well, what if I was looking at the house through rose-colored glasses? What if it's really a gutted wreck with pee-yellow siding?

"Jack?"

"Yeah?" he asks, fishing a Rainbow Wok menu from the drawer by the phone.

"It really is a great house, isn't it?"

He looks at me for a long moment. Then he smiles a little, shaking his head. "It was a great house, Trace."

Relieved, I say, "I thought so."

"You're the one who talked me into it...don't tell me you're talking yourself out of it now?"

"No!" I say firmly. "Not at all."

But that is kind of what happened when we got married. I was gung ho for it until we were halfway to the altar, at which point I started to second-guess whether Jack was the right person for me after all. It's a long, involved story that has to do with Buckley, my hair and a Pre-Cana course, so I won't get into it again.

The important thing is that we did get married, and Jack is the right person for me, and all my misgivings were completely unfounded.

I'm sure it'll turn out to be the same way with Operation Fresh Start.

Mental Note: *you love change. You thrive on it. Remember?*

"So what do you want?" Jack asks, perusing the menu.

Suddenly overcome with sheer exhaustion, I say, "I don't care. Surprise me."

"Surprise you?" he echoes incredulously. *"You?"*

"Why not?" I shrug and head into the bedroom, painful pumps in hand.

Actually, I know *why not.*

Because as I said, I am the ultimate control freak. I like to be the one who decides what I'm going to eat. And wear, for that matter, I think as I sit on the edge of the bed to strip off these holey nylons.

For example, if I had my way, I'd never put on another pair of panty hose as long as I live.

But in Manhattan's corporate world, you just can't avoid it.

Which is why—as much as I have been longing to own this house in Glenhaven Park—something other than *The next time I have a gut feeling about anything, do me a favor and slap me* is ringing in my ears tonight.

I also hear Jack's voice.

Tracey has to last forever at Blaire Barnett if we're going to buy this house, because we can't afford it without her salary.

Forever is an awfully long time…even when a person is living happily ever after in her dream house.

7

"Hello?" My mother answers the phone on the first ring, as usual.

"Hi, it's me."

"Stefania!"

At least, I *thought* that was my mother answering the phone.

"Ma?"

"Mary Beth?"

Okay, it's definitely my mother. Mary Beth is my older sister and she and my mother speak at least three or four times a day, even though they live a few blocks apart.

But who the hell is Stefania?

"No, Ma, it's me! Tracey."

"Tracey! I knew you'd call! See, Frank?" she says to my

father, who is obviously somewhere in the vicinity, which is strange at this hour on a weekday. "What did I tell you? Tracey is calling to wish us a Happy Saint Joseph's Day!"

Uh-oh again.

Is it March 19?

I glance at the date on Kate's e-mail. Yup. March 19, all right.

Saint Joseph's Day. No wonder my father is home on a weekday at this hour—it's almost noon—which means I'd better make this snappy. I've got a lunch meeting in the eighth-floor conference room.

"Pop told me you wouldn't call," my mother is telling me somewhat smugly. "He was just saying that people in New York City don't even celebrate Saint Joseph's Day."

Well, I can't speak for the other eight million New Yorkers, but I, for one, forgot all about the most gala Spadolini holiday next to Christmas.

"I'm sure they do celebrate it, Ma. We have Italians here, remember? We even have Little Italy."

"That's not real," she all but snaps.

I bite my tongue, telling myself she's just cranky because I live almost five hundred miles away. She still hasn't gotten over my cross-state flight from the nest. The rest of the family dutifully lives within shouting distance.

I think my mother's secretly harboring the hope that I'll get over this nonsense and come home, Jack in tow. Nothing would make her happier than to have us set up house in Brookside.

Which makes me wonder why I thought it was a good idea to call and share our happy house news.

I wouldn't have if I'd remembered what day it is, because Connie Spadolini is undoubtedly teetering on the verge of exhaustion and in no mood to hear that my downstate sojourn is about to become more permanent than ever before.

Before I get into all that, though…

"Ma, who's Stefania?" I ask, wondering if she's not just exhausted, but also delirious, because I can't think of a single Stefania who would call my parents' house and greet my mother, *Hi, it's me.*

Come to think of it, I can't think of a single Stefania, period.

Unless she meant Father Stefan, the priest at our church. But his voice sounds nothing like mine, and anyway, she calls him Father Stefan—Father, for short. No nicknames.

"Stefania," my mother tells me, "is Josie Lupinelli's cousin—she's visiting from Krakow."

Krakow—that's not even in Italy.

Wait—is it?

Geography isn't my forte, but I'm sure it's not.

"Josie Lupinelli has a cousin in Poland?" I ask. I manage not to add, *One who's cozy enough to call you and say,* Hi, it's me *without a trace of an accent, because if she had an accent, you wouldn't be mistaking her for me, your own daughter, would you, now?*

"Of course she does, Tracey. Josie's Polish."

"Josephine Lupinelli is Polish," I repeat, just to be sure, considering that Josie has a distinctly Mediterranean look. In other words, she's about four-eight, has an olive complexion, dark, soulful eyes and a mustache darker than my aunt Aggie's. (I'm allowed to say that because I'd have one, too, if it weren't for wax.)

Mental Note: check mirror to see if it's time for waxing appointment.

Now that I'm married, I don't spend nearly as much time analyzing my appearance as I once did. A quick glance, and I'm usually good to go.

Sometimes, the old facial hair creeps up on me and I don't even notice it until I catch a glimpse of Keith Hernandez on the street and realize it's not Keith, it's me, reflected in a store window.

"Josie Lupinelli is half-Polish," my mother concedes. "She's Tatarkiewicz from home."

It takes me a second to translate that phrase into good old American English.

In Spadolinish, it means Josie's maiden name was Tatarkiewicz.

Which doesn't sound Italian to me, so…okay.

Still…

"How come Josie's cousin from Poland is calling you on the phone?" I ask my mother.

"I don't know—to see what she can bring, maybe? She has very good manners. Very old-fashioned, very polite. And she's only nineteen."

"Good for her," I say somewhat curtly. "What she can bring where?"

"Over here. Where else? For the Saint Joseph's Table."

"She's invited? We don't even know her!"

"We know her."

Is it just my imagination, or does my mother put slight emphasis on the *we?* If she did, then she's trying to tell me that I am no longer considered a part of the family back in Brookside.

Okay, maybe that's a little extreme on my part. Maybe I'm just feeling understandably jealous of this old-fashioned, polite Polish interloper. I can't help it.

My mother goes on to tell me briefly about Stefania's background, but I don't listen.

An e-mail from Kate just clicked in on my desktop computer, and the subject line reads:

HELP!

E-mails from Kate frequently bear that subject line, so no need for premature concern. Usually, she just wants to know if you remember the name of the lipstick shade that looked so fabulous on her at Saks on Saturday, or where she can buy Veuve Clicquot at 8:00 a.m. because she has a fierce Bellini craving.

Hmm. This one says:

Meet me for drinks after work. What time are you free?

Uh-oh.

Sounds kind of terse. Something may be amiss in Kateland.

Though just how seriously amiss can't be discerned electronically. The last time I was summoned via e-mail for emergency cocktails, it was because Lancôme had discontinued her favorite Le Rouge Absolu Satin Romance lipstick.

"So anyway, Ma," I say, realizing she's concluded her bio of Stefania of Krakow, "Happy Saint Joseph's Day. You, too, Dad," I call a little louder. As if he can hear me. As if he can hear anything.

I type out a quick reply to Kate's e-mail as my mother shouts, "Frank, Tracey says Happy Saint Joseph's Day. Frank! Frank!"

Back on the line, she informs me with a sigh, "He's deaf lately."

Yeah, well, forty years working in a steel plant will do that to a person.

Poor Pop.

Poor Ma.

I guarantee she's been working herself ragged for at least a week now, preparing the traditional meatless feast for, oh, seven or eight dozen hungry people. Not that she'll have that many at her annual Saint Joseph's Table, but she always makes enough food to feed an army of famished soldiers—preferably the Good Christian kind.

Traditionally, you were supposed to invite people less fortunate to your Table, such as widows, orphans and paupers.

Those are in short supply, even in my hometown, so who knows, maybe Josie Lupinelli's cousin from Krakow is an impoverished widow. Or orphan. Whatever.

Too bad Jack and I can't attend this year, because we are certainly impoverished, according to the budget he set up on an Excel spreadsheet last night.

Until now, we've pretty much just spent what we needed to on whatever we needed.

Now we have a monthly allotment for everything from postage stamps to gasoline for the car we're going to have to buy. When Jack suggested that our monthly dining-out/take-out/entertainment budget be set at a hundred dollars, I pointed out that this only allowed twenty-five bucks a week, and that the two of us can't even see a movie with popcorn and Sno caps for that price.

"We're going to have to sacrifice some things to make room for others," he said.

He wound up raising the dining-out/take-out/entertainment budget to a hundred and fifty, taking the extra money out of the monthly clothing budget—three hundred dollars for both of us. Jack insisted that was plenty, and I was too mentally and emotionally exhausted to point out that a decent suit for him would leave me wearing last season's jeans well into the next three months.

Anyway, an impromptu flight to Brookside for Saint Joseph's Day certainly isn't in the budget, so that's not going to happen this year.

My mother always invites my brothers, their wives and kids; my sister (divorced—shh!) and her two kids; assorted friends, relatives, parishioners and random locals of Sicilian descent; and of course my grandmother, the token widow, who is still going strong in her eighties, looking fabulous for her age—and knows it—and loves it when you know it, too.

The Table is adorned with flowers, candles and religious statuary including a toddler-size plastic Saint Joseph whose bare feet are usually positioned in the vicinity of my plate. Father Stefan says a long blessing and then there's a toast, followed by hearty cheers of *"Viva San Giuseppe,"* which means Long Live Saint Joseph.

As the meal goes on *Viva San Giuseppe* is shouted out whenever anyone is moved to say it, and everyone has to put down their fork, lift a glass and chime in.

The more wine everyone consumes, the more prone they are to shouting, *"Viva San Giuseppe!"*

It's kind of like a college drinking game, only with church ladies and better food.

"What is that tapping?" my mother—who is not deaf by any means—wants to know.

"Oh—sorry. It's just my keyboard. I'm at work." I pause to quickly scan the e-mail I just typed, then hit Send.

I probably can't get out of here until after 8. Tomorrow is better, my boss is out of town.

"You're at work on Saint Joseph's Day," my mother acknowledges sadly.

Imagine her profound sorrow if she knew I had to go in on Easter Sunday last year, to get ready for a Monday-morning Client presentation.

My father and brothers—who have all at some point stoically worked through the flu, various injuries and the early stages of their wives' labor—all take off on Saint Joseph's Day. They go to early mass, of course, then spend most of the day setting up tables, carrying heavy platters and getting their hands slapped by my mother for stealing samples.

"So what are you making for the Table this year, Ma?"

"The usual—fried sardines, lentils with linguini, pasta fagiole, stuffed artichokes, fried cardone, stuffed calamari, fava," she rattles off, stops for a breath and resumes, "spaghetti with garlic and oil, zucchini frittata, fried mushrooms and cauliflower, asparagus frittata…"

Yeah, there's a lot of fried and/or stuffed stuff on Saint

Joseph's Day. But back in Brookside, people aren't opposed to that. In fact, they embrace it.

Which would be a healthy attitude if they weren't all so…unhealthy. Overweight, high blood pressure, high cholesterol, heart conditions—it seems like every time I call home, I hear about someone else who's been added to the endless intercessions list at Sunday mass.

"What about the breads, Ma?"

"The breads? I've been doing breads all week. The breads are done."

The breads are individual, egg-glazed, anise-flavored loaves of slightly sweetened dough shaped like a cross or Saint Joseph's staff or beard. It's great sliced thinly and toasted the next day, with butter.

"What'd you make for dessert?"

"Pignlate, sfinge and cannoli," my mother reports in a *What else?* tone.

You know, when I was a kid, I longed for the kind of house where the cupboards are stocked with Oreos. But my mother made our cookies and pastries from scratch. Nary a chocolate chip or snickerdoodle emerged from her oven in all those years, and God forbid a Dunkin' Donut should ever cross her threshold. She made old-fashioned Italian cookies and pastries that use ingredients like almond paste or figs; her one chocolate-cookie recipe calls for raisins and cloves.

Don't get me wrong; they're delicious. I have the Italian

chocolate-cookie recipe on an index card *from the kitchen of Connie Spadolini* and have shared it at the request of countless enamored friends.

But when you're trying to survive middle school, hanging out with latchkey kids who eat Oreos and Lay's Barbecue Potato Chips after school, you just want to fit in. You don't appreciate unique cookies or—in lieu of chips and French onion dip—hard cheese, salami and those garlicky green olives that smell to high heaven.

No, you don't want to expose your Working Mother Oreo Household friends to your house where your mom is always, *always* at home (aside from church or her standing weekly appointment to have her hair "done" at Shear Magique), cooking and cleaning and praying for people's souls.

Flash forward a good decade and a half: what I wouldn't give to be in that cluttered kitchen back in Brookside, biting into a hot, crisp, powdered-sugar-encrusted *sfinge*—which is pretty much cream-puff dough fried in a vat of hot oil, an age-old Saint Joseph's Day tradition.

For a moment, I'm so entrenched in homesick nostalgia that I forget why I really called my mother.

Then—oh, yeah.

"Hey, Ma, guess what?" I ask before remembering that I vowed never to say that to her again.

For this reason:

"You're pregnant!"

I sigh inwardly. "Why does everyone—" especially Connie Spadolini "—think I'm having a baby whenever I say I have news?"

"Because that's the best news there is," comes the simple reply amid running water and clattering pans.

"That depends on how you look at it, Ma." I can't resist saying, "If I were thirteen and unwed, would it be the best news?"

"That's different. And you don't kid around about stuff like that, Tracey," she says, undoubtedly saying a quick little prayer for my perennially touch-and-go soul.

"Sorry, Ma. So do you want to know the news even though it's not about another grandchild?"

It isn't as if she doesn't already have eight grandchildren and another on the way (my sister-in-law Katie is pregnant again).

"Of course I want to hear your news—wait a second." Sounding frustrated, she calls to my father, "No, Frank, I said get the *big* platter. The one we got from Fat Naso and Marie for our wedding.... No, the other one. Yes. That's it. Tracey? Are you there? What's your news?"

Talk about anticlimactic.

Still, I manage to summon a "Jack and I bought a house!"

Either I've stunned her into silence, or she's got a mouthful of something.

The latter, I realize, when I hear her chew and swallow before saying, "Oh, good! Where is it?"

I know that somewhere deep down inside, Connie honestly believes I might actually be moving back to Brookside. *Surprise, Ma!*

See, the thing is, no good news I ever give her is going to be the good news she wants to hear, which tends to diminish the pleasure in delivering the good news every time.

"It's in the suburbs," I tell her.

Pause. "Closer to home or farther away from home?"

By home, of course, she means Brookside.

I know better than to point out that A) Brookside is no longer my home and hasn't been in years, and B) Brookside is still a good four hundred-some miles away from Glenhaven Park.

"Um…closer, Ma. Definitely closer." By about thirty miles. "And it's a great house, old, with four bedrooms, so we'll have plenty of room for company. You guys will all have to come and visit us."

"That is neat," my mother says. "Frank, the kids bought a house!…Frank! Frank! I said the kids bought a house!"

An e-mail pops up in my in-box, from Kate again.

Tonight, please, whatever time. Really need to see you. Just call me when you're leaving and I'll meet you at the Campbell Apartment.

Uh-oh. It sounds kind of desperate.

Of course, even in her time of need, Kate thrives on fabulousness.

The Campbell Apartment is an amazingly atmospheric bar tucked away above the Vanderbilt Avenue entrance to Grand Central Station. Back in the Roaring Twenties, it was the private digs of a New York tycoon who was presumably named Campbell. It was uncovered about a decade ago, like some long-forgotten mausoleum.

Now it's been restored to its former Jazz Age glory with an ornately painted twenty-five-foot ceiling, a massive fireplace and lots of vintage furniture. The place is steeped in elegance with dim lighting and cocktails that easily cost twice as much per drink as a dinner entrée at Brookside's nicest restaurant. There's a strict dress code and someone suitably stern and dazzlingly intimidating stationed at the door to make sure potential patrons are properly swanky.

Luckily, I'm wearing a decent dark suit that can be swanked up if I remove the white blouse, change from low pumps to heels and add the decent silver necklace and earrings I keep hidden under the paper clip tray in my desk drawer for fashion emergencies.

I check my wallet and see that I've got enough cash for one glass of wine or a fancy cocktail, and the Budget Master will be none the wiser.

"Tracey, Pop says congratulations," my mother tells me.

"Really?"

"Yes, and he said make sure you don't buy the first house you look at."

I sigh inwardly.

I do a lot of that when talking long-distance to my mother. And even more when we talk in person.

"Ma, we already bought it, and anyway, this isn't the first house we looked at."

"Frank, this isn't the first house the kids looked at. Frank! I said, she says this isn't the first house they looked at!"

You know, after this conversation, I'm going to need a drink later.

Okay, see you then, I type back to Kate. Then, P.S., WE GOT THE HOUSE!!!!!!

"Pop wants to know how many houses you looked at," Connie Spadolini informs me.

"At least half a dozen," I say, which is almost the truth.

"Frank! They saw half a dozen houses. At least."

I hear the rumble of my father's voice, and then my mother tells me, "He says that's the same thing as the first house."

"No, it isn't. What does that even mean?"

"Do you want to talk to Pop? You know how cautious he is. He just wants you to be careful with your money."

"No, I'm at work right now," I remind her quickly as another e-mail clicks in from Kate.

All it says is: Great.

Does she mean great about my meeting her tonight, or great about us getting the house? "I really have to go," I tell my mother, noting the time on the e-mail.

"Are you cooking *sfinge* at home tonight?" she asks hopefully.

No, but I'll be drinking wine at the Campbell Apartment. Maybe so much wine I'll be moved to shout out *Viva San Giuseppe* a few times.

8

One look at Kate's face when she comes striding into the Campbell Apartment—cell phone in hand as though she's just hung up from a disturbing call—and it's clear there will be no revelry tonight, wine-fueled, or otherwise.

At least, not in this particular red-upholstered nook.

"Sorry I'm late." She sits beside me on the couch, in chic, sleeveless black, and is obviously distracted.

Has the personal chef quit? Did Mini-Kate cause bodily harm to the new nanny?

"It's okay. I was late, too. I just got here."

"Bad day at work?"

"As usual." Good thing I don't feel like talking about it,

because it's obvious that Kate isn't in the mood to be an ear or a shoulder. I have a feeling she needs both from me.

"Can I get something for you ladies?" The cocktail waitress arrives, also in chic, sleeveless black and just as distracted as Kate.

Without consulting me, Kate promptly orders two Prohibition Punches.

"I was actually going to have pinot grigio," I say.

"Go ahead, Tracey."

"What—oh."

The Prohibition Punches are both for her, further proof that we're not here to celebrate Saint Joseph's Day or discuss my new house.

Though Kate does say, as she tucks her cell phone back into a gi-normous designer handbag, "Listen, congratulations on getting the house. You must be so excited."

"We are. Definitely. We close around Memorial Day."

She smiles briefly. "That's so great."

But I can tell she doesn't want to hear about my plans for painting the ugly kitchen cabinets or planting a garden like my mother's.

"I don't know what I'll do without you," she says, and I wonder fleetingly if that's why she looks so upset.

Nah. My moving to the suburbs doesn't seem like a two-drink dilemma...unless you talk to Raphael, who practically hung up on me when I told him the house news earlier.

He blamed it on Georgie, his soon-to-be-son: "Congratulations, Tracey, Georgie needs the phone, gotta go."

Who knows? Maybe Georgie really did need the phone, though he's all of seven years old.

Or maybe Raphael is sulking.

I'm pretty sure he's just sulking.

I'm also sure he'll get over it.

Mental Note: e-mail Raphael tomorrow to see if we can get together Saturday night. He can't hang up on e-mail.

"I'll still be in the city every day for work," I remind Kate.

"Not on weekends."

"Knowing my job, weekends, too."

"It won't be the same, though."

"Nothing ever stays the same, Kate."

"Tracey, I know that. Believe me. I know." There's a tremulous note in her voice, and she looks away.

"What's going on with you?" I ask, and brace myself for the answer.

"It's Billy," she says, and my heart sinks.

I knew it.

He's having an affair. Damn him.

Then again, do you think maybe it's not what I thought? Wouldn't that be just too cliché?

But what else would bring this tragic pallor to Kate's flawless skin? Maybe Billy is dying of some horrible disease or just got a job transfer to Minot, North Dakota, or something.

"Billy's having an affair."

Mental Note: clichés are clichés because they're true.

"Oh, Kate." I grab both her hands. They're cold and bony and shaking like crazy. "What did he say?"

"He didn't say anything."

"You caught him with another woman?"

"No!"

Oh, right. That was me.

"It's just…I feel like he's different. Like he doesn't love me anymore. He's so wrapped up in his e-mail or text messages or whatever it is that he's always checking for on his BlackBerry, and he's been working out a lot more, and spending less time with me and Katie, and getting home really late at night," she says in a rush. Her Southern twang is always much more pronounced when she gets worked up like this. "He always says he was at work or out with clients but…I don't know if I believe him. Actually, I don't. I don't believe him. But it's not like I have anything to go on."

No…but I do.

The moment of truth has arrived.

Here is where I can either tell Kate she's jumping to conclusions and that none of those things—even added together—necessarily mean Billy's having an affair.

Or I can tell her what I saw on Horatio Street.

Even though I didn't really see anything explicit.

To tell, or not to tell. If it were me, would I want to know?

Hell, yes.

Anyway, she already knows. Just like I do.

I take a deep breath. "Kate, I saw Billy out really late

one night a few weeks ago in the Meatpacking District with a woman."

She wrenches her hands out of mine to press them against her throat, sucks in a lot of air, and her eyes get huge. "Who was she?"

"I have no idea."

"Why didn't you tell me this before?"

"I don't know…I guess I just didn't think much of it at the time." Big fat lie.

I hate myself for not telling her before.

I hate that Ass-wipe Billy even more, though, for putting me in this position.

"Oh, God. What was she wearing, Tracey?"

"A business suit," I say, wishing that sounded reassuring. "Maybe she was a colleague of his."

"Was she tall and skinny with shoulder-length dark curly hair?" she asks, and I nod reluctantly. "Did she have super-white teeth and a mole on her shoulder and a slight British accent even though she's not from freaking Britain at all and probably has never even been there?"

Hmm. Methinks these aren't just random questions.

"I—I mean, I didn't see her shoulder. Or her teeth. Or hear her voice. They were far away."

"What were they doing?" Kate's voice is barely controlled hysteria, and she rakes a hand through her blond hair.

"Nothing, just walking down the street. They got into a cab."

"Together?"

I nod.

"Shit. Did it head downtown or up?"

No way around this. "Down."

"I knew it." Kate shakes her head, tears in her eyes.

"Kate—"

"I know who she is. Marlise, from his old job. She lives in Battery Park City. I met her at the office Christmas party and she was dressed like a dirty little ho in some strapless thing."

I—who incidentally met my husband while dressed like a dirty little ho at the office Christmas party—am not sure quite what to say to that, except, "Maybe it wasn't her."

"It definitely was. But if it wasn't," she adds with the logic of a spurned wife, "it was *someone.* Some woman. Not me."

"It could have been business."

Wait, why are you doing this? Inner Tracey demands. *You know what Billy's up to. You've known it since the second you saw him that night.*

"It wasn't business," Kate snaps, and I don't blame her.

"Where's the waitress with our drinks?" I ask, thinking that'll somehow help.

Which is the same reason I'm instinctively trying—at least verbally—to give Billy the benefit of the doubt.

I'm not trying to protect him, I'm trying to protect Kate. I want to make her feel better, even if it's just momentary. Even if her future is clear as Grey Goose: she's going to be one of those brittle, beautiful, wealthy single mothers who populate the cavernous, lonely apartments in the city's most exclusive neighborhoods after their husbands move on and move in with other women, other families.

I wonder if Marlise has a husband and children.

I wonder if Kate will be better off without Billy.

I wish I could say yes, because I can't stand the SOB, but Kate loves him and on some level, they do suit each other. They come from similar backgrounds, appreciate the same things—things that might not matter to other people. Like labels and good bourbon and fine art and ridiculously extravagant tchotchkes in the Neiman Marcus Christmas catalog.

Besides, on her own, Kate would be—well, maybe not helpless, exactly, but she did go from being daddy's girl to sorority girl to coddled wife. Of course, Billy did his coddling not with cuddling but with cash, hiring others to do things like cook for her and massage her, things Jack does for me.

The truth is, without Billy, Kate would be miserable. Even more miserable than she is right now.

"What am I going to do, Tracey?" she asks, her beautiful aquamarine eyes so flooded with tears that I hope her colored contacts don't raft down her cheeks.

"Confront him?"

She nods. "I'll tell him you saw him with—"

"No, wait, Kate—don't drag me into this."

"But you're the one who saw him, not me."

"Yes, but he didn't see me. And I didn't really see anything."

"You saw my husband get into a cab with another woman in the middle of the night and head in the opposite direction of home."

"Well, if you're going to bring it up to him, tell him someone saw him. Don't mention that it was me."

"Why do you even care?"

Because something tells me she and Billy are going to patch things up no matter what he was up to, and I'm the one he'll resent for the rest of his life.

Not that he's my favorite person, or that I'm his.

"I probably shouldn't care," I admit to Kate, "but it would make things pretty uncomfortable when I see him."

"You think you'll be uncomfortable? What about me? I'm the one he's cheating on. You know what? I really wish I'd slept with Gabriel when I had my chance."

"Who's Gabriel?"

"My old personal trainer, remember?"

Vaguely. But I tend to tune her out when she starts talking about the gym. Which, by the way, is a private one, on the third floor of her house. Billy had it put in just for her; he prefers to go to some athletic club—also private, but presumably filled with buff and beautiful people. Women.

"You had a chance to sleep with Gabriel?" I ask Kate.

She nods and delicately blows her nose in a lace handkerchief. "We were together every single day for hours, all flushed and sweaty, when I was trying to lose my baby weight."

Her baby weight was all of ten pounds, and it took her maybe two weeks to lose it, which is why I might hate Kate if I didn't love her. And I just can't see her flushed and sweaty, even in a gym setting.

"Did he make a move on you?" I ask.

"No, but he wanted to. I could tell."

I don't doubt her. "But I think you were right not to do anything about it, Kate. That would only bring you down to Billy's level. You're better than that."

Our drinks arrive at long last. She chugs hers, then has another. I switch to seltzer, thinking one of us had better keep her wits about her if we're both getting home safely tonight.

I walk Kate the few blocks down Park Avenue, back to her brick town house on Thirty-eighth. She cries the entire time. She's more sad than angry now. I wish she were angry, because I feel like that would give her more strength.

I'm hoping Billy the Bastard won't be there when we arrive, because I don't know what will happen if he is. In Kate's condition, she might confront him, and I don't want to be in the middle of it.

He isn't there, though. Just Katie, who's asleep in the nursery, and the nanny, who, Kate tells me, is upstairs in her quarters.

There was a time when I fantasized about living in a place like this, one that has a nursery and "quarters" for the live-in help. Kate's house is spotless, sterile, plush, hushed, same as always (unless the Screaming Jesus is awake, in which case there is no hush). There's nothing lived-in about it. I used to think the baby was going to change that, but this just isn't the kind of house where you step over Tinkertoys or find crumbs on the coffee table.

Our house—mine and Jack's—will never be like this. Thank God.

It's hard to believe I used to covet Kate's beautiful home, filled with rare antiques and heirloom rugs and expensive art.

Now, as I leave her alone there, tearfully running a bath in her marble bathroom with custom-built cabinetry, I find myself thinking I'll take ugly old cupboards any day, even if I never do get around to painting them.

Our new house has a lived-in, loved-in feeling that all the money in the world can't buy.

Our old apartment, when I get there, also has something all the money in the world can't buy—or, for that matter, make go away: Mitch.

He's sprawled on our barely three-month-old couch wearing sweats, a bowl of popcorn balanced on his stomach. Jack is in his favorite chair, leaning elbows on knees toward the TV, where a basketball game is obviously in a pivotal moment.

It takes both of them a few seconds to even realize I'm there.

"Hi, Tracey!" Mitch sits up and has the grace to look vaguely guilty for having parked his sock feet on the cushion where I normally sit. "Here, want to sit down?"

Uh, not there.

In fact, not anywhere. It's late, and all I want to do right now is go to bed. With my husband, but I have a feeling that's not going to happen anytime before midnight.

"No, thanks," I say. "I'm just going to go to bed in a minute. It's been a long day."

"Hey, while we have you here," Mitch says as I kiss the top of Jack's head, "have you seen Jack's jockstrap?"

"Um…no?"

"What the heck did you do with it, bro?" Mitch asks Jack, who shrugs.

To me, Mitch says helpfully, "He couldn't find it."

"No kidding."

"We were going to play racquetball, but Jack didn't want his junk flopping around," Mitch informs me without so much as a cringe.

"That's understandable." I am so cringing inwardly—and noticing that Jack is paying no attention whatsoever to this conversation.

"So much for racquetball, so here we are," Mitch concludes.

"Yeah," I say, "here you are. Bummer."

He nods in agreement, obviously thinking I'm referring the missing jockstrap.

I ruffle Jack's hair to get his attention.

"So what was up with Kate?" he asks, eyes fastened to the screen.

If Mitch wasn't here, I'd tell him what was up with Kate. In fact, I wish Mitch weren't here so I could tell him, because I'm feeling pretty bummed and burdened.

"She just wanted to celebrate our new house with me."

"Really? I thought you said it seemed like something was going on with her. I figured you were going to come home and tell me Billy's cheating or something."

"Why would you figure that?" I ask, and my voice sounds unnaturally high.

Jack shrugs, still maddeningly focused on the television. "No reason."

"There must be some reason."

With a sigh, he grabs the TiVo remote and freeze-frames the screen mid-jump shot.

"Hey!" Mitch bellows, and I want to tell him to go home and watch his own TV, but I don't.

I ignore him and say to Jack, "Did you know Billy was having an affair?"

Oops.

"Billy's having an affair?"

I glance at Mitch. Yeah, he's listening in, munching popcorn as if he's in the front row at the multiplex.

"I didn't say Billy was having an affair," I tell Jack. "That was you."

"No, it was you, too."

"No, it wasn't." Good thing there's no conversational TiVo remote that would allow Jack to rewind and replay the whole exchange.

"You did say it, Tracey," Mitch puts in, and I want to put a big couch pillow over his stupid head and sit on it.

I shake my head and walk toward the bedroom, saying over my shoulder, "Billy is not having an affair."

"Billy's having an affair," I tell Jack the next morning as we walk to the subway on the way to work. It rained in the night and it's trash-pickup day, so everything smells like wet garbage. Nice.

"What!" Jack gapes at me. "I thought you said he wasn't."

"I did say he wasn't."

"So...what happened? I didn't hear the phone ring in the night, and you didn't check your e-mail. Was this news bulletin somehow telepathically beamed into your brain while you were sleeping?"

"No, I knew about it last night, but I didn't tell you because Mitch was there." I pause, wondering whether now is the right time to bring up the fact that freaking Mitch is freaking always there.

I decide against it, for two reasons.

The first: we're moving away from Mitch in about sixty-four days (okay, *exactly* sixty-four days; I counted).

The other: Jack has been ultrasensitive lately about Mitch.

He seems to have gotten it into his head that I think Mitch is a pain in the keister.

Okay, maybe I put that into his head.

And I only said it when I found out that Mitch had found and polished off the Garden of Eatin' Salsa Reds I had been hoarding in a remote cupboard.

I'm really hoping absence will make my heart grow fonder, but until we move, Mitch being a fixture in our lives is a sore subject that I'd rather not get into again with my husband.

"Remember when you asked me last night if Billy was cheating on Kate?" I ask Jack as we step over an oil-slicked river of gutter water on the corner of Lexington Avenue. "What made you say that?"

"No specific reason. Just a vibe I got from him when we were out the other night."

So I'm not the only one with a vibe.

Though, of course, I've got something more significant than a vibe. I've got cold hard evidence.

I tell Jack about how I saw Billy in the Meatpacking District with some woman the night I went to Raphael's.

"I hope you didn't tell Kate about that," is his response.

"Why?"

"Because you don't need to get into the middle of their marital problems. Trust me, you can't win."

Stopping at a crosswalk, we both jump back as a Yellow Cab whips around the corner dangerously close to the curb, splashing gutter water over our ankles. All in a day's walk here in Manhattan.

God, I can't wait to get out of here.

"Don't you think I owe it to Kate to tell her what I saw?" I ask Jack as the sign changes to Walk and we cross the street.

"You didn't *see* anything. You said so yourself."

"I saw him with another woman."

"You don't know what was going on."

"Even you think he's having an affair."

"What I think doesn't matter. Neither does what you think. I'm telling you, Tracey, I've been through a divorce with my parents. Don't say anything to Kate about that night."

"Too late. I told her."

Jack just shakes his head.

For a few moments, we walk on in silence.

"I'm starting to think it's a good thing we're moving soon." That didn't come from me. I'm not just starting to think it's a good thing we're moving; I've thought so from day one.

"I can't believe you just said that," I tell Jack.

"Don't you think things are getting a little claustrophobic around here?"

"Definitely—but I didn't think you did."

"Yeah," Jack says, "I do."

"I didn't think you were ready to move."

"I didn't think so, either. Sometimes I think if it weren't

for you lighting a fire under me, I'd never make any changes in my life."

"I don't know about that, but you'd still be living in your dumpy Brooklyn apartment with Mike Middleford."

He's Jack's former roommate, who was also my former boss, a minor stumbling block on our path to true love. I was initially reluctant to date Jack because I was afraid of running into my boss in his underwear.

The funny thing is, it did eventually happen, but by that time, Mike and I were more like old pals and he was well on his way to getting fired from Blaire Barnett anyway. Not, thank God, for reasons that had anything whatsoever to do with me, or his tighty whities.

Last we heard, Mike was still—or was it again?—unemployed and living in Jersey with his wife, Dianne, and a couple of kids.

Funny how you manage to lose touch with the people who once shared so much of your life, right down to your address.

Thinking of Mike, Yvonne and Thor, Sonja, and even my long-ago ex-boyfriend, Will McCraw, I can't help but wonder who else is going to fade from our lives as the years march on. Especially if we're no longer living in the heart of the city.

Like I told Kate last night—or maybe Kate told me—nothing ever stays the same. Life is all about change.

Wasn't I the one who was telling Jack just days ago that he should embrace it?

His family has certainly embraced it.

When his sister Kathleen heard we were moving, she had the twins call us and leave an a cappella singing message on our answering machine, which was sweet.

Kind of.

Okay, it was also kind of awful: they had written the unintelligible lyrics themselves, either set to the tune of "Here Comes Santa Claus" or Iron Butterfly's "In-A-Gadda-Da-Vida"; it was impossible to tell which.

They ended the message with one of them—I'm sure it was Ashley—saying, "You're going to love living here, Aunt Tracey and Uncle Jack, and just think, now you get to see us all the time!"

Yeah. Just think.

Jack's sister Jeannie, a court reporter who lives with her husband, Greg, in Putnam County, called to offer their help in fixing up our house. That's just like her: she's working full-time to put Greg through law school, is six months pregnant, and they're in the midst of dealing with their own fixer-upper. I found myself volunteering to help her and Greg paint the room for the baby and babysit when the time comes—not that Jeannie would ever take me up on it. She's the opposite of Kathleen, who probably would have also asked me to build a bookshelf and be their wet nurse.

Jack's sister Rachel, who got married last year and lives about fifteen minutes from Glenhaven Park, is excited that we'll be living nearby and said she and her husband, Nolan, can't wait to show us around. She's my favorite sister-in-law and I really like her husband, though Jack thinks he's too competitive. I'm sure it's all in his head because I've always found Nolan perfectly nice—not that we've ever spent much time with him. It was a whirlwind courtship and marriage. I'm looking forward to getting to know him better and spending more time with Rachel.

As for Jack's youngest sister, Emily, who's single and works in the fashion industry, she's in Paris on business. I e-mailed her to tell her about the move and received an e-mail back that said, "Wah! I can't believe you're leaving the city. What am I going to do without you guys?"

Which is pretty ironic, considering that Emily lives a scant seven blocks from us in Manhattan yet we haven't seen her since the holidays. She's caught up in clubbing and hob-nobbing with the socialite-heiress-debutante-rehab crowd; needless to say, Jack and I don't fit in.

We'll slip much more smoothly into the suburban lives of the rest of the family, I'm sure.

Well…pretty sure.

I mean, it's not like they'll expect us to see them every day, right?

Of course not. That would be my family.

Jack's family is much more hands off, thank God. Even Kathleen doesn't bother us, for the most part.

Then again, we've always lived miles away and Kathleen hates the city. It's near the top of a long list of things that exhaust her. The devilmint twins, I'm sure, are number one.

But when you're married, family comes with the territory, right?

Right.

And God knows Jack has put up with his share of stress from the Spadolini contingent. A lesser man would have bailed the first time he came out of the bathroom at my parents' house—way back before we were even engaged—to be greeted by Connie Spadolini asking, "Well? Did you poop?"

I, of course, was mortified. But Jack, who had been having stomach problems that morning, didn't bat an eye. He thought it was sweet that my mother was so concerned for his well-being.

I can't imagine Wilma Candell ever asking me, upon exiting her bathroom, whether I pooped.

For that matter, I can't imagine Wilma Candell pooping.

Yes, Jack and I certainly do come from different worlds.

As we walk down the stairs to the subway, I slip my hand into his.

He looks at me. "What?"

"Nothing. I just really love you."

"I just really love you, too."

He just really does.

Even though I've gone and turned our lives completely upside down.

I'm not saying that's a bad thing. I'm not saying I no longer want to move, or that the house isn't our dream house. I'm just saying it's not going to be easy to leave another phase of our lives behind.

But moving doesn't have to mean losing touch with our city friends. There are people like Kate, and Buckley, and Raphael and Latisha, who I know will be a part of our lives forever.

No matter what, I vow fiercely, and try to ignore a little shred of foreboding.

9

Tomorrow is the long-awaited Closing Day on our brand-new Dream House.

Today is the long-dreaded Purge Day on our cluttered old apartment.

Jack and I have both taken a couple of personal days off from work for the move. Mitch wanted to do the same, but I convinced him it wasn't necessary. Lately, he's been hanging around even more than usual—if that's possible. The last thing I want is him looking over my shoulder as I sort through my underwear drawer, trying to figure out what stays and what goes.

In the interest of a fresh start—and not inflating the moving company's hourly rate by having them pack and transport a lot of stuff we don't need—Jack and I have made a pact to throw away every single thing that is not absolutely essential.

That seems pretty cut-and-dried, doesn't it?

It might be, if we had the same definition of *essential.*

Jack says *essential* is anything a person can't live without.

I say *essential* is anything a person can't live without and/or anything that a person once believed he/she—okay, mostly *she*—couldn't live without.

This includes but is not limited to dog-earred Judy Blume books; mixed tapes dating back to middle school; Cipro antibiotics in case there's another anthrax scare (label says it expired in 2003, but I figure expired Cipro is better than no Cipro at all); an old address book; lots of small hotel-size bottles of shampoo, conditioner, mouthwash, lotion and shower caps (no, I don't use shower caps, but you never know when you might have a houseguest who will need one); three dozen take-out chopsticks in paper sleeves; two tall stacks of recycled plastic Chinese soup containers (I conceded and threw the third stack away); and certain trendy clothing items that will undoubtedly be making a reappearance in *Glamour* any season now. Leggings, anyone?

This collection *excludes* mementos of Will McCraw, whom I once believed I couldn't live without.

Not only do I no longer think about Will, I no longer have the urge to keep anything that might trigger unwanted thoughts of Will. In the course of today's purge, I've thrown away countless letters from Will, old programs from productions starring Will (though I did keep the hapless eye-candy review, tee hee) and even some old photos of me with Will, which I'll admit were pretty easy to part with considering that I was a good fifty pounds heavier when I was dating him.

I have also dutifully thrown away a lot of candy and gum wrappers, stray socks without partners, expired credit cards and a few nearly empty containers from the fridge. Yes, I've kept many other nearly empty containers—like my favorite Abraham's baba ghanoush, which I'm not sure I'll be able to find in Glenhaven Park. And yes, I kept a few single socks, as well as a select number of partnerless earrings I plan to wear if A) their partners ever surface, or B) that asymmetrical-earring look ever comes back into vogue.

I'm not saying that would be a good thing. Just that if it does happen, I'll be equipped.

Meanwhile, Jack has been pitching mercilessly from the second he got out of bed this morning. It's like he awoke with a mission: to rid our world of several perfectly good, expensive cardigan sweaters; a bunch of hardcover novels he claims to have already read; a pile of CDs he says he never listens to—true, but who says he might not want to listen to them someday?; even his old cell phone, which I pluck from the top of the garbage bag when I see it.

"What are you doing?" Jack asks, looking up from my kitchen junk drawer.

"You can't just throw away a phone."

"Why not? I have no use for it."

I wait to answer him until a deafening wailing siren has passed by somewhere outside and below.

"For one thing, it's bad citizenship."

"Huh?"

"It's not environmentally responsible. It's just going to sit in a landfill and poison the earth." I'm actually not a hundred percent sure of that but I thought I saw something about it on *Dateline,* or maybe that was computers. "And for another thing, all your contact information is in there."

"So? It doesn't even have a battery."

"What's to stop an identity thief from getting a battery, powering up the phone and becoming Jack Candell?"

He snorts. "All that's in it are a bunch of old phone numbers."

"Or so you think. That's what the identity thief is counting on." I look up as, overhead, one of the circus freaks takes a ceiling-fixture-jarring dive.

Ignoring it, Jack asks, "You honestly think an identity thief is going to rifle through that bag of garbage looking for a cell phone when he can just as easily steal someone's wallet for a lot less trouble?"

"Yes. It happens all the time. I saw that on *Dateline,* too," I add for good measure. I can't be sure, but it's likely. I see a lot of things on *Dateline.*

Jack grumbles something and goes back to the junk

drawer, which is not likely to be spared, since it's filled with…well, junk.

Watching him dispose of several flat strips of twist ties, I vow to rescue them from the garbage as soon as he turns his back. You can never have too many twist ties.

Meanwhile, I start emptying the cabinet under the sink, which contains two recycling bins, several of those no-frills glass vases you get when the florist delivers a bouquet, and a whole lot of cleaning supplies.

"Wait, why are you throwing those away?" Jack asks as I carry half a dozen beer bottles toward the trash bag. "We can return them for the deposit."

"No, they were Coronas from that Cinco de Mayo dinner." We had Buckley here that night. Jack had originally thought we should have a bigger guest list, but I (privately) decided we should limit it to just people who aren't Mitch, and people who are psyched about our upcoming move.

Buckley is seriously the only one of our friends who fits that bill—although I probably shouldn't say he's psyched, exactly. More like, not offended by it. I'm sure he would be psyched if he weren't so distracted by the second novel he's trying to write.

I'm still not feeling the love from the others: Kate, Raphael, Latisha. I'm sure they'll all come around, and of course they're all busy with their own stuff these days.

Too busy to help us purge and pack, that's for sure. Well, Buckley said he would stop by, but he has yet to show.

I guess I don't really blame Kate for not wanting to pitch in. She and Billy are officially on the rocks. She confronted him about Marlise—I didn't have the heart to ask her whether or not she mentioned my seeing him with her—and he not only promptly admitted to the affair, but asked Kate for a divorce.

Which she refused him, if you can believe that. Instead, she dragged him to marriage counseling. I picture their sessions as Kate crying her eyes out to some impartial stranger while a detached Billy text messages his girlfriend.

The sad thing is, according to Kate, I'm not all that far off the mark.

"Corona bottles," Jack is saying, "are recyclable. Now who's a bad citizen?"

"Sure as hell not me. There are old limes inside, see?"

"Can't you get them out?"

"No, they're all moldy."

"Yeah, but we can still put them into the bottle-recycling machine at the supermarket. It doesn't care about moldy limes."

"Talk about bad citizenship…do you really want moldy limes ground into your recycled products?"

"I'm sure the ground-up glass is cleaned before it's turned into…what is it turned into, anyway?"

"I have no idea. But these are disgusting and I'm throwing them away."

"A second ago you were worried about saving the planet

from my old cell phone. Now you're tossing bottles that are supposed to be recyclable."

"I sure am." I pitch them into the trash with a clatter. "Mold overrules recyclable."

"If you found a quarter, would you throw that away?"

"That's different."

"No, it isn't. We can't afford to throw away money these days."

Uh-oh. Here's the austerity budget again, rearing its ugly head. We've been on it for over two months now, and it hasn't been quite as bad as I expected.

Yet ever since we signed the contract for the house—which was right around the time Jack's father's lawyer informed him that the contested will is going to be hung up indefinitely—Jack's been quietly freaking out about money. Never mind that the bank concluded that we can afford the new house, even without the inheritance.

Jack keeps asking—usually in the wee small hours of the morning—what we're going to do if one of us loses our job.

That's not unheard of in our industry. Agencies lose accounts and have to do massive layoffs all the time. They fire people, too. Legend has it that some underling once left a comma out of a presentation document, and the group director was fired. Whenever someone makes a stupid mistake, the Client expects to see someone's head roll as a result—preferably someone more significant and satisfying than the errant underling.

Ironically, it took me this long to figure out that there really was an upside to underlingdom. When the powers that be don't know you even exist, and you're not making any money, you have a hell of a lot less to lose.

But one of the agency's premier accounts, McMurray-White, is up for review. They're a huge Midwestern packaged-goods company, and the makers of Abate Laxatives, among many other products.

If the agency loses the account, massive layoffs are inevitable. I—as low man on the Creative totem pole—would lose my job for sure. That would have been a godsend, pre-house mortgage.

Jack, who also works on their business, has more seniority and other accounts, but who knows? Sometimes everybody goes, not just people who work only on that account.

If Jack or I get laid off, our monthly mortgage payment would be in instant jeopardy.

"Fine," I tell Jack, and retrieve the beer bottles, with their white-fuzz-covered, blackened lime wedges from the garbage. "We can recycle them. But you deal with it, please."

"I will." He tosses a handful of hot-mustard and duck-sauce packets, then asks, "Why do we have cherry-tomato-seed packets in this drawer?"

"They came in the mail, some promotional thing, a few years ago. I saved them."

"Because…?"

"Because I was going to plant them."

"Where, in the rug?"

"Wait, don't throw those away. They're for my garden." At Jack's dubious look, I say, "Why do you always look at me that way when I mention my garden?"

"Because you don't *have* a garden?"

"I will as soon as we move."

"I know, it's just...you keep talking about it, and reading about it..." He eyes the stack of gardening magazines I've accumulated in the past few months. "Do you want to throw some of those away?"

"No! I haven't actually read any of them yet. I've been too busy. But I will."

"Yeah...what's up with it, though, Trace?"

I tell him about my mother and the hot August afternoons.

"Yeah, but you can always buy fresh tomatoes and basil and flowers any time of year. You do now."

"It's not the same. The tomatoes were so sweet and that deep red color."

"You can get sweet, deep red tomatoes now. On the vine, even."

He just doesn't understand. I try to explain. "But they're not warm from the sun. They always tasted better warm from the sun."

"Okay, okay, whatever. I get it."

But he doesn't.

Seeing my scowl, he adds defensively, "I just never knew you had such a hankering to make things grow."

To be honest, I didn't, either. It's a relatively new phenomenon. For all I know, it's displaced maternal longing. Or maybe there's just something about all this concrete that makes me long to plant something and watch it grow. Or maybe I'm just feeling nostalgic and homesick for my mother and the tomato salads of my childhood.

"I guess I just have a green thumb like my mother," I tell Jack, who doesn't look convinced. "We're Sicilian, after all."

The thing is...

My mother, when I spoke to her the other night, didn't sound so good. She admitted she hadn't been feeling well, either.

I'm not a worrier—

Okay, I *am* a worrier, but usually not about my mother, who is invincible.

But that conversation made me feel uneasy. I really need to plan a trip back to Brookside as soon as possible so that I can see for myself how she is.

Not that I'm not a hundred percent certain she's fine, but...

"So you're really going to plant a garden, huh?" Jack smiles.

"Yes, and don't laugh at me."

"I'm not laughing. I'm picturing you out in the sun, picking tomatoes. I think that's sweet. Come here." He pulls me into his arms and presses his forehead against mine.

I laugh. "What are you doing?"

"Want to take a break from purging? We still have our bed, don't we? You didn't chuck it into the trash?"

"Nope."

Jack and I both agree on that, at least—that furniture is essential.

It's in the definition of furniture that we run into trouble.

I would say anything made of wood. Like our oak sleigh bed, which was my first major adult purchase, back when I was slightly single during my first summer in the city.

Jack would include plastic (the stacked milk crates he uses as a bedside table), rubber (an airbed that may or may not have a hole) and cardboard (the aforementioned CD cabinet he bought at Wal-Mart), all of which I'm plotting to throw into the trash as the day wears on.

"Come on." Jack pulls my hand toward the bedroom.

"What about Buckley?"

"What about him?"

"He's supposed to be coming over."

"Well, it's not like he can just walk in on us," Jack points out, and he's right.

All this building security is a definite plus. When we move into our house, people can show up right outside our window and peer in at us.

Not that I expect that to happen.

But I suppose it could.

Somewhere overhead, the circus freaks' interior designer drags an armoire across the floor. Or something like that.

Glancing up, Jack knits his brow and asks, "What do you think they're really doing up there?"

"I told you. Redecorating or disposing of dead bodies. Whatever. Just think, after today, it won't matter. We'll be home sweet home." Reaching our bed, I shove overboard a heap of clothes on hangers.

Jack sits on the edge of the mattress and pulls me down beside him. "I don't want you to get your hopes up too high, Trace."

"What do you mean?"

"I feel like you think this house is the answer to all our problems."

"Well, it's the answer to the circus-freak problem, and the roach problem, and the street-noise problem, and the M.C. problem—" Yes, the Mad Crapper is still on the loose, inching ever closer to our doormat. "Unless you're the M.C.," I add, and ask Jack, "You're not, are you?"

"No."

"Good."

"Are you?"

"No."

"Good."

We smile briefly at each other.

Then Jack says, "I just want you to be realistic. We're buying a total fixer-upper, and we haven't even seen it since we walked through it with Verna over two months ago."

Nothing is going to burst my bubble, dammit!

"We had it professionally inspected," I remind him, "and it was structurally fine. Do you think the foundation has crumbled and termites have gotten to it since we saw it?"

"No..."

"I mean, I suppose Hank and Marge could have hung more bad wallpaper, but we can deal with that, right?"

"Right."

"Be happy for us, Jack."

"I *am* happy for us."

"Everything's going to be fine. I promise you."

"You sound pretty sure about that."

"I am."

And I'm right.

For about a week, anyway.

That's how long we have before the shit hits the fan in a way even the Mad Crapper's wildest dreams couldn't conjure.

But I don't know that just yet, so I'm feeling pretty content by the time Jack and I, sated, stroll back to our abandoned project, just in time for Jimmy to call upstairs to announce Buckley's belated arrival.

He blows in the door with a bottle of champagne, flushed cheeks and a "Sorry I'm late, guys. Look what I brought."

Leave it to Buckley to think of toasting our little apartment's last hurrah.

Except that he didn't.

"Guess what? Are you sitting down?" He looks at me and Jack. "No, you are not. Sit down. You have to sit down."

We look around the cluttered room.

"There's nowhere to sit," Jack points out. "What's up? Wait, I know. You're pregnant."

Buckley flashes him a distracted grin. "Seriously, sit, you guys."

"Is everyone all right?" I ask Buckley, because when people tell you to sit down, something big is going on.

It's not my mother, is it? I want to ask. *Please don't let it be my mother.*

Which is ridiculous, and I need to get a grip.

Mental Note: if something were wrong with my mother, it wouldn't be Buckley who'd show up to tell us, with a bottle of champagne in hand, no less.

Okay. So my mother is still obviously hanging in there.

But something is definitely up. Something big and good.

"Paramount just optioned my book for seven figures," shouts Buckley, who never, ever shouts.

Jack lets out a *whoop* and slaps him on the back.

"Oh my God! Buckley!" I hurtle myself at him, squealing. "This is amazing!"

"I know. I can't believe it. I feel dazed." He *looks* dazed, all wide-eyed and glowing. "They want me to collaborate on the screenplay."

"You're going to write a screenplay? Do you even know how?"

"For a million bucks, I'll figure it out."

"When did all this happen?"

"Just now. Today. That's why I'm late," he says breathlessly as Jack produces three champagne flutes from a high cupboard. "I had to tell my mom, and my sister, and then I had to call this Realtor my agent suggested—"

"You're already shopping for mansions?" I ask. "Maybe you can find one in Glenhaven Park. Then we can be neighbors! Although," I add teasingly, "I didn't see any mansions on our block. But I'm sure there are—"

Then I catch sight of the look on Buckley's face.

Uh-oh. "What?" I ask.

"The Realtor is helping me find a place—not a mansion, though—in L.A."

"Buckley! No!" Jack gives me a look, which I ignore. I can't help it. I don't want Buckley to move to the West Coast any more than…

Any more than Raphael and Kate want me to move to the suburbs, I suppose.

"It's part of the screenwriting deal," Buckley explains. "I have to be out there by next month."

"For good?"

He hesitates. "For now."

"Well, we're really happy for you, Buckley," Jack says, putting a champagne flute into my hand. "Right, Trace?"

"Right."

Jack gives me another look. I guess I sound less than enthusiastic.

You know, I thought Jack was the one who hated change,

but he seems okay with all of this. Maybe it's me. Maybe, for all my big plans, I'm the one who would just as soon stay put in the end, and keep things just the way they are, forever.

Maybe I hate change.

Maybe I don't want to let go, after all.

Maybe I just want to hold on tight.

In that spirit, I give Buckley a big, heartfelt hug. "You know I'm going to miss you like crazy."

"I'm going to miss you, too."

"But this is a great opportunity for you."

"Yeah," he says, beaming. "It really is. Thanks, Tracey."

He sounds a little strangled. Realizing I'm crushing his lungs, I release him. "Just promise me one thing."

"What is it?"

"If you get nominated for a screenwriting Academy Award, and you don't have a date because your starlet girlfriend is away in rehab and your mother and sister are busy, take me to the Oscars. That's all I ask. Oh, and give me a cut of your goody bag."

Buckley breaks into a big grin. "Deal. If you make a deal with me in return."

"What's that?"

"Don't mention this to Raphael just yet. You know how he is."

I nod solemnly. I absolutely know how he is: obsessive about anything remotely Hollywood related. If he finds out Buckley is moving to la-la land and hobnobbing with people of TMZ-video ilk, he'll figure out a way to tag along as, I don't know, Buckley's houseboy or something.

Jack pours the champagne so that we can toast Buckley's amazing success, and Hollywood and Glenhaven Park, standing in our living room this one last time all together.

"To happy endings," Buckley says.

"And new beginnings," Jack adds.

I don't say anything at all.

I can't, because there's a huge lump in my throat.

10

Well, it's official.

Jack and I have just closed on the house. We are now home owners.

For such a landmark occasion, the closing itself is pretty understated. Not that I expect to step off the train in Glenhaven Park and be met by the mayor, streamers and a marching band to escort us down the main drag to the lawyer's office.

But when you think about the milestones in your life—first communions, weddings, childbirth—they are usually surrounded by ritualistic fanfare.

Buying a house is as low-key as a trip to the dentist, from the clipboard sign-in and bad magazines in the waiting room to the parting gift—not a new toothbrush, but a refrigerator magnet calendar.

Of course, the dentist involves considerably more gore (if you have the misfortune to inherit the bad Spadolini teeth, as I did), considerably less paperwork and a mere ten-dollar co-pay. As opposed to a mountain of contracts and about fifty thousand times the co-pay. And let me tell you, all that *ch-ching, ch-ching* is far more nerve-shattering than the dreaded high-pitched hum of the drill firing up.

The highlight of the closing is meeting Hank and Marge, who turn out to be exactly as charming and folksy as I imagined. They show up holding hands and wearing hats and suits, à la 1948 and tell us how happy they are to be selling their house to a nice young couple like us.

We promise them we'll take good care of it, and we are all hugging and a little misty-eyed by the time the whole thing is over.

"What now?" I ask Jack, back out on the street less than an hour later, depleted checkbook and keys in pocket. "Should we go check out the house again? Or go out and celebrate?"

"We don't have time for that—or money, for that matter," proclaims the Budget Master. "We have about twenty-four hours to get out of our apartment, and we're nowhere near ready."

This is true.

It seems a little anticlimactic to take the train straight back to our apartment in the city to finish packing, but that's what we do.

Good thing, because it takes forever.

Somewhere in the midst of all that, I spoke to my sister, who said she had talked my mother into going to the doctor this coming week for a checkup.

Mary Beth sounded worried. Which shouldn't have bothered me, because Mary Beth frequently sounds worried. But I'm worried, too: the invincible Connie Spadolini has been feeling uncharacteristically fatigued, and Mary Beth said she doesn't look good, either.

I'm going to try to get up there in the next week or two to see for myself.

What if something is seriously wrong with my mother?

Riddled with uncertainty, I pushed the thought from my head and concentrated on packing.

By the wee hours, we have run out of boxes. I am bleary-eyed and haphazardly throwing stuff into big black Hefty bags, hoping I'm hitting the ones that are meant to be moved, as opposed to the ones that are meant to be tossed.

For all I know, my shoes and belts are lying at the base of the building's garbage chute—possibly in a fresh Mad Crapper load—and we're transporting to Glenhaven Park a bag filled with expired condiments and old newspapers.

At long last, we collapse into bed on this, our last night in the city that never sleeps.

We manage to get all of two hours' shut-eye before the

alarm goes off at 5:00 a.m., and I awaken swamped in ambivalence.

Not just about the daunting day ahead, but the equally daunting lifetime ahead in Glenhaven Park.

Even now, I am not a hundred percent sure we're doing the right thing.

Which I'll admit is ironic, since the doing is pretty much done.

As I lie here in the dark listening to Jack whistling Jimmy Buffet's "Grapefruit–Juicy Fruit" in the shower, I think back to how the whole thing started on the rainy night I'd had it up to there with city life.

And, call me crazy, but I really have to wonder…

Is this suburban home-buying thing the real-estate equivalent of my plot to have a baby just to get a few months off from work?

Why didn't sensible Jack stop me this time, like he did before?

Why is he whistling, dammit?

What is *wrong* with him?

What is wrong with *me?*

I think I just finally snapped under the pressure of living in Manhattan and working in a major ad agency. I'll bet it happens to everyone, sooner or later.

But couldn't Jack have seen that I had gone off the deep end?

Couldn't he have thrown me a lifeline instead of jumping right in with me?

This whole thing is insane.

One minute, I've had it up to here with urban stress; the next, we own a four-bedroom fixer-upper in the middle of nowhere.

In retrospect, I'm thinking that a weekend at a charming bed-and-breakfast might have done the trick.

Well, it's too late now.

At this point, maybe I should just be glad that a baby isn't involved.

Guess what?

Jack got called into the office for a mandatory department meeting, probably some late-breaking Client crisis, leaving me to tie up loose ends and supervise the pair of moving men we hired.

Doesn't it just figure?

He promised he'll try to be home by lunchtime. It's a quarter of twelve now, and the movers have already worked their way through the kitchen and most of the living room.

I hate to say it, because I don't want to jinx myself, but…

So far, so good. Really.

"Yeah, hi, listen, I need a straw," announces a burly—aren't they all?—mover, sticking his head into the nearly empty bedroom, where I am hurriedly shoving the last of our dirty laundry into the last Hefty bag.

"You need a what? A straw?" He must be taking a lunch break. Unfortunately for him, the collection of fast-food straws from our junk drawer went the way of all those Chinese condiment packets.

"No," he says, "a *saw.*"

I stop shoving the laundry and stare at him. "A *saw?*"

He grunts a "yup."

See, the thing is, when it comes to moving, I'm not exactly a pro. I've never hired movers before, and I've moved only three times in my life, not counting college (which I don't count, because it was ages ago and didn't involve furniture): into the Queens sublet for my first summer in New York, into my East Village studio two months later, and then here, with Jack.

So I have no idea: Do movers routinely need saws?

If so, for what?

I'm not sure, but something tells me anything that involves a saw and a moving man can't be positive.

Maybe he's joined forces with the serial killer upstairs and needs to dispose of a body.

Maybe I heard him wrong.

I don't know how I could have, though. Aside from "straw," "saw" doesn't sound like anything that isn't used to cut something into pieces, unless he swallowed the first syllable and it was "see."

"What did you say you needed?" I ask, hoping it was a seesaw. Not that I have one of those handy or can imagine why he might need it.

"A *saw.*" He has the nerve to look pissed off at *me.*

"Mind if I ask what you might want to do with it, if I had one?" I'm pretty sure we don't, but if we did, it would be packed in one of the trillion sealed boxes in the next room.

"The couch won't fit out the doorway."

"So you want to saw the doorway?" I ask, horrified. The super would freak.

"No! Geez, no."

"Good. For a second there I thought—"

"We need to saw the legs off the couch. Well, maybe just one leg. We'll have to see."

"What?" I stare at him.

He nods.

Where the hell is Jack? Why is he not here to deal with this?

"How can the couch not fit out the door? How do you think we got it *in* the door? It's not like it was a kit we assembled in our living room." I am indignant, and naturally neglect to mention that, all right, some of our furniture might have been a kit. And made of cardboard. But we got rid of that the other day.

The couch—which, you recall, is new, and nice, and custom upholstered—is one of the few "real" pieces of furniture we own.

The burly mover, whom I will now be calling B.M. for short, shrugs. "I don't know how you got it in. All I know is that we can't get it out. We've been twisting it and turning it every which way and we can't afford to waste any more time. We need a saw. You can pop the leg back on later."

Is he nuts? He makes it sound like Lego.

"I need to call my husband," I inform him, pulling my cell phone from the pocket of my jeans. "Give me a second."

B.M. reluctantly leaves the room.

Naturally, Jack's cell phone rings right into voice mail. Maybe he's on the subway.

More likely, he's still at work, since lunchtime rolls around late in the day, if at all, at Blair Barnett. I dial his line there.

"Jack Candell's office."

"Sally, it's Tracey. I need to talk to him. Is he there?"

Wouldn't it be great if she said he's already on his way home?

It would be, but great just isn't in the cards today.

"He's here, but he just went into another meeting."

My heart sinks. Just went into? That means he won't be coming home any time soon. "Can you please let him know I need to talk to him? It's really important."

"It's a big meeting, Tracey. The whole department. Something's up. I can't interrupt unless it's life or death. Is it life or death?" she adds hopefully.

My turn to hesitate.

No, I don't suppose mangling a couch qualifies as a death. More like an amputation.

I tell Sally to please have Jack call me the second he's available, hang up and call Buckley. Out of everyone I know besides Jack, he's the most reliable voice of reason in my life.

Buckley has come running to my rescue more times in the past than I care to count.

He's seen me at my absolute worst: in my fat jeans, crying, drunk, naked, with puke in my hair. Not all of those things at once—not as far as I recall, anyway.

The point is, nothing throws Buckley—at least, not where I'm concerned—and I'm sure he'll come running over here.

It occurs to me, as the phone rings on the other end, that this is probably the last time I'll ever be able to count on Buckley to save me in a pinch. Tomorrow, I'll be living forty-some miles away, and in a few weeks, he'll be living on the opposite coast.

What am I going to do without him?

I guess I'm about to find out, because I get his voice mail. Figures. He's probably power lunching at Michael's with Steven Spielberg.

Now what?

I consider calling Latisha and Raphael, but they'll both be at work and distracted.

Dialing Kate's number, I hope she's home.

But when she answers on the second ring, I wonder why I called her, of all people. Her life is a wreck. She doesn't need one more thing to worry about.

Not that I can imagine Kate stressing, for very long, about my legless couch. In her world, when a B.M. saws a leg off your couch, you buy a new couch.

In her world, actually, I'd be willing to bet no one threatens to saw legs off couches in the first place.

In fact, things like this only seem to happen in my world.

"Hey—what's up? I thought you were moving today," Kate says.

"I am. I mean, I'm about to. But the movers said they need a saw to cut the leg off the couch because they can't get it through the door."

"Of the new house?"

"Of the old apartment. Which we got it into."

"What the hay-ell? How can that be?"

"I have no idea. Kate, what should I do?"

"I'll call Billy and ask him," says Kate, an old-fashioned Southern belle who leaves the big decisions to the lying, cheating man in her life.

"No, that's okay. Don't bother Billy with it."

"What does Jack think?"

"Jack isn't here," I tell her, feeling exasperated and overwhelmed and helpless on the verge of tears.

Come on. Get a grip.

That, of course, is Inner Tracey, disgusted.

You're a strong, independent woman, aren't you? Can't you figure this out on your own?

"Where's Jack?" Kate is asking. "Why are you moving all by yourself?"

"Jack's at work."

Pause. "Are you sure?"

"Yes!" Sigh.

Did I mention that Kate now believes all married men are lying, cheating bastards?

"Listen, Kate, I'm sorry I bothered you... I'll call you from the new place over the weekend and make plans for you to visit as soon as we get the guest bedroom set up. You can be the inaugural houseguest."

"Really, Tracey? It would do us a world of good to get out of the city. Maybe Billy can take a long weekend in June."

Billy? I guess I assumed he wouldn't be coming. He's the last inaugural houseguest I want in our brand-new home.

But apparently, he and Kate are still a package deal, so I assure her they're welcome anytime, along with the Screaming Jesus, of course.

Then I tell her I've got to go deal with the couch thing, because I am strong and independent and I can do this on my own.

Feeling a little like a Dr. Quinn, Medicine Woman, I gather up my skirts and march off to the new frontier.

(Okay, the living room, and I'm not really wearing skirts. I just threw that in for effect.)

The two B.M.s are sitting on the couch with their feet up on boxes, taking a breather. Both barely out of their teens, in smudged T-shirts, with bulging tattooed biceps and five-o'clock shadow, they seem a little—well, threatening isn't the right word. More like intimidating.

But I'm Dr. Quinn, and they can't scare me.

B.M. #1, who asked for the saw, straightens a little but keeps his feet on the box and asks, "Well?"

"I checked with my husband. We don't have a saw."

"No?"

"No. Guess you'll just have to try to get it out in one piece." Which, pardon me if I'm wrong, is the whole point. I mean, isn't this why we hired professionals? Anyone can just show up, hack things into little pieces and carry them out, right?

B.M. #1 looks at B.M. #2. They both look down at the couch, then over at the door.

"Ain't gonna happen," B.M. #2 says flatly.

B.M. #1 nods and shrugs. "You're gonna hafta go borrow a saw. Or buy one."

There are so many things wrong with this scenario that I'm speechless.

But what can I do?

I can A) tell the B.M.s to get lost and wait for Jack to get home before figuring out our next steps…

Or I can B) grab my purse and march down to the closest hardware store—not that I have any idea where one even is—and borrow or buy a saw.

A is tempting. But we told the super we'd be out of here by tonight. By the time Jack actually gets here, and we figure out our next steps, which will either involve hiring new movers or renting a van and doing it ourselves, we'll find ourselves camping out in the lobby—prime Mad Crapper territory—overnight.

I have to choose B by default.

I can't reach the super to see if I can borrow his saw, and wouldn't you know the doorman doesn't have one handy.

While marching to the hardware store, I try Jack's cell again. Then his office. Then Buckley.

No luck.

But I guess this is good practice for when I'm on my own in the wilds of suburbia. Did I mention I'm no longer convinced this move is the right thing to do?

"What kind of saw do you need?" asks the hardware-store guy.

"I don't know…I guess just a regular old saw to cut the legs off a couch."

"You're going to cut the legs off your couch?"

"No. My moving men are."

"What kind of moving men cut the legs off a couch?"

Wouldn't we all like to know.

I buy the damn saw and book it back home, where the B.M.s have finished emptying the apartment of everything but the couch.

"Here's the saw." I hand it over and retreat to the bedroom like my friend Lori did during her son's bris. I just can't bear to watch.

After closing the door to block out the sound, I dial Jack's cell phone again.

Miracle of miracles, he picks up.

"Where have you been?" I ask.

"In a meeting, and it was—"

"Listen, Jack, things are crazy here," I cut in. "Where are you?"

"On my way to the subway. Why? What's wrong?"

"The movers are at this very moment cutting at least one leg off our new couch, that's what's wrong."

"What!"

"They said it won't fit through the door, so they have to saw the leg off."

"Please say you're kidding."

"I wish I were."

"They brought a saw?"

"No."

"Where'd they get a saw?"

"It's ours."

"We don't have a saw."

"We do now," I say reluctantly.

There's a moment of silence. Then Jack says evenly, "Tracey, listen to me. You need to stop them. Now."

"They can't get the couch out if they don't saw off the leg." I'm on the verge of tears.

"We got it in with four legs."

"I know, but they said—"

"Just tell them to stop!"

I throw open the door, all set to shout, "Halt!"

Too late.

The movers—and the couch—have disappeared, leaving only a forlorn wooden stump and some sawdust behind.

"They already did it," I tell Jack miserably. "What are we going to do?"

He doesn't say anything, and if I didn't hear the background noise of the street on the other end of the line, I'd think he'd hung up on me for the first time in our relationship.

When he does speak, he says, "Listen, we have some stuff to talk about."

His tone is so deadly serious that my first thought is he's leaving me. He's leaving me because I let the movers cut the leg off our couch.

"Jack," I say, and swallow hard. "Are you—?"

"I'm talking about our jobs. I was about to tell you when you brought up the couch."

So it's our jobs, and not our marriage, that are at stake here. I start to heave a sigh of relief, then remember the damn mortgage.

"What about our jobs?" I ask Jack in dread.

"For starters, the agency lost the McMurray-White account."

"What? No!"

"Yes."

"We're going to lose our jobs, aren't we?"

Long pause.

"You are," Jack says. "There are massive layoffs happening right now. It's a bloodbath up there, Tracey."

"Did they fire you?"

Another long pause.

I wait, standing in our barren apartment, holding my breath and wondering how, in the grand scheme of life, we can possibly find ourselves unemployed on the very day we're moving into our new house. I mean, what kind of cruel twist of fate is this?

Then Jack says, "No, they didn't fire me. Our department is spinning off into a new company. Fresh Media. I just got promoted to vice president and group director."

I'm floored. So floored that I sink to…the floor, since there's no where else to sit.

"Tracey? Are you there?"

"Yes," I say, my thoughts reeling. "So…let me get this straight. You got promoted, and I'm about to get laid off?"

"I think so. Maybe not."

"I am too, Jack!" I say a little shrilly. "What are we going to do now?"

"Just promise me you won't obsess about losing your job all weekend. We have enough going on."

"You think?" I ask, and tuck the hacked-off couch leg into my pocket.

11

At dusk, standing on our very own rocking-chair porch—void of rocking chairs—Jack and I watch the moving van drive away through the rain.

About eight hours ago, we said goodbye to our old apartment and followed the moving van up to Westchester in the new—well, used with low mileage—car we bought a few weeks ago. There was plenty of Memorial Day weekend traffic, and it's taken hours for the B.M.s to unload the van.

Jack and I tried to organize the boxes and furniture as it all came in the door, but the last thing I knew, several cartons containing our clothes were in the basement, and the pots and pans were in one of the bathrooms.

The beautiful couch is in the living room, listing to one corner like a sinking raft.

That's not why I suddenly find myself crying, though.

At least, I don't think it is.

Maybe it's cumulative, who knows?

All I know is that, standing here on the rocking-chairless porch of my new—well, used—Sears Catalog House, I am not quietly weeping.

No, I am loudly and abruptly bawling, like a toddler who's just slammed her tender noggin on the edge of the coffee table.

Jack, standing beside me in ancient jeans and a faded Yankees T-shirt and a backward baseball cap, looks alarmed.

"What?" he asks, clutching my upper arm. "What's wrong?"

"I don't know."

"Calm down…is it the job thing?"

"No." If anything, now that it's sunk in, I'm kind of relieved that I'll probably be getting fired when I go in on Tuesday. Jack got a raise with the promotion. It doesn't make up for my salary, but it is a good chunk of it.

"Why are you crying, Trace?"

"Because I'm homesick," I wail as the truth hits me.

Here is the best thing about my husband: he does not slap me across the face and tell me to snap out of it like Cher in *Moonstruck*.

Not Jack. He just shrugs, used to me by now.

"Yeah," he says, and puts an arm around me, "you'll get over it. Hey, look—there's a family of deer!"

I turn to see Bambi and a couple of fawns gently nuzzling the blossoming rhododendron beside the porch. I instantly feel better. It's as if they've come to welcome us—though they're not paying any attention to us whatsoever. I walk all the way to the edge of the porch and lean over the railing, mere feet from them.

"Hi, guys. Aren't you beautiful?"

I swear I could pet them and they wouldn't flinch.

"I can't believe they're so tame," I tell Jack, still sniffling a little. "It's like we're living on our own private wildlife sanctuary, isn't it?"

The biggest deer takes a huge bite of rhododendron blossom.

"Jack?" I say, eyeing the ravaged branch. "Do you see this? These deer are eating the flowers."

"Yeah. They're herbivores."

"What about my garden? Are they going to eat that when I plant it?"

Jack just shrugs. "Come on, we have a lot to do."

I follow Jack into the house, wiping my nose on the shoulder of my T-shirt. I know, but I have no idea where the tissues are. I have no idea where anything is.

The minute we set foot into the house, my misgivings flood back.

I have no idea what we're doing here, in an unfamiliar,

empty (aside from a trillion boxes, a legless couch and some measly sticks of cheap furniture that look out of place), echoey house that smells of strangers and stale cigarette smoke.

Particularly depressing, for some reason, are the nail holes and unfaded paint rectangles on walls where a lifetime of another family's portraits once hung. Hank and Marge's family portraits.

Right. Because this is Hank and Marge's house; not ours.

Except that it isn't.

It's our house.

Hank and Marge are no doubt settling into their cushy, newly built condo in Putnam County, and their bank is cashing the biggest check anyone has ever written.

Okay, maybe that's a tiny exaggeration, but that's certainly how it felt when we were writing it.

And all those other checks. And signing our names over and over again, on contracts requiring us to pay an astronomical amount of money every month for the rest of our lives.

Okay, maybe that's another tiny exaggeration. We'll be paying off the house for the next thirty years. Which feels like the rest of our lives because from there, it's basically just a downhill slide to death.

I know. See? I told you I was depressed.

"Do you realize that we won't have a month without a mortgage payment until we're sixty?" I ask Jack as our footsteps echo across the scuffed linoleum in the kitchen. "We'll be old coots by then. I can't stand thinking about it."

"I'll be sixty. You won't," he says with reasonable Jackness, stepping around a big cardboard carton marked FRAGILE—PLATES AND GLASSES. He feels around for a switch and turns on a light, banishing some—but not all—of the late-day gloom. "You'll only be fifty-nine. That's not an old coot."

Wondering what a coot is, anyway, I tell Jack, "Fifty-nine is definitely in the old-coot realm."

"Not to someone who's sixty. You'll just be a spring chicken compared to me."

"Speaking of chicken, I'm starving." I open the fridge, not sure why I'm bothering, since it will of course contain nothing other than strangers' old food smells.

Wrong.

"Oh, ick," I say wearily—and with some surprise, because the house, despite being well worn and lived in, was left pretty much spotless. "Hank and Marge didn't clean out the fridge before they left."

Staring at the plastic-covered plates on the top shelf, I feel as if I'm going to cry again. What is wrong with me?

I guess it's just exhaustion, hunger and emotional upheaval taking their toll. That, and my inexplicable, be-careful-what-you-wish-for post-move homesickness. Throw in worry about my mother's weird fatigue, my looming unemployment and impending old cootdom, and is it any wonder I'm not crumpled on the floor?

"If you get a garbage bag," I tell Jack with a sigh, "I'll dump this old food in."

"That would be a great idea," Jack says, "if we had an empty garbage bag. We should've thought to bring some with us."

Yeah, and we should've thought to stay put where we were.

But it's too late for should'ves now, isn't it?

Eyeing a Saran-wrapped platter, I realize there's a label or something stuck to it. I lean closer and see that it's not a label, it's a note.

Dear Tracey and Jack: Here is a little something for your first night in the new house. Enjoy, and congratulations! Love, Hank and Marge

"Oh my God, Jack, look! This isn't old food…it's new food!"

It appears that those old coots, God bless 'em, have left us an entire meal: sandwiches and salads and pastries. There's even a bag of plastic utensils, plates and napkins.

Jack and I fill plates and sit cross-legged on the living-room floor, chowing down in the light of a single bulb from a shadeless lamp.

"You know what?" I ask Jack around a mouthful of egg salad. "I feel better."

"Not so homesick anymore?"

I pause a moment, and I listen.

No sirens. No honking horns. Not a sound from above but the gentle spring rain pattering on the roof.

Our roof.

"How can I be homesick," I ask Jack, reaching across our two plates and putting my arms around his neck, "when I'm home?"

Jack smiles and kisses my forehead. "I'm glad to hear you say—"

He breaks off as suddenly a weird light beams into the room, flashing through the window, which has no blinds or shades or curtains.

"What is that?" I ask.

Of course I am immediately thinking of alien abductions, a possibility I never worried about in the city.

Seriously, where's a UFO going to land in Manhattan?

But there's plenty of space here in the suburbs, and fewer people to hear a victim's screams. For all I know, I'm about to be beamed up to a flying saucer on my very first night in the suburbs, which would really suck, but the way things are going, would you really be surprised?

"It's a car." Jack has gotten up and gone over to the window. "My mother's car."

Another set of lights beam into the room.

"And here comes Bob and Kathleen," Jack adds.

"What? They're here? All of them? The twins?"

He nods.

Frankly, I'd much rather be abducted by aliens.

"Why didn't you tell me they were coming?" I ask, getting to my feet and trying to dust off the seat of my ragged jeans, which by now are covered in grime, nicely matching my snot-soaked tee.

"Are you kidding me? I didn't know they were coming!"

"Knock-knock!" Wilma is calling cheerfully through the screen door.

I usually hate when people say "knock-knock."

But I adore Wilma, so I call back cheerfully, "Come on in!" even though the last thing I feel like doing right now is entertaining company.

This is, after all, part of the reason we moved to the suburbs, right? To be closer to family.

And here they all are, streaming through the door and weaving their way around the boxes: Wilma, carrying a huge bouquet of flowers; Bob, still wearing a suit from work; Kathleen, wearing a frail and exhausted pallor; and the devilment twins, who hug us hello at Wilma's prompting, then ask if they can watch something called *The Last Mimzy* on TV.

"The cable won't be hooked up until next week," I tell them.

"But we have to see the rest of *The Last Mimzy!* Mom said we could watch it here!"

"I'm sorry, guys," I say before I remember that Kathleen doesn't like anyone calling them guys.

They're girls, she's always correcting people, to which I want to say, *You should take what you can get.They could be called so much worse.*

The wretched little beasts—see?—glare at me in unison, then promptly disappear into another room as if they own the place.

"Well, this place is just charming!" Wilma declares, looking around, and at the moment, it is so not charming that I'm not sure if I want to hug her or Cher-slap her.

"What happened to your couch?" Bob, who is already walking around like an inspector, naturally zeros in on that.

"Tracey let the movers saw off the leg to get it out the door," Jack says, and I am sure I want to Cher-slap him.

"I didn't *let* them," I protest. "They just did it."

"You went out and bought them the saw," Jack points out, which makes me wonder if he might not be harboring a teensy little bit of resentment after all.

"They told me to get them a saw!" I snap. "We were paying them by the hour. And I couldn't get ahold of you. What was I supposed to do?"

Jack shrugs. "Nothing. I'm just saying."

As if sensing we're both worn a little thin, Wilma says, "We probably shouldn't have stopped in, but we just couldn't resist. These are for you, Tracey." She thrusts the flowers into my arms.

"Oh…uh, thank you!"

Don't get me wrong, ordinarily I love flowers.

But ordinarily, I can reach right under the sink, pull out a no-frills florist vase, fill it with water and voilà: instant centerpiece.

Not only do we not have a table for the centerpiece, but Jack deemed vases nonessential, and all of ours are now, presumably, en route to a landfill somewhere.

"I don't know what I was thinking," Wilma says, reading my mind. "I should have brought something to put those in."

"Oh, no, it's fine," I tell her. "I'll just set them here..." On the counter, to die a slow, wilting death in their cellophane wrapper.

Talk about depressing.

"Do you want a tour of the house?" asks Jack.

"That's why we're here." Bob opens a closet door and pokes his head in.

"*And* to help you with the unpacking," Wilma adds.

At that, Kathleen all but throws the back of her hand limply against her forehead and swoons. "Well, it's late and we have the girls, and Bob is still dressed from work, so I'm not sure how much unpacking we can do..."

"It's okay," I say, trying to block out the image of the girls manhandling my wedding china. Meanwhile, Bob is *tap-tap-tapping* on the inner closet wall and mumbling something uncomplimentary. "We'll be fine on our own."

"Yeah, and we're not in any rush," Jack says. "I have a feeling it's going to take weeks before we're settled in."

"Weeks? Try years," Bob says, bouncing a little on a creaky floorboard, like he's testing it. "*We* still have boxes we haven't unpacked. Listen, you're going to want to do something about this floor."

"Yeah, we're going to refinish it at some point," Jack tells him.

"Refinish it? Try replacing it. You see the way that board is coming up over there? It's warped. The whole thing is going to blow."

I stare at the floorboard, trying to picture it blowing. What does that mean, exactly? Someone steps on it, and it turns to splinters?

"I don't like the wiring, either," Bob announces.

Which begs the question, when, exactly, did you inspect the wiring, Bob?

"I hate to say it—" Bob sighs "—but you crazy kids might have gotten more than you bargained for with this place."

"Bob!" my mother-in-law scolds him. "I love the new house. It has great potential."

"I don't mean anything bad, Wilma. I just feel like they're in way over their heads. Yeah, the place has great potential, but right now it's a death trap, and the infrastructure is for shit."

"Don't talk that way in front of the girls," Kathleen scolds him automatically, then asks, "Where *are* the girls?"

Everyone shrugs.

"Girls! Girls!" Kathleen is immediately frantic. "Where are you?"

No reply.

"Oh my God!" Kathleen clutches Bob's arm, as if she's convinced the death trap of doom has devoured her little darlings. "Do something! Find them!"

"Girls!" Bob hurries into the next room, with the rest of us at his heels, except Kathleen, who has presumably collapsed from the stress. "Where are you?"

They're not in the next room.

I'll tell you where they are: they're upstairs, playing dress-up with a garbage bag full of my work clothes.

"That is just too cute!" Wilma exclaims as Ashley parades around wearing my one good silk blouse wrapped around her head like a turban. "Who are you supposed to be? An adorable little swami? Look, she's an adorable little swami!"

Naturally, Ashley, who has no idea what a swami is—God only knows what she was supposed to be, but it wasn't that—goes into her interpretation of an adorable-little-swami routine. Which involves gymnastics and off-key singing and makes no sense whatsoever.

Wilma is riveted, applauding throughout and singing along with the unintelligible lyrics, and I want to shake her.

"You have to do that for the talent show!" Bob declares when the clueless swami is wrapping things up with a cartwheel that snags my good blouse on a loose nail head sticking out of the floorboard.

Rrrrrrriiiiiiipppp.

"Uh-oh," Jack says, and looks at me. "Was that yours?"

Before I can answer, Ashley lands on her feet with a little bounce and reports, "It was in the rag bag."

"Do you have another one so we can both be little swamis in the talent show?" Beatrice demands.

"Sorry, Bea, I'm fresh out," I say, trying not to let my eyes bulge too much as I watch Ashley examine the tear in my blouse.

Beatrice's face screws up as if she's going to cry, and Bob hurriedly assures her that he'll take her out ASAP and buy her a nice new rag to wear on her head in the talent show.

"Are you coming to see us in the talent show?" Ashley wants to know.

"Of course they are," Wilma tells her. "Aunt Tracey and Uncle Jack will be able to come to all your performances now that they're living up here. Isn't this going to be fun?"

"Good times," I murmur, wondering why I ever thought Jack's family was sane compared to mine.

All our relatives are raving lunatics. Every last one of them.

Including Wilma, who has just pulled a pitch pipe out of her pocket and is asking the girls to sing the swami song lyrics again, louder and with feeling.

Back in the kitchen, Kathleen is weak with relief at the sight of her babies, unharmed. To Bob, she says, "I told you we shouldn't go anywhere without Sam to keep an eye on the girls."

"Next time, we'll bring Sam," he agrees.

Or—here's an idea—leave the dueling swamis at home, I want to suggest. *How about that? Or—here's a better one—don't drop in again until we've redone the entire house.*

Jack gives them all a tour while I try to make headway in the kitchen, looking for the coffeemaker, Maxwell House, filters and cups for tomorrow morning. I don't find any of those things, but I do come across a single earring—which may or may not be one whose partner I packed somewhere else—Jack's long-missing jockstrap and a framed photo of us when we first started dating.

Droplets of moisture got under the glass and melded the photo to it, and it started to tear when I tried to peel it off once. Too bad, because it's a great picture.

We look so young and happy and carefree in it.

Now we're just a couple of old-coots-to-be with a mortgage and an hour-in-each-direction daily commute to jobs we may or may not have for much longer.

I stare at the picture and Barbra Streisand sings in my head, "Can it be that it was all so simple then," and I swear to God, I'm about to start bawling into Jack's jockstrap.

But then I hear footsteps on the stairs. I shove the picture in a drawer before Jack and the in-laws come trooping back into the kitchen, fresh from their tour.

"You really have to fix the loose towel bar in the bathroom before it falls on someone's head and kills them," Bob is saying to Jack.

"Like who? A dwarf?" Jack asks, and I get the impression he's wishing the towel bar—or, say, boulder—would fall on Bob's head.

"Tracey…are you crying?" Wilma asks, looking closely at me.

"No! It's just the dust, I've been putting stuff away…"

"You look exhausted," she says kindly. "Why don't you two call it a night and come sleep at my house on the pullout. You don't even have beds set up here."

She's right. There's a mattress and box spring and slats and headboard, none of which are in the same room or even on the same floor. I'm sure we packed the sheets and pillows somewhere. Unless we didn't, and threw them away.

Mental Note: you are delirious.

"Come home with me," Wilma says, "and tomorrow, we'll get the whole family to come back and help you make short work of these boxes."

At that, Kathleen suddenly remembers they have an extraordinarily busy day tomorrow.

I don't believe it for a minute, but I'm more than happy to see her hustle Bob and the twins out the door with a promise to call us about buying tickets to some community-theater production the twins are in. Not the talent show. The talent show is something else, as is the variety show they're in next month.

The twins have more upcoming performances than Céline Dion, and we are clearly expected to attend all of them.

"So, what do you say?" Wilma asks, left alone with us.

"Should we leave now, and come back in the morning? I can organize your cupboards for you. I love organizing things."

I look at Jack, hoping he's thinking what I'm thinking.

Wilma means well, but I want to organize my own cupboards.

And I want to sleep in my own bed in my own house.

Wilma jangles her car keys expectantly.

Jack shakes his head slightly.

I shake mine, just as slightly, back at him.

"Thanks for the offer, Wilma," I say, "but this is the first night in our new house, so we'll stay."

Jack smiles at me.

I smile back.

His mother leaves us with hugs and congratulations and a promise to come back tomorrow to help. Then we're alone together in our own little house, standing in our own cozy living room…surrounded by utter shambles.

Jack has his arm around me and I lean my head against his chest.

"Well?" he says.

"Well, what?"

"What the hell is a mimzy?" he asks, and I crack up.

Then I say, "We forgot to tell your mother about your promotion."

"We'll have plenty of time for that." Jack yawns. "So do you still feel like this is home?"

I think of the photo in the drawer, and Barbra.

Can it be that it was all so simple then?

Looking back, I remember when my mother had me convinced Jack was a smooth operator, and the fights we had every time somebody else that wasn't us got married, and the Christmas when he gave me a Chia Pet instead of an engagement ring, and the time he told me, at Pre-Cana, that he loved me for my hair.

It was never simple.

It will never be simple.

"I feel like this can be home," I tell Jack, "eventually. I think we're going to love it here. Eventually. I think—" I try to stifle another loud yawn.

"You're beat. So am I. Come on, let's go put our bed together and christen our new bedroom."

"Let's go put our bed together and go to bed. And sleep," I add pointedly, seeing the hopeful glint in Jack's eye. "I'm bone tired."

We head for the stairs. "Got any idea where we packed the CDs?" Jack asks on the way.

"CDs? Why?"

"I was thinking a little U2 might be good background music while we put the bed together."

"Ha. Nice try. I have no idea where the CDs are. But I'm sure we'll find them eventually."

Just as I'm sure everything is going to be okay here in suburbia…

Eventually.

* * *

The next morning as Jack and I are tearing through boxes and bags trying to find our toothbrushes, we hear an actual knock—as opposed to a vocal *"knock-knock"*—at the door.

"Who do you think it is?" I ask Jack, who has bed head, razor stubble, morning breath, and is wearing only boxer shorts.

"How am I supposed to know?" he asks crankily.

(My ordinarily good-natured, easygoing Jack doesn't do well without his morning coffee. We've located everything but the filters, so we're caffeine deprived until one of us gets brushed, washed, dressed and down to the local Starbucks. Hopefully there *is* a local Starbucks. There has to be, right? Right? Don't scare me like that.)

More knocking.

"Hurry—you have to get the door," Jack tells me.

"Me? I can't answer it like this! Look at me!"

"I am looking at you. You're wearing sweats. I'm wearing underwear. Guess who wins?"

Guess who loses is more like it, and the answer, of course, is me.

I make my way down the stairs, nearly tripping a few times over stuff that's strewn in my path. We really have to get organized with the unpacking. Good thing we have a long holiday weekend stretching ahead of us. By Tuesday morning, I'm sure the house will be in order and this nightmare of rain-soaked cardboard and damp Hefty bags will be behind us.

Whoever's at the door is still knocking, somewhat impatiently.

Turns out—and I can't believe I never noticed this until now—there is no window on the front door; it's just solid wood.

Geez, where's a good old-fashioned peephole when you need one?

In the city, that's where—hopefully, along with all the ax murderers and home invaders.

Here in suburbia, people apparently open their doors blindly and take their chances.

Mental Note: add front door with peephole—or better yet, glass windowpane—to shopping list.

I look around for a suitable weapon. Mace, meat cleaver, andiron…

No, no and no.

What I do see, lying on top of a nearby box, is the hacked-off couch leg. It'll have to do in a pinch. I grab it.

Telling myself that Jack is going to feel mighty guilty if I'm raped by a masked intruder, I hold my breath and turn the knob. If attacked, in lieu of bopping him over the head with this small stump of fine, polished wood, I suppose I can always release my breath, which is guaranteed to send a would-be rapist running for the hills.

But it isn't a masked rapist.

It's Angelina Jolie.

Or at least, a very convincing look-alike in gi-normous movie-star sunglasses, a tight white T-shirt and black yoga pants that you need to be super toned to wear because they show every bulge. (She has none, of course.)

"Oh, you *are* home! I was just about to leave."

"We're home," I say jovially, and pat my bed head self-consciously.

"Welcome to the neighborhood. I'm Cornelia Gates Fairchild."

Huh. That is some name, don't you think?

"Tracey Candell," I return, after considering—and dismissing—the insertion of Spadolini. Somehow it doesn't flow the way her name does. "Do you live on the street?"

"Two doors down. This is for you." She hands me a Saran-wrapped loaf, which, let me tell you, is a heck of a lot heavier than it looks. "It's organic-gluten-free-quinoa-millet-and-buckwheat."

It's what?

"Thank you!" I say, as if it's exactly what I was hoping for, trying hard not to breathe foul oral fumes in her direction. "That's so sweet of you."

"You're welcome. Do you have kids?" she asks, and I see her trying to sneak a peek over my shoulder at the interior of the house.

"Oh…no. Do you?"

"Four."

Four kids? I never would have—

"Pippa is five, Henry is three, Louisa is two and Aubrey is two weeks."

Two weeks?

Okay, there is no way this woman gave birth A) to four children, and B) two weeks ago. I guess little Aubrey is adopted. I bet they all are. Maybe she's got a Benetton family like Angelina Jolie.

Wait…*is* she Angelina?

Hard to tell. She really might be.

She could be using an alias, for herself and the kids. Laying low in the suburbs, away from the paparazzi glare.

Hey, wouldn't it be cool if she were Angelina Jolie, and we could be buds? Raphael would be all over that. I bet he wouldn't think the suburbs are bourgeois then. He and Donatello would be house hunting here faster than you can say Perez Hilton.

"Do you want to come in for coffee?" I may be a little starstruck myself, and thus willing to overlook the fact that I *have* no coffee.

"Decaf?"

"Sorry."

"No, thanks," she says, "I'm nursing. And anyway, I should be going. My husband and I want to get our tennis match in before the baby wakes up."

So let me get this straight. She's nursing, so she did give

birth, yet is without bulges a mere fortnight later, plays tennis and obviously has a babysitter. I hate her.

Unless she's Angelina Jolie, in which case I can't help but want to befriend her.

"What's your husband's name?" she asks me.

"Jack."

"Uh-huh. What does Jack do?"

"He's in advertising," I say, and can't bring myself to return the questions about her husband. It's not that I don't care what his name is (she could be using an alias for Brad), or that I don't care what he does—although if he's not Brad I don't care what he does—but that seems like an odd question to ask someone you just met.

"Oh, advertising," she says, and I can't tell what, exactly, she means by the *oh*. Her tone isn't dismissive, but she doesn't seem overly impressed, either.

Not that I *care* whether she's impressed by Jack's job. Though I suppose I could have mentioned he's a vice president now. After all, I'm really proud of him and I feel bad that his promotion kind of got lost in the shuffle.

Meanwhile, Cornelia/Angelina is surely going to ask what I do, and I'm positive she'll be doubly unimpressed when I tell her.

But she doesn't ask. She just says, "My husband, Whitney, is a financial analyst."

"Oh, financial analyst," I say. Leave it to me to somehow come off sounding both impressed and fascinated.

"Do you do yoga?" she asks doubtfully, eyeing my sweats as though making sure they aren't concealing a sylphlike physique.

"No."

"You should start! We have the best new instructor down at Modern Buddha. You should come to the beginners' class. You should check with the studio, but I think it's Mondays, Wednesdays and Fridays at eleven."

"A.M.?" I ask, thinking she's just delivered an awful lot of shoulds.

She laughs. "Of course, a.m."

"The thing is…I work."

"You *do?*"

I nod.

"Where?"

"The city."

"You're going to commute?"

"That's the plan." I try to sound flip.

Cornelia/Angelina all but wrinkles her nose and neglects to ask what it is that I do for a living. She just says, "Well, I really do have to get going," in a perfectly polite way, but managing to sound as if I'm trying to keep her here.

"Thanks for the bread," I say, because anything in loaf form tends to look like bread, though I wonder if something that's organic-gluten-free-quinoa-millet-and-buckwheat does, indeed, qualify as bread.

"Enjoy."

With a wave, she's off to tennis.

Jack is waiting at the top of the stairs in his underwear. "Well? Who was it?"

"Well, at first I thought it might be Angelina Jolie, but now I'm not so sure."

Mildly nonplussed, Jack asks, "Huh?"

"She brought us this as a welcome to the neighborhood."

"What is it? Bread?"

"I'm not sure."

"Well, that was nice. Our first friend."

"I guess so."

Suddenly, I desperately miss Raphael, and Kate, and Buckley and…

Actually, not Mitch.

Not yet, anyway. But at this rate, you never know.

"By the way…" Jack holds up something that looks like a long, metal rod.

"What is that?"

"The towel bar from the bathroom."

"What happened to it?"

"It was loose. I tried to fix it."

"Good job," I crack, and he scowls.

"Sorry," I say. "Can you put it back on?"

"No, it snapped off. We'll have to get a new one."

"Put it on the list." We started making a list this morning of items we need from the hardware store. It seems there are quite a few things around here that need tweaking, replacement or repair. I can't help but wonder how we're going to do all this...and who's going to do it.

Looking at unkempt Jack standing there holding a broken towel bar, I have a hard time picturing him transforming himself into a savvy do-it-yourselfer anytime in the near future.

I hate to say it...and I won't, aloud...but Bob may have been right.

We two crazy kids may have gotten more than we bargained for.

12

Do you know how long it takes to unpack and settle into a house (as opposed to an apartment)?

I'll let you know…someday. I hope. Possibly this year, but I wouldn't bank on it. It's taking Jack and me forever to put away our clothes and work our way through the boxes of household stuff, figuring out where stuff should go.

The thing is, with a house, you know you're going to be there forever, so you want to do everything right.

I figured by now we'd have had a chance to explore our new hometown, and I really wanted to go to the Memorial Day parade they were having today. But the weather's been a washout, and I haven't left the house since we arrived here on Friday, other than a quick run to the nearest grocery store for kitchen staples like bread, milk and Little Debbies.

Remember that loaf-brick-thing Cornelia/Angelina dropped off the other day? It wasn't edible. It was dense and had a seedy texture and a weird flavor, like fermented sprouts or something. If I didn't know better, I'd think she was trying to poison us.

Come to think of it, I *don't* know better. Maybe I should have saved the evidence for a forensic team. Unfortunately, it's somewhere in one of the billion trash bags we've filled and dumped at the curb over the last forty-eight hours.

Jack has gone back and forth to the hardware store countless times since Saturday morning. He has also managed to crack a ceramic bathroom tile trying to replace the towel bar, fall off a ladder, sit on a bag filled with lightbulbs and bend the hinge on a kitchen-cabinet door while trying to make it close more tightly.

Now it doesn't close at all.

The one thing I really need him to fix—the couch leg—is the one thing he doesn't want to touch.

He said he wants to wait a bit and see if the moving company is going to pay for it, since we put in a claim. On our own, we can't afford to hire a professional furniture repairman, much less buy a new couch.

Considering Jack's overall domestic klutziness, I guess it's better that he won't even attempt a temporary fix.

I've been trying to overlook what a disaster he's been

around the house so far; I figure he's probably just stressed out and overtired.

Personally, I'm just anxious to get through all the mundane tasks, like putting up plastic shower-curtain liners on rings that keep unpopping, and start with the fun stuff, like the painting and decorating and planting my garden. I picked up a bunch of seed packets in the supermarket yesterday: more tomatoes, of course…a few varieties. Also eggplant, cucumber and peppers, basil and dill, zinnias and bachelor buttons and forget-me-nots. All the same kind of stuff my mother has growing in her garden.

I keep looking longingly out the window at the spot where I'm going to plant the seeds, just as soon as I have a chance. Hopefully next weekend. I'm itching to get my fingers into the dirt.

I guess it's good, in a way, that I've been too busy to dwell on the possibility of my getting fired when I show up for work tomorrow. But it's definitely been lingering in the back of my mind, and so has my mother's health. She claimed she was feeling better when I spoke to her yesterday, but I wouldn't expect her to tell me if she wasn't.

She mostly wanted to talk about the house, and I promised I'd bring pictures when we go up to visit. I also reminded her that we have plenty of room for houseguests, so she and my father will have to come down soon.

"We'd love to," she said, but when I pressed her for a date, she was noncommittal.

My parents aren't big on travel. In fact, they've only visited me in New York once, for the engagement party Wilma threw for me and Jack. I know they weren't thrilled with Manhattan, but I think they'll like to see me settled in a real house, in a beautiful little town like Glenhaven Park (though of course they'd be happier if it were Brookside).

In any case, it's been an exhausting long weekend and I'm glad we got an extra day to work on the house.

When my cell phone vibrates in my back pocket after dark on Monday night, I'm plugged into my iPod, listening to a good, satisfyingly loud and pounding Kanye West tune, in the midst of lining the shelves of the linen closet with contact paper I cut to size.

At least, I thought I cut it to size.

Either the contact paper shrunk or the shelves expanded. I didn't find out until I had peeled off the backing. Now it's stuck to everything but the shelf, and I'm not in the mood to answer my phone.

It's probably Kate again.

She called me about an hour ago, crying about Billy, who decided to take off for the Hamptons for the remainder of the long weekend, without her. She asked if I could come over.

Either she forgot that I moved, or she expected me to jump on the next train. When I told her I couldn't, she seemed miffed. Then she poured out her heart, leaving me feel utterly helpless. There's just not much I can do from here. I did my best to be a supportive friend and not bad-mouth Billy, but let me tell you, the whole conversation sucked the life out of me.

Or I suppose it could be Latisha calling again, too. She's checked in several times over the weekend to talk about the layoffs. She kept her job, but a bunch of people in her department are gone, as well as just about everyone in mine.

Crosby Courts included. Seeing her axed would have thrilled me not so long ago, but not anymore.

Crosby's demise is like a death knell for my own job security.

It's ironic that I would have given just about anything to get out of Blair Barnett just a few short months ago. But things have changed. This isn't how I want it to end—on their terms, not my own. This isn't when I want it to end—when we have a mortgage, a car and a house that needs more work than we ever anticipated.

Jack and I can really use my salary now that we're home owners, and I don't know what we'll do if we lose it.

The phone stops ringing. Good.

When it starts up again a minute later, I sigh, turn off the iPod and pop the headphones out of my ears. I have to answer it.

After all, it could be Jack. He had to go out to pick up Taco Bell for us for a late dinner because the only take-out place in town that delivers is the pizza parlor—which, by the way, isn't great. We already tried it. The delivery took over an hour—unheard of in the city—and the pizza arrived cold.

What if something terrible happened to Jack?

Or what if he can't remember whether I wanted the Chalupa Supreme or the Gordita Supreme? He kept getting mixed up. At this point, I'm so famished I'll gladly take both, plus a Chili Cheese Nachos BellGrande.

Checking the caller-ID window on my phone, I see that it says UNKNOWN.

So it's not Jack.

What if it's the hospital emergency room? Would that come up UNKNOWN?

I have no idea, and I hope I never find out.

Heart pounding, I say, "Hello?"

"Tracey? It's Mary Beth."

"Oh! Hi." Thank God. "What's up?"

The contact paper just got stuck in my hair, and I tug gingerly at it. Ouch.

"I'm at the hospital emergency room."

"What!" I instantly feel sick to my stomach. "What happened? Is it Ma?"

"She fainted and Pop called an ambulance."

An ambulance. *Oh my God oh my God oh my God…*

"What's wrong with her?" I ask Mary Beth, pacing along the hall, contact paper dangling from my head and now stuck to my iPod earbuds as well.

"She's okay now. They don't know what happened. They're running some tests."

"Is she conscious?"

"Of course she's conscious. She was only unconscious for a minute."

"Can I talk to her?"

"She doesn't know I'm calling you. You know how she doesn't like anyone to make a fuss over her, and she hates doctors, so she just wants to get out of here. She keeps telling them to let her go home because she left a pot of minestrone on the stove."

Yeah, that's my mother. But thank God it sounds like she's okay—for now.

Still…something has to be seriously wrong for her to pass out, right?

I stop pacing and lean against the wall, feeling weak and worried.

Naturally, the contact paper sticks to the wall as well as to my hair and the headphones.

Damn, damn, damn.

I give it a hard yank, then cry out in pain as a big chunk of hair rips out of my skull.

"Tracey, my God, get ahold of yourself," says Mary Beth, who obviously thinks I'm screaming in agony about my mother. "I'm sure she'll be fine."

"Really?"

"Really."

"Well, I've got to come up there." Now the contact paper is stuck to my sleeve.

"That's a good idea. Come up next weekend. By then—"

"Next weekend! I was thinking Jack and I could be there by morning if we leave now."

"Tracey, it's not an emergency."

"She's in the emergency room. How is that not an emergency?"

"I just thought you should know. I didn't want to worry you…"

Sure she did. If you don't want to worry someone, you don't call them until you have something conclusive to say. Something other than that Ma is lying on a gurney drawing her last breath, for all I know.

"I just don't think you should drop everything and come. That'll scare Ma. She'll think she's dying and nobody's telling her."

"*Is* she dying and nobody's telling her?" Or me?

"No! I just told you, I'm sure she'll be fine. I'm sure it was just a hot flash. I've been telling her she needs to do something about her hormone levels."

Did I mention Mary Beth isn't a gynecologist?

"Who else is at the hospital with you?" I ask, hoping to get one of my brothers on the phone.

"Just Pop and Stefania."

Stefania is there? Why?

Fighting an unreasonable wave of envy, I remind myself that this isn't about Stefania taking my place in the family. This is about my mother, in the hospital.

I open my mouth and a sob escapes.

"Tracey, don't worry. She's okay. I shouldn't have called you."

"No, I'm glad you did." I sniffle.

"Listen, I have to get back in there."

"Let me know what the tests show, okay? Promise?"

Mary Beth promises, and we hang up.

I make my way forlornly through the empty house, trying to unstick the contact paper, longing for familiarity and finding none. To hell with the new house and the fresh start.

All I want right now is to go home. Home to Brookside.

I want my mommy.

I don't sleep at all Monday night.

Mary Beth called back to say that the tests were inconclusive and they have to do more, but they let my mother go home from the hospital. I fought the urge to call her there.

"She doesn't know you know," Mary Beth told me. "She said not to tell you."

Picturing Stefania bringing my mother hot soup and fluffing her pillows, I informed Mary Beth that I would be visiting as soon as I can get there.

On Tuesday morning, Jack and I board the Metro-North train for our first-ever commute to the city. So much for my fantasy of cozily riding together to the city, sipping coffee and sharing the paper. We can't even find seats in the same car. The train is jammed.

At least it's on time, as always.

Then again, I find myself wishing the train had stalled in the tunnel for a change. I dread what I'm going to find when I get to the office.

In the lobby, as we wait for the elevators among a much smaller crowd than usual, Jack gives my hand a squeeze. "It's going to be okay," he says.

"I'm about to get fired, Jack. How is that okay?"

"You don't know that."

"Yes, I do. I feel it in my gut."

He doesn't argue. "Just keep your head up and don't forget to copy your hard drive onto that flash drive I gave you." He's so matter-of-fact about the whole damn thing you'd think he wasn't freaking out inside about the impending loss of income.

But I know he is. He didn't sleep either last night, and he didn't even want to have sex, which is ordinarily his favorite insomnia antidote.

I get off the elevator alone on my floor, and see that there's no receptionist. Not a good sign. Did she get the ax, too? The place is like a ghost town.

I make my way to my office, where I immediately spot the yellow Post-it note stuck to my computer screen.

See Me—Jim

Jim is the creative director.

Trust me: there is no more ominous phrase in the corporate world than *See Me.*

So that's it, then. My fate has just been sealed.

I death march down the deserted hallway like a doomed queen to the guillotine. Remembering what Jack said, I hold my about-to-be axed head high.

Mental Note: you have become quite the pessimist lately, haven't you?

That's true. I mean, why am I automatically jumping to the worst conclusion? It's like yesterday when I thought my mother must be dying.

Maybe I'm not about to be fired after all. Maybe Jim just wants to update me on the layoffs and promote me to assistant creative director.

Yeah.

That's not what happens.

Jim, looking somber, tells me to take a seat and informs me that they're going to have to let me go.

Turns out I would have made a lousy doomed queen, because not only do I forget to keep my head high, but I pretty much collapse in a puddle of tears, dripping all over Jim's desk.

"I'm sorry, Tracey," he says, handing me tissues and a folder from human resources. "This outlines your severance package. It's been a pleasure working with you, and if you ever need a reference, I'll be happy to provide one. Good luck."

And just like that, my corporate life is over.

Goodbye, Madison Avenue copywriter.

Hello, suburban housewife.

★ ★ ★

After tearfully calling Jack with the bad news, furtively copying my hard drive onto the flash drive, sorrowfully packing up my office and stoically meeting with human resources, I head home alone to Glenhaven Park.

The train is just about empty going north midmorning on a workday, and I get a triple seat to myself. The others on board appear to be students, blue-collar or medical workers just ending their shifts in the city and household staff about to start theirs in tony Westchester towns like Chappaqua and Bedford and Glenhaven Park.

I don't really fit in on the train.

I no longer fit in in the city, for that matter.

Nor in Glenhaven Park.

As I trudge across the deserted commuter parking lot, I realize that I no longer have a life, and it's all I can do not to cry.

Now what? I wonder as I slip behind the steering wheel.

I even feel out of place here in the car. Until now, Jack's done all the driving.

For years, living in Manhattan, I've relied on public transportation to get myself around. My driving skills are definitely a little rusty.

Hesitant to turn on the engine just yet, I decide to call Jack and let him know I've arrived safely in Glenhaven Park. He was a little harried when we spoke earlier—things are chaotic in the Media Department today because of the restructuring.

I can't reach Jack. Or Sally, who was laid off on Friday.

Poor Sally.

Poor me.

I do reach Buckley, who sounds frantic when he answers the phone. "What's up?" he asks. "How's the new house?"

"I just lost my job." I manage not to cry, but I feel like I'm going to.

"Are you serious?"

"Yes…what am I going to do?"

"Geez, Tracey, I'm really sorry. That sucks." He sounds a little breathless.

"Where are you?"

"LAX. I just landed and I've got to grab my bags and find the driver the studio sent for me. I've got a meeting in an hour and then this Realtor's going to show me some stuff."

Well, I guess that says it all, doesn't it?

He's riding around in limos, shopping for mansions and meeting with studio executives on the West Coast, and I'm sitting jobless in a Hyundai reluctant to go home to my fixer-upper on the East Coast.

"Let me let you go," I tell Buckley, who doesn't protest.

"I'll call you later," he promises distractedly.

"You don't have to. I'll talk to you when you get back. You are coming back, right?"

"Of course." Pause. He's still panting like he's jogging. "I've got to get all my stuff."

Right. Buckley is moving away.

I hang up and consider calling Raphael to cry on his shoulder about my job loss. But he's still pissy about the move. He'll probably tell me I had it coming because I already had one foot out of Manhattan.

When I talked to him on Saturday and mentioned the amputated couch leg, he had a one-word, unsympathetic comment. "Karma."

Which I foolishly asked him to clarify, inviting him to pontificate on all the reasons I shouldn't have left the city. When he tried to make the mutilated couch a metaphor for our friendship, I told him I had to go hang my wet laundry on the clothesline.

Okay, so I didn't have wet laundry and I certainly don't have a clothesline in my new backyard. But it was strangely satisfying to feed his suburban stereotype. I should have thrown in a car pool and a Mary Kay party I had to attend.

So, no calling Raphael. Not for a while.

Feeling utterly alone and abandoned, I reluctantly turn the key in the ignition.

There's still an aching lump in my throat, and it seems to be swelling by the second as I back out of the spot.

Especially when a passing car honks its horn as if I'm going to plow right into it.

Okay, maybe I actually was going to plow right into it. In my defense, it came out of nowhere, and was speeding.

Shaken, I turn toward the business district.

Freshly fired and cast adrift in suburbia, I'm in no hurry

to go to an empty house, where—still without cable—there won't be much to do besides unpack boxes and wallow in misery. I can't even raid the cupboards for a satisfying junk-food fix; Jack and I polished off the Little Debbies last night.

Maybe I'll linger here on the main drag for a while, explore my new hometown and figure out the lay of the land.

Driving down the main drag in the sunshine, I feel a little better. Lots of people are out and about on this beautiful weekday morning—albeit no one I can relate to on sight.

The sidewalks are filled with upscale-looking mommies and nannies and mannies pushing strollers and holding toddlers' hands. It's like a kiddie promenade, and I have to wonder again, seriously…

What the hell am I doing here?

Maybe I should have hung around in the city and waited for Jack after all. I considered it, but without an office or apartment there, I wasn't sure quite where to go to pass six or seven hours.

I'm not sure quite where to go here, either, though…until I drive past Bug in a Rug and spot that huge rag doll in the window and an empty parking space right out front.

I impulsively pull into it, and the front tires hit the curb with a jolt. Oops.

I'm sure I'll get the hang of this driving stuff again. What choice do I have? It's not like there are buses and cabs here, unless you count the luxury short bus that shuttles senior citizens around town.

Everyone else seems to rely on their Mercedes-Benz or Jaguar or Lexus or Hummer, from the looks of the lineup of cars parked along the street.

I call Jack again. Still not there.

"Where are you?" I say into his voice mail, trying not to whine. "I'm back in Westchester, but I stopped off to buy my niece that big doll for her birthday. Call me when you get this. Love you."

I'm halfway to the door of the boutique before I remember to turn back, aim the key remote at the car and press the button. The remote chirps, confirming that it's locked, which makes me feel vaguely ridiculous.

I mean, it's not as if I think a gang of street thugs is staking it out around here in broad daylight. "Hey, Lefty, we gotta get our hands on that smokin' pea-green Hyundai."

I bet I could leave it unlocked with the keys in the ignition—running—and no one would go near it.

In the window of Bug in a Rug, my niece's future birthday present seems to beckon me in, saying, *Please buy me and give me a beautiful home with a sweet little girl who will cuddle me to sleep every night.*

Perfect; Hayley will love this doll.

They're celebrating her birthday in Brookside next weekend. Jack and I had been hoping to drive up for it, but now he doesn't think he can get away from work. I'm thinking maybe I'll go alone, since time off is no longer an issue for me.

Even though the immediate danger has passed with my mom, I just want to see for myself that she's okay, and maybe get a chance to talk to her doctors about those tests.

Then again, a four-hundred-and-fifty-five-mile solo road trip might be an ambitious undertaking for someone who has difficulty pulling into and out of parking spots.

As I enter the children's boutique, a little bell attached to the door dings merrily. The place is hushed, with classical music playing in the background, and smells of potpourri and cinnamon candles. Very inviting.

Behind the counter, a woman with a tight bun and tiny reading glasses perched at the sharp point of her nose looks up with a not-quite-as-inviting-as-you'd-expect expression.

"Hello," she says warily.

"Hi!" I say in my friendliest voice, which comes out booming and practically rattles the cute little glass figurines on the shelf beside me.

She seems to wince. Maybe she's trying to smile, but her bun is too tight. I decide to give her the benefit of the doubt.

"Can I help you with anything?"

Might as well cut to the chase. It's not like I'm here to browse, and even if I wanted to, I get the feeling she wouldn't want my grubby hands pawing through her clothing racks with their delicate pastel pink and blue garments—although, at a glance, I see that they aren't pink and blue and pastel at all.

There seem to be a lot of unusual shades, like chartreuse and pumpkin, and even a leopard-print onesie thrown in for good measure.

Clearly, this isn't your average children's boutique. I think I need to just get the giant doll and get out.

"I love the rag doll in the window," I tell Bunhead. "Can I see where you have them?"

"Them?"

"The dolls."

"There's only one. And it's one of a kind."

"Oh! That's nice." Hayley will be the only kid in the world to have one. What could be better? "Can I please see her?"

"Her?"

"The doll." I imagine Bunhead had a Barbie-deprived childhood and feel vaguely sorry for her.

"Of course." Again with the wince.

Okay, I strongly dislike her, Barbie-deprived or not. I can't help it.

She seems so put out, practically grumbling as she opens a drawer and hunts through it for God only knows what. Maybe I need to sign a special waiver before I get to take a closer look at the doll, whose expression, I'm starting to think, I might have misread on my way in.

I think what she's saying is *Please buy me and get me the hell away from this horrid woman.*

"There they are," Bunhead mutters and removes a set of keys from the drawer.

Turns out the doll is chained and padlocked to her cute little wooden chair. *Sweet Jesus, get me out of here,* she screams silently as Bunhead hoists her from the window and lugs her across the store.

She deposits her on the counter with a grunt and turns expectantly to me.

"She's adorable," I tell the woman, running my hands down one of the doll's arms, and then the other, then feeling around at the back of her neck for a price tag.

"It's very delicate," Bunhead informs me, emphasis on the *It,* and I can tell she's itching to slap my hands away.

I'm starting to think, much as I hate to leave her behind in chains, that I might not be able to afford this doll. Especially without a job. I did get a pretty decent severance package, but I can't go around squandering it on fancy toys.

I all but do a strip search looking for a price, to no avail, so I have to ask, reluctantly, "How much is she?"

"Seven ninety-nine," is the incredible reply.

"You're kidding!"

"Plus tax," Bunhead adds crisply.

Who'd have thought you could buy a doll like this for less than ten bucks?

See? I told you everything was ridiculously expensive in

Manhattan. It's going to be so nice to live in a place where things are reasonably priced—not just giant rag dolls, I'm assuming, but everything else.

Except, oddly enough, for houses.

But I guess that's real estate for you.

"I'll take her," I tell Bunhead. "My niece will love her."

I pat the doll's arm, telling her silently, *Don't you worry, I'll have you out of here in no time.*

The woman looks pleasantly surprised. She actually smiles as she asks where I want the doll sent.

"You mean you'll ship her directly to my niece?" I ask, fishing in my bag for my wallet.

"Oh, absolutely. We'll gift wrap her, of course, and pack her securely."

Ah, note how quickly *it* changed to *her* now that we have a sale.

"That would be great."

"Yes, she'll be in very good hands," says Bunhead, my new BFF.

I see that I only have a couple of fives and some ones in my wallet. "Um, how much is shipping?" I ask, thinking I might have to put it on my credit card.

"A hundred even for second business—day service, and you know what? I'll throw in the gift wrapping for free."

Free gift wrapping?

What a bargain!

A hundred even?

What a…

Wait—what?

"A hundred *dollars?*" I ask, incredulous that shipping costs almost ten times what the doll herself costs. "I, uh, don't need second-day service. My niece's birthday isn't until—"

I break off as a terrible thought occurs to me.

Did she say seven ninety-nine?

Or did she say seven hundred and ninety-nine?

As in dollars. Hundreds of.

Yeah. I think so, too.

But I can't bring myself to even ask her, now that we're BFFs.

"On second thought, you know what?" I say smoothly, as though I just had a better idea than dropping a grand right here on the spot. "I think I'm going to wait and get her a little closer to my niece's birthday."

Bunhead looks only slightly disappointed. "When is her birthday?"

"October," I lie.

"Well, we can certainly have her all set to go and send her out whenever you like. Will that be cash or charge?"

Nice try, Bunhead. Do I look like the kind of person who carries around seven hundred ninety-nine plus tax plus shipping in cash?

I'm already backing toward the door as I say, "You know what? I'll be back."

Not.

I cast one final apologetic glance at the doll, whose expression I really did misread.

Now she seems to be taunting me, saying, *I didn't want to live in zee shoddy home of your niece in zee first place.*

Yes, she has a French accent now. And fangs.

Back out on the street, I try to call Jack again, desperately needing a familiar, loving voice. Still no answer on his cell or office phone. I leave another message, trying to sound perky and breezy and upbeat, which I'm sure he won't buy for a second.

I debate getting into the car and heading straight back to the house to wallow and unpack, but decide that's just too depressing.

Instead, I decide to go over to Pie in the Sky, buy a pie and take it home and eat the whole thing myself before wallowing and unpacking.

Because that's not the least bit depressing.

But what's a girl to do when her world is a shambles?

I climb the stairs to the bakery, which smells mouthwateringly of hot pastry and sugary fruit filling.

"Hello," says the good-looking thirty-something guy behind the counter, infinitely more friendly than Bunhead from the get-go. "How can I help you today?"

"I want to buy a pie," I say brilliantly.

Duh. Isn't that why most people come to a pie shop?

"Our flavor of the week, which is always ten percent off, is strawberry," he informs me, then gestures at the glass case filled with mouthwatering pies and tarts. "Those are our other flavors."

Let me tell you, the Mississippi Mud pie is pretty darned tempting, and so is the Southern Pecan. I'd like to say, "One of everything, please."

But after the doll episode this is a no-brainer: the flavor of the week is the only bargain here at ten percent off. I tell the Pie Man I'll take a strawberry pie.

As I stand at the counter watching him put it into a nice, glossy white box and tie it up with waxed red string, I can't help but worry a little about the price.

Then again, it's a pie. How much can it possibly be?

I'll tell you how much.

"Forty-nine fifty," the Pie Man tells me, sliding the pie across the counter toward me.

Okay, compared to the doll, it's practically a steal.

Still…fifty bucks for a pie?

WTF, Pie Man?

"Is it…I thought it was ten percent off?" I say, convincing myself that forty-five bucks is slightly more palatable.

Slightly.

"That's including the ten percent off," he informs me ever so gently, at which point I take the pie out of the box and smush it in his face like Curly.

Okay, not really.

I want to, though.

Almost as badly as I want to buy and eat the entire pie in a single sitting.

I give the Pie Man a taut smile and my American Express card, and five minutes later I am pulling into my driveway, wondering how we can afford to own a house here when we can't even afford to buy a toy here.

But I'm sure the doll incident was a fluke. After all, something like that can happen anywhere.

Well, not anywhere.

In Brookside, the doll would have been seven ninety-nine. With free gift wrapping and free shipping. But who cares? I don't want to live in Brookside. And I don't want to live in Manhattan.

I want to live right here.

Here in the overpriced and eerily quiet suburbs.

There are no signs of life at our neighbors' houses. On one side is a working couple with older kids; on the other, a younger couple with toddlers; directly across the street, a retired couple who reportedly travels a lot.

I wonder which house belongs to Cornelia/Angelina. She said two doors down, which means it's either an adorable cottage with a picket fence or a stately brick colonial reminiscent of Jack's childhood home, on a smaller scale.

I'll go with stately over adorable. I should probably drop her a note in the mailbox for the unpalatable baked good at some point. And—oh, guess what? Now I'm free for that

11:00 a.m. beginners yoga class. Which I might look into. Just as soon as I scarf down this pie.

It sure is quiet around here, I note as I walk toward the house. Other than my footsteps, there's not a sound but chirping birds and the distant hum of a lawn mower.

It's peaceful in a dangerous kind of way.

Or maybe more like dangerous in a peaceful kind of way.

I check the house to make sure there are no serial killers hiding in the closets and under the bed, then hunt through the clutter on the kitchen counter until I find a plastic take-out spork. We still haven't figured out where—or whether—we packed our silverware.

Before sitting down with pie and spork, I try Jack again.

This time, he picks up.

"Hey," he says, "are you okay?"

"I'm fine."

"You don't sound fine."

"I will be. I stopped off on the way home and bought a fifty-dollar pie and I'm going to eat the whole thing by myself."

Pause. "Did you say fifty dollars?"

"Yeah. I know it's not in the budget, but I needed it. And just think, we'll be saving, like, three hundred without having to buy a commuter train ticket for me for June!"

"That's six pies," Jack says dryly. "Did you get the doll for Hayley?"

"I changed my mind. I think Hayley's outgrown dolls."

"She's two."

Oh. Right.

"If you must know," I tell Jack a bit huffily, "the doll was more than our gift budget for the entire year."

"Gotcha," Jack says, and I hear another phone ringing in the background. "Listen, I have to go."

"Okay. Hey, maybe I'll get some groceries into the house and make dinner."

"I don't think I'll be home till really late, with everything that's going on here."

"Oh."

Right.

Overnight, he has a life—a life in the city—and I don't have one anywhere.

An hour later, I'm on my hands and knees puking up strawberry pie in the upstairs bathroom—no, I'm not bulimic, just sick as a dog—and I hear a voice downstairs calling, "Knock-knock!"

It's Wilma, looking as if she just stepped out of a catalog, as always, well pressed and well accessorized.

How the heck did she get in here? I know I locked the door right before I checked the house for stray serial killers.

It turns out Jack made her a key a few days ago. What a sweet thing for a son to do.

What a lousy thing for a husband to do.

Turns out Jack also called his mother just now and sent her running over here because he's worried about me. What a sweet thing for a husband to do. What a sweet thing for a mother-in-law to do.

Yeah, right.

Jack and Wilma are suddenly getting on my last nerve, bless their hearts.

"I thought the worst when I saw the car in the driveway and there was no answer," Wilma tells me.

The worst?

Which is...what?

Polishing off a second pie?

Hanging from a noose affixed to a deer-ravaged limb of a Mature Planting?

Skipping town in a boxcar with Jack's pay raise?

"I'm fine," I assure my mother-in-law. "Really. I mean, I didn't want to lose my job, but it's actually kind of a relief to know that I don't have to get up at dawn and ride the train back and forth to the city every day."

She nods dubiously, and I wonder if she's thinking I'm thinking *now I can launch my evil plan to mooch off your hard-working son for the rest of my life.*

I'm sure she isn't, because like I've said a thousand times, Wilma isn't your typical mother-in-law. I feel as though she loves me just as much as she loves Jack, which probably isn't true, but I enjoy pretending it is.

So I should be nice to her right now, even if I'm about as glad to see her as I am to feel the threat of another barf-orama stirring in my gut.

Wilma sets her red patent-leather purse gingerly on the listing couch—the only surface that isn't already covered with stuff—and watches it slide right off.

"Oopsy!" She catches it before it hits the floor.

Oopsy? I think.

"Here," I say, "let me take that for you."

She hands it over and I look around for a place to put it.

"Sweetie," she says as I hang the straps of her bag over a doorknob, "between the move and losing your job and worrying about your mother, you've been through hell these past few days. How is your mom, by the way?"

I tell Wilma she's home and waiting for more tests, and that I'm planning to drive up there to see her.

"When?"

"This week," I say spontaneously. After all, what else have I got to do?

"By yourself?"

"Sure, I'll be fine. It's not that bad a drive."

"Isn't it five hundred miles?"

"Almost…"

"Aren't there a couple of mountain ranges between here and there?"

"Ye-es."

"You shouldn't go alone," Wilma tells me.

"Jack can't take off work, and I really kind of need to see my mother." I can't help but feel a little prickly.

"I understand," Wilma says, and pats my shoulder. "I'll go with you."

The remnants of the cherry pie lurch sickeningly in my stomach. "You…will?"

She nods decisively. "What else have I got to do?"

"That's really…sweet of you, Wilma, but…" I fight the urge to shut my eyes to block out the disturbing memory of my grandmother, clad in hot-pink hot pants she bought at the Montgomery Ward, thrusting a crocheted toilet-paper cozy into Wilma's hands.

No, it's not my worst nightmare.

It actually happened, at the engagement party a few years back.

Wilma was gracious, as always, and she really hit it off with my family, but…well, she was distracted by the other guests, plus that was on her own turf.

Somehow, I have a hard time picturing her in the land of zau-zage connections.

True, she flew up to Brookside for the wedding, but that was a wedding. There wasn't much time for informal familial interaction.

"We'll go on a road trip together, just us girls," she tells me. "Like Thelma and Louise. Won't that be fun?"

I'll admit it's been a while since I saw the movie, but didn't Thelma and Louise drive off a cliff and die?

Sure, one of them got to sleep with Brad Pitt first. But in the Tracey and Wilma version, that's not going to be me, so…

"You really don't have to drive all that way with me, Wilma. Seriously, it's such a long trip."

"Oh, it's fine. You can't go alone. I know Jack just won't have it."

As it turns out, he just won't.

"You should go," he says. "It would be good for you, and you haven't seen your family in months."

"I know, but I hate to leave you here alone in a strange place."

"I can ask Mitch to come up. He's been bugging me about it."

I'm sure he has. It's been a whole…what? Four days since we've moved?

"He can help me do a few things around the house, too," Jack informs me, gesturing at the general chaos that still surrounds us. "He might know what to do about the couch."

"Mitch? Is he handy?"

"Sure," Jack says vaguely.

"I don't know…"

"Listen, I'm sure you and Mom will have a great time, just a couple of gals on the open road."

When I give him a dubious look, he asks, all innocent, "What?"

"You know what."

"Come on, Tracey. It'll be good. You love my mother."

I do. And I love my family. And, seriously, the old highway's a-callin': I really do need to get away from my non-life for a few days.

Still…

"Trust me," says my husband, "a road trip to Brookside with my mom is just what the doctor ordered."

Turns out he's right.

He just neglects to mention that the doctor's name is Kevorkian.

13

Did I mention that I adore my mother-in-law?

I did?

Good.

Then you won't think I'm entirely heartless when I say that the woman is a complete moron.

How could I never have noticed this fatal flaw before? Was I so blinded by Wilma's maternal affection and fashion forwardness that I just didn't notice her lack of...well, brain cells?

Don't get me wrong...in her element, Wilma is divine. The Hostess with the Mostess, the Life of the Party, the Savvy Shopper, the Style Maven, the Doting Matriarch.

Out of her element, she's a Blithering Nincompoop.

I get my first inkling about forty minutes into our big road trip, when I'm barreling along in six lanes of traffic and ask her to check the map to see which exit I take to get onto Route 86 west.

"I don't know," she says from behind the crinkling, billowing map. "How do I figure that out?"

I try to explain, but she doesn't seem to get it. Nor does she seem to realize that it's important that we figure this out, or we will wind up in Connecticut.

Which we do.

Which sets us back a good hour.

Nor does Wilma get how to put a new CD into the car stereo—"Oopsy! I think I jammed it in too hard and now it won't come out!"—or work the condiment pumps at the Burger King where we stop for lunch—"Oopsy! Sorry about that mustard, ma'am."

When we stop for gas, she insists on paying, and pumping…though she hasn't a clue how to do it and I have to get out and show her. She sets the gas-tank cap on the roof of the car, and that's the last I see of it, aside from a fleeting glimpse of it hurtling into oblivion as we merge back onto the highway at sixty-five miles an hour.

Oh, and Wilma has a freakishly small bladder. She must. Why else would the woman have to pee every hour, regardless of whether there's a public restroom anywhere within a twenty-mile radius of the exit? At one point, we meander across the state line into Pennsylvania on a two-lane road lined by cow pastures, because Wilma begged me to stop, even though there were no facilities listed at the exit sign.

"That doesn't mean there isn't a restaurant or gas station," she told me.

Um...yes, it pretty much does.

Not only that, but she brought a walk-in suitcase that presumably contains everything from bathing suits to parkas, and for all I know, a rubber raft and snow skis. Yet she keeps asking me if I think she'll be too cold, or too warm, or too dressy, or too casual.

Kathleen calls her on her cell phone for the duration of the drive, apparently helpless just knowing her mother has temporarily left the tristate area. She keeps putting the twins on to whine about how much they miss her, and Wilma, predictably, gets all choked up and feels guilty.

Yup. Here we are, just a couple of gals on the open road, and all I can think is that Thelma and Louise had the right idea when they drove off that cliff. I'm not sure which of them was at the wheel when it happened, but I'm positive the other one had Ashley and Beatrice on speakerphone, saying, "Sing something for Aunt Tracey, girls. She's driving and she said she wants to hear some beautiful music."

Mental Note: shoot Wilma, then self.

The seven-hour trip takes more than ten, and it's after dark when we finally pull into my parents' driveway.

The whole family is gathered there, waiting to greet me,

as they always are when I come home for a visit. My parents, siblings, in-laws, nieces, nephews, grandmother…

And a total stranger.

"Tracey, Wilma, this is Stefania," someone says, and a blond stranger throws her arms around first me, then Wilma.

"It is so nice meeting you," she says in broken English. "We have been wait!"

We?

Well, well, well. Isn't that cozy.

"Nice meeting you, too," I say politely, noticing that she's wearing fuzzy pink slippers.

I mean…it's kind of unusual for a dinner guest to show up in fuzzy pink slippers, isn't it? Or any slippers at all, for that matter.

Yes, that *would* be unusual…

But since—as I am about to discover—Stefania has just moved in with my parents, she isn't technically a guest here.

I am.

Wilma is, too.

But Stefania? Nope, she's one of the family, padding around in her slippers like she owns the place, even asking me if she can get me something to drink.

Yes, that's right: she's moved in. I learn that bit of news from my favorite sister-in-law, Sara, before we've even made our way entirely into the house.

It seems that Josie Lupinelli's son is home from college, and presumably wanted his room back. So instead of sending her back to Krakow, Josie shuttled her on over to my parents', who were glad to have her.

They put her in my old room, of course.

Meaning I'll be bunking with Wilma in my brothers' old room down the hall.

"I can't believe no one told me Ma and Pop are taking in boarders!" I hiss at Sara, trying not to sound pissy.

"She's not a boarder, she's a friend."

Maybe…but it seems odd that my parents are hanging around with nineteen-year-old internationals when they could be…

What?

Hanging around with you?

Yeah. That's it. I'm jealous. I hate that I am, but I can't help it.

Maybe it's because I've always been the youngest kid in the family. I guess this is what it must have felt like for my siblings whenever my parents brought home a new baby to fuss over.

Except that Stefania's not a baby, and I don't even live here anymore.

Gazing at my parents, I notice that my mother does look a little pale and drawn, and my father has more gray around the temples.

They're getting older. And I miss them desperately.

We walk into the house, which smells—as always—like your favorite Italian restaurant, and is filled with a mishmash of old and new (as in, purchased in this millennium) furniture and a lifetime of mementos. Framed photographs are everywhere: some brand-new and some decades old, some snapshots and some professional portraits. My nieces' and nephews' toys are everywhere, and so are the kids themselves, crawling, running, climbing, bouncing on cushions.

It's chaotic and it's cluttered and it's home.

No, it isn't. You have your own house now. Remember?

"Ma," I say impulsively, turning to her, "you should drive back with me when I leave on Sunday. You could have a nice change of scenery, see the new house, spend a few days."

"Tracey, you just moved. You aren't set up for houseguests. Do you even have guest-room furniture?"

"Of course," I say, wondering if a blow-up air mattress that may or may not have a hole counts. "Anyway, you would take our bedroom."

"I couldn't do that. And you probably haven't unpacked yet, so…"

She's right. I haven't. There are still boxes everywhere.

Still…

"Jack and I would love it if you came, Ma. We have plenty of room."

"Not this time," my mother says, patting my shoulder. "You have your mother-in-law with you for the drive, anyway."

"Yes, but we'd love to take you back with us, too. Just a few gals on the open road…wouldn't it be fun?"

"Some other time," my mother says. "When Pop can come, too."

"I'm sure he'd be fine here without you for a few days, Ma."

She shakes her head. That just isn't how things are done in my family. The women don't go off on road trips and leave the men high and dry.

I sigh inwardly, knowing it's never going to change; it is what it is. Why can't I accept that?

Why do I step over the threshold here and instantly feel so wistful, so guilty, so frustrated, so jealous?

"It's been so nice having Stefania around," my sister-in-law Katie comments to me as we work our way into the living room. "Too bad her visa is expiring. She has to go back to Poland in two weeks."

Well, hallelujah.

"Really?" I say aloud. "That's a shame."

"It is, because she's been a big help with Ma. With all the rest of us having to work during the day, there's no one to be here with her if anything else should happen, God forbid," Katie goes on, and I feel guiltier by the second.

I mean, I'm no longer working during the day. If I lived here in Brookside, I could be the one spending time with my mother.

But you don't live here in Brookside…remember?

Yeah, but what if—God forbid—something happens to my mother? Will I look back with regret? Will I wish that I had never moved to the opposite end of the state?

Part of me thinks that's ridiculous; after all, kids are supposed to grow up, cut the apron strings, move on, right?

It's just in my family, no one else has really done that. My grown siblings all depend on each other and my parents, their daily lives so interwoven that sometimes I marvel that they don't all just live under the same roof.

And whenever I visit, I get sucked right back into the Spadolini mind-set, complete with longing and guilt.

I turn my attention back to my mother who, aside from being a little pale, looks pretty much the same as always.

I hugged her harder than ever and had to fight back the tears when I first saw her come out onto the front steps in her sauce-stained apron.

Now, watching her chat with Wilma, I tell myself there's nothing wrong with her.

I believe that wholeheartedly…

Until Mary Beth drags me into the empty kitchen, where pots are bubbling on the stove and casserole pans are heating in the oven.

"Listen, Tracey…we found out there's something wrong with Ma."

My blood runs cold. "What is it? Cancer?"

"No…"

"Her heart?"

"No. She got the test results back…"

Oh, no. Oh, God. Please don't let anything happen to my mother.

I brace myself.

"It looks like she has type two diabetes," Mary Beth says gravely.

I'm not sure whether to be relieved or concerned. I mean, diabetes doesn't sound like an instant death sentence. But I'm sure it's not good. "What does that mean?"

Mary Beth fills me in: it basically means my mother's body isn't producing enough insulin, which causes a glucose buildup in the blood. In the long run it can have serious complications. For now, the doctor wants my mother to lose weight, change her diet, get more rest and start exercising.

"What did she say about that?" I ask my sister.

"She called the doctor a *mamaluke.*"

Oy.

But that's my mother. She hates doctors. She and my father both think they're all a bunch of quacks. In their world, you can heal just about anything with a novena, chicken soup or a little whiskey.

"Ma said she's not going to change a thing." Mary Beth sighs. "She spent yesterday weeding her garden and she made *pizza-frite* last night."

That's fried bread dough, which my mother slathers in butter, then tops with sugar and cinnamon and canned fruit-pie filling.

"I'll talk to her," I say, eyeing the heaping platters of homemade food waiting on the countertops. No way is my mother going to be able to lose weight until she stops acting like a one-woman Food Network.

And rest? I have never seen the woman sit in a chair unless it's to eat or knit or have her hair done.

"Good luck." Mary Beth shakes her head. "She only hears what she wants to hear."

We continue to discuss my mother's health until she bustles into the kitchen a few minutes later.

Seeing her, I want to grab her and hug her hard again, or beg her to come back to Westchester with me so that I can take care of her, or scold her for calling the doctor a *mamaluke.*

But before I can do any of those things, she commands, "Let's start taking things out of the oven. Everyone's hungry."

"Where's my mother-in-law?" I ask her.

"In the dining room talking to Grandma."

Uh-oh.

I grab the nearest platter, which is piled high with homemade zau-zage calzones. "I'll bring this in."

Hustling it into the dining room, I find Grandma lifting her turquoise satin blouse and exposing her left breast to Wilma.

Dear God, it's worse than I imagined in my wildest dreams.

"See? It's right there, by the nipple," Grandma is saying loudly—I've noticed that her voice seems to rise a decibel with every birthday she celebrates.

"Grandma! What are you doing?" I shove the platter onto the table and rush over, thankful that at least no one else is in the room, and wishing Wilma weren't here, either. I don't dare look at her.

"I was just telling your mother-in-law that I've got a rash from my new brassiere."

But why, Grandma? Why were you telling her that?

"What brassiere?" I ask weakly instead, and remind her, "You aren't actually wearing a brassiere."

I wonder if she's finally gone senile. Let me tell you, it's been a long time coming. She's in her mid-eighties now, and she's had a good ride, but—

"I *know* I'm not wearing a brassiere. Because the fancy push-up one I ordered from Sears catalog gave me this itchy red rash, see?" She thrusts her boob—which I'm sure was once pert, but now sags like a tennis ball in a gym sock—in my direction. I can't help but notice that she really could use a push-up bra.

Still…

Seeing Wilma, poor thing, looking slightly faint, I say brightly, "Sears! That reminds me—you have to hear about our house, Grandma. It's from Sears catalog, too. Why don't you put your boob away and I'll tell you all about it."

"Tracey! *Boob* is not ladylike," she scolds.

Neither is exposing yours to visiting houseguests, I want to remind her.

But at least she's lowered her top and is tucking it back

into the waistband of her jeans, which rides right in the vicinity of her rib cage. Yes, she's wearing jeans. High-waisted, dark, soft, shiny denim pleated jeans. With hooker high heels. Her hair, these days tinted a brassy shade of blond, is piled high on her head and she's wearing makeup, including blue eye shadow.

For a moment, I wish she were a regular grandma: a sweet, gray-haired lady in a housedress and scuffies with a pocketful of Root Beer Barrels.

Don't get me wrong. I love my grandmother. She's just...a character on a good day, a total fruitcake on a bad one. It's like her appropriateness filter has disintegrated. Maybe that's a sign of age.

Suddenly, I feel more bittersweet sorrow than embarrassment.

Grandma's not going to be here forever.

My mother isn't, either.

Even this familiar house will one day be sold to someone new, the way Hank and Marge's house was sold to me and Jack.

That's my home now, my own home, almost five hundred miles away. That's my life now. Someday, I'm going to be the matriarch bustling around in an apron or—God forbid—showing my boob to my granddaughter's mother-in-law.

"What kind of brassiere do you wear, Wilhelmina?" Grandma asks.

Oh, for the love of God.

"You know what, Wilma," I say quickly, "you must be exhausted after that road trip. Do you want me to bring you upstairs so you can freshen up before we eat?"

"That would be nice," she says gratefully.

"I'm sorry about my grandmother," I whisper to her as we leave the room.

She dismisses that with a flutter of her manicured hand. "Oh, we've all had eccentric grandmothers."

Somehow, I doubt that, but it's kind of her to say.

We pass Stefania on our way to the stairs. "Hi! Hi, Tracey! Hi, Wilma!" Waving, she gives us a big, America-is-good kind of smile, and for about two seconds I feel bad for resenting her.

Then I remember that she's sleeping in my room, and I'm bunking with Wilma down the hall.

"How's it going, Stefania?" I say, and add evilly, "Why don't you go keep my grandmother company. She's in the dining room."

"Okay! Okay, Tracey!" Off she goes.

"She's a nice girl," Wilma comments as we ascend the stairs.

"She is."

"I just love your family. They're all so warm and welcoming. And I love watching your parents together," she adds somewhat wistfully. "It reminds me of you and Jack."

And of all that she missed, having been married to—and divorced from—my late father-in-law.

Poor Wilma. I feel really bad about wanting to drive her off a cliff.

Until—over the homemade tiramisu my mother made for dessert—she transforms my immediate future into a living hell.

She doesn't do it single-handedly, by any means, and it all begins innocently enough, right after I finish describing the new house to everyone in as much detail as I can without boring them to tears.

That's the great thing about family—mine, anyway. You can share stuff with them—like long stories and vacation photos—and they don't glaze over and tune you out the way your friends or coworkers might.

"How many bedrooms did you say it has, Tracey?" asks my brother Joey.

"Four."

"Tracey asked me to drive back down there with her on Sunday," my mother announces. "But of course, I can't."

Naturally, they all concur; of course she can't.

However…

"I'll come," my grandmother says, and I nearly choke on my Diet Pepsi.

My mother rolls her eyes. "Ma, you can't do that."

"Why not?"

"How would you get home, Ma?" my father wants to know.

"I could fly."

"Alone?" Mary Beth shakes her head. She would never in a million years get on a plane alone.

Grandma shrugs. "Why not?"

"It's dangerous, Ma." That's my mother.

Ordinarily, I'd correct her. But if she wants to let my grandmother think she'd be taking her life in her hands visiting me, who am I to stop her?

"If I croak in a plane crash, I croak in a plane crash, Connie," Grandma responds with a what-are-you-going-to-do shrug. "I'd love to go back to New York City again."

"Oh, New York City," Stefania speaks up. "I love to see New York City. Statue of Liberty is there, yes?"

"Yes," I admit, but clarify—for everyone's benefit—"I don't actually *live* in New York City anymore. I live far away from New York City now."

"Not that far away," Wilma says with a laugh. "It's just a short train ride to Grand Central."

"Grand Central Station? We were there!" Grandma says. "When we came down for the engagement party. Woo-hoo! You should see it, Stefania. The ceiling is painted in constellations. It's just gorgeous."

"I love to see ceiling," Stefania says agreeably. "Woo-hoo!"

"Remember when we went to the top of the Empire State Building, Joey?" Sara asks my brother. "What a neat place. It's too bad little Joey was too young to remember. We'll have to come down and visit you guys someday, Tracey, if you really do have room."

"Oh, they do," Wilma assures her.

"I love to see Empire State Building!" That's Stefania again, of course.

"You should come, too, then," Wilma tells her. "That way, you two can fly back together and no one has to worry about Grandma on a plane alone."

Shut up, Wilma! Who was worried? Was anyone worried? I wasn't worried. Even Grandma wasn't worried. If she croaks, she croaks.

"But, Ma, don't you need Stefania here to help you since you've been sick?" I ask in desperation—and that, of course, is the final nail in the coffin.

Connie Spadolini is not sick and she does not need help.

"Of course not. Don't be ridiculous, Tracey." My mother turns to Stefania. "You have to see New York City before you go back to Krakow."

"She doesn't *have* to...I mean, it's not like a law or something." I laugh nervously. No one else does. I try another tactic. "Maybe she doesn't want to do all that traveling. With an overseas trip coming up, she'd be exhausted."

"I love to traveling!" Stefania says energetically.

"Tracey and Jack will show you all around the city," Wilma tells her. "There's so much to see. You'll have a terrific time."

Wait, what? I don't want to play tour guide to Stefania and Grandma. And I seriously doubt that Jack will want to play tour guide to Stefania and Grandma.

But it's too late.

Everything's settled.

They're coming, and from where I sit, there's not a damn thing I can do about it.

From where Jack sits—probably on a cardboard box at the moment—there is.

"Just tell them it's not a good time for us to have company," he advises into the phone when I call him that night from my parents' basement. No, not a finished basement, but the kind with clammy stone walls and cobwebs and spiders.

It's pretty much the only place in this house where no one can possibly overhear a conversation. Everyone is upstairs, asleep.

Oh, and guess what? My mother-in-law snores like a trucker. Go figure.

"I can't tell them it's not a good time for us to have company," I inform Jack, "because I already told my mother it was a perfect time for us to have company."

"Why would you do that?"

"Because I wanted *her* to come. Just her." Remembering that he doesn't know about Ma's diagnosis, I fill him in quickly.

"That's not good, Trace. She really has to start taking care of herself."

"I know…but you know her. She says she won't change her diet, and she won't exercise."

"That's not good," he says again.

"I know it isn't good. Nothing about it is good." I wish he were here or I were there, because I really could use a hug.

"Doesn't she realize how serious this is?"

"She's stubborn," I remind him. "They all are, here. It's like they're living in their own little world, on their own terms. I have about forty-eight hours to make her see that she's got to change and get on a good diet and exercise program."

"It's not up to you, Tracey."

"No one else is taking control."

"Because she's a grown woman. And so are you. She has her life, and you have yours. You can't—"

"She's my mother, and she's sick!"

"I know, but what are you going to do? Kidnap her and send her to a health spa for a year?"

Jack is right. I know he is.

And I know I'm a control freak. I can't help it.

"You have to let go, Trace," he tells me gently.

"Why does it seem like that's all I've been doing lately? Letting go?"

"Because it is. And, yeah, it's been a rough stretch," he tells me. "You'll get through it. We both will. Everything will turn out to be fine."

Sometimes I really wonder.

"I love you, Jack," I tell him with a lump in my throat.

"I love you, too," he says.

And that, I think, feeling infinitely better, is all I really need to get through anything.

14

Well…almost anything.

If you thought the ride to Brookside was bad, imagine the return trip.

Actually, you don't have to imagine it.

Let me tell you all about it.

Grandma sits in front, because she gets carsick—or so she claims.

Turns out, Stefania gets carsick, too.

All over poor chic Wilma and the beige upholstered backseat of my Hyundai.

It happens only twenty minutes into the trip, which has me seriously considering a U-turn.

"No, no, I am fine," Stefania says wanly, mopping her face

with a tissue Wilma handed her. "I love to see New York City!"

"It's a long trip, though, Stefania..."

"No, I am great!" she insists, then gags and gulps.

"Maybe you should let Stefania sit up front," Wilma, looking green herself, suggests to my grandmother, who is eyeing the mess in the backseat.

Grandma glances down at her brand-new white Dress Barn pantsuit, purchased just for today's trip. "I'm sure she'll be fine back there," she decides. "Won't you, Stefania?"

"I am great. Let's go! Woo-hoo!"

What is there to do but drive on, breathing fresh vomit fumes?

"I know! Let's sing show tunes," Wilma suggests. "That always helps."

Huh? That *never* helps.

But she and Grandma are off on a Rodgers and Hammerstein medley before you can say *Oklahoma*.

The singing subsides only when I stop at the next rest area so that Stefania can go into the bathroom and clean herself up.

While she's in there, I swab out the backseat the best I can with a couple of fast-food napkins that were in the glove compartment, but it's still disgusting.

Owning a car is definitely overrated. What I wouldn't give to be back on the good old subway, where there may be plenty of other people spewing bodily fluids, but at least it's not my job to clean it up.

Back on the road, Wilma and Grandma launch into all the songs from *South Pacific,* which naturally reminds me of my Tahitian honeymoon.

Why, oh why, didn't Jack and I stay there while we had the chance? Now that we have a mortgage and I'm unemployed, we'll be lucky if we manage to get back there before our fiftieth anniversary. Or ever.

I mean, think about it: how many seniors do you see jetting off to Tahiti for a second honeymoon? And how much fun can they possibly have? Even if Jack and I do manage a return visit before we croak—as Grandma so eloquently puts it—who's to say I won't be going around exposing my right boob to strangers, talking about my brassiere rash?

How depressing, the way time marches on and everything—and everyone—changes.

Why didn't I ever worry about any of this until lately?

Is it because life seems so much more serious when you buy a house and move away from all your friends?

Is it because my identity was connected to my job, and my social life, and even the nonstop pace of the city?

Who am I now, other than Jack's wife?

Is this it? Is this all there is?

"Join in, Tracey," Grandma commands during "Some Enchanted Evening." "You know the words. Come on, even Stefania's singing."

When she's not dry heaving. And—P.S.—she doesn't know the lyrics. She barely speaks English, for God's sake.

Under happier circumstances, I'm sure I'd think she's a good sport. But in my glum mood, I find her spunk annoying.

Luckily—well, depending on how you look at it—the *South Pacific* medley comes to a crashing halt when we have to make yet another premature stop so that Wilma—who insisted at the previous stop that she didn't need to use the ladies' room—can use the ladies' room.

And—no, I am not exaggerating—we stop again a half hour after that so that Stefania can upchuck again. At least this time, she makes it to the toilet.

"Are you sure you're okay?" I ask when she emerges from the stall, looking shaken.

"I am great!" she more or less snaps at me, and who can blame her?

Here she is in a foreign country, poor girl, trapped in a car with a couple of Broadway-belting babes and a lousy driver in the midst of an identity crisis.

I find myself softening a little.

When she said she wanted to see New York, I'm sure this wasn't what she had in mind.

I definitely owe her a bells-and-whistles sightseeing tour of Manhattan. Ordinarily, I avoid tourist traps, but now that I haven't set foot in the city for nearly a week, I find myself craving certain things. Maybe not a double-decker tour bus down Fifth Avenue, though.

Maybe it'll be good to have her and Grandma around for

a few days. I mean, what else have I got to do? Besides unpack boxes and try to find my way around a strange town and wonder about the meaning of life. My own, anyway.

The trip drags on, and on, and on; we're just four gals on the open road, singing, puking, stopping to pee so often that I'm thinking of raiding my grandmother's luggage for Depends and making Wilma put them on.

Kathleen calls Wilma's cell phone so many times that I instill a new rule: all cell phones in the car must be turned off for the duration of the trip.

Of course, there are only two cell phones: Wilma's and mine.

Before turning it off, I call Jack to tell him where we are and that we'll be a little late or, more likely, a lot late. I don't want him to worry.

His phone bounces right into voice mail. He probably forgot to charge it again. I leave him a message.

As we head out of the Catskills and start to close in on the metro area, it's dark and of course it starts to rain, and the traffic builds until there are blinding headlights and speeding cars everywhere.

The others have long since sung themselves hoarse, thank God, so at least I can focus on not getting us all killed.

Still, after a particularly close call with a dump truck that had to be doing eighty, I ask, "Does anyone else want to drive the rest of the way?"

Stefania pipes right up with a claim that she's not allowed

to drive in this country. I'm not sure I believe her, but then, I'm not sure I want to put my life—sorry as it is—into the hands of someone who learned to drive just a few years ago at most, and quite possibly on the opposite side of the road.

"I would, but I have night blindness," Wilma tells me.

Yeah, don't we all. With a clenched jaw, I hit the brakes as a tractor trailer changes lanes without signaling, cutting me off.

They all scream like they're taking the downhill plunge on the Dragon Coaster.

"I'll drive!" That, of course, comes from Grandma.

I happen to know my mother made her give up her license a few years ago after she came home one afternoon with bright yellow paint on the dented fender of her Caprice Classic and no clue how it got there.

There are no Yellow Cabs in Brookside. I'm convinced that somewhere, there's a school bus that's a little worse for the wear.

"It's okay, Grandma," I tell her wearily, "I'll drive. We're almost there, anyway. There's only another hour or so to go."

Yeah, that would be true, say, on a sunny, midafternoon midweek day in March. But on a rainy Sunday night on the first official weekend of summer, when everyone and their brother is returning to the tristate area after a weekend away, one hour takes three.

When at last I pull up in front of Wilma's condo, she pretty much bolts from the car. I bet she'd be content to leave her oversize luggage behind if I didn't drag it through the rain to her door.

"Thank you, Tracey," she says. "Have a wonderful week with Grandma and Stefania."

"If you want to come into the city with us one day—"

"Oh," she says, "I don't think I'll be able to do that. I've got a lot going on."

Wow. Is it possible that she's as over me as I am over her?

Too much togetherness is never a good idea, no matter how much you adore someone. All I want is to get back to normal with Jack.

Except…

There isn't any normal. Not anymore. We live in a strange place, and I don't have a job, and Jack has a hugely important job that kept him at the office most of the weekend, and now I have to contend with Grandma and Stefania and, oh yeah, a three-legged couch.

Can your life be any more abnormal, Tracey? you may be wondering.

Why, yes, dear reader, I assure you it can.

Because I lead the pack into my new house to be greeted by—no, not Jack—but the Screaming Jesus.

At first, I don't even recognize the wailing toddler in a red beret standing by the back door, and assume that A) there are multiple chapeau-wearing Screaming Jesuses in the world, and B) I've got the wrong house—an honest mistake when one is new to the neighborhood, right?

Right.

Unfortunately for me I've got the right house, and there

is only one Screaming Jesus, and she's here, and—my God, she stinks to high heaven.

Jack materializes to greet me with a quick, fierce hug.

"Welcome home," he shouts above the din. "Look who just popped in for a visit!"

"Hi, Tracey," a raccoon-eyed Kate says miserably, huddled in a chair in the corner of the kitchen.

"Kate? What are you doing h—"

"I'm Tracey's grandma," cuts in Grandma, who, like Glen Close in *Fatal Attraction,* will not be ignored. She sashays over in her high-heeled white pumps to shake hands.

Kate sniffles and manages a tiny, "We met at the wedding."

Jack to the rescue: "Grandma, you look so beautiful! Come on in, we're so glad you're here." He gives her a hug, then turns to Stefania and introduces himself.

"Very nice to be meeting you," she tells him as the Screaming Jesus continues to scream and stink up the room and Kate sobs, "Billy left me. And the nanny quit."

"Oh, Kate…" I wrap my arms around her. "I am so, so sorry."

"What am I going to *do-o-o-o-o-o-o?*"

I feel my own eyes filling up with tears. "I'm sorry," I say again helplessly.

"Aaaaahhhh!" screams the Screaming Jesus, whose beret miraculously stays jauntily perched on her blond head as she tears around the room with a loaded diaper. Yes, folks, we have our very own Mad Crapper right here in the suburbs.

My grandmother winces and looks down at her, then up at me. “Who *is* this unhappy little French girl?”

“Grandma, Stefania, that’s little Katie, Kate’s daughter,” I tell them across Kate’s blond head. “She’s two. And she’s not French.”

But—*mon Dieu!*—is she unhappy!

“Can she chew gum?” Grandma asks Kate, rummaging around in her old-lady purse.

“No…I’m afraid she’ll choke.”

“How about a jawbreaker?” Grandma produces a lint-covered one.

“No!”

Grandma goes on searching, Katie continues howling and Kate resumes sobbing as Jack and I exchange a resigned glance.

Then Stefania reaches down and plucks Katie off her feet and carries her into the other room. Moments later, the screaming subsides and we hear Stefania crooning something in Polish.

A moment later, she sticks her head into the kitchen, holding the now-cooing but still-ripe tot. “You have diaper?”

Kate wordlessly hands over the chic black bag hanging on the back of her chair. No quilted pastel paisley diaper bag for this mom.

“Thank you.” Stefania disappears again.

“Who *is* that person?” Kate asks, looking discombobulated.

“She’s Stefania,” I say with a shrug and notice, out of the corner of my eye, that my grandmother has begun opening and closing cupboard doors, snooping.

See what I mean? Filter gone.

“Grandma, let me show you around the house,” Jack says quickly, and sweeps her from the room.

I sink into a chair next to Kate and squeeze her hand. “Tell me what happened.”

She wipes her streaming eyes and manages to choke out, “Billy said he doesn’t love me anymore. He loves that… person.”

“Marlise?”

“I can’t even say her name. He said he wants a divorce. Do I have to give him a divorce, Tracey?”

“You mean…legally?”

She nods.

Good question.

Does she have to give him a divorce?

I sure as hell would—no doubt about that.

And she definitely should—no doubt about that, either.

But—*have to?*

“I…don’t know.” I shake my head.

“If I don’t have to, then I’m not going to.”

“But, Kate, do you really want to force him to stay if he doesn’t want to?”

“Yes! I don’t want to be divorced. Anything’s better than being divorced.”

"That's not true. You deserve better than Billy, Kate. Look, remember when I was head over heels in love with Will? And you kept trying to make me see him for what he really was?"

"He was an ass. And gay."

"He wasn't gay. He was definitely an ass. But I couldn't see it because I thought I was in love with him."

"This is different. We're married. We have a child."

Kate's right. It is different. I have no experience with divorce or single motherhood. Just an ancient breakup with a heterosexual ass.

What am I supposed to tell her?

How am I supposed to help her?

All I have to offer is an ear, and a shoulder and a spare bedroom without a bed.

"I'm glad you came here," I say, hugging her again.

"I didn't know what else to do. And I can't go back home without him. I don't want to be there if he's not."

"You can stay here as long as you want."

She wipes tears from her swollen eyes. "Thanks, Tracey."

I leave her to pull herself together and go look for the rest of the gang.

I can hear voices and my grandmother's tap-tapping heels overhead. Before I reach the stairway, I spot the couch.

Which—can it be my imagination?—is no longer listing, but seems to have sunk a few inches since I last saw it.

I step closer, turn on another lamp.

It *is* a few inches lower.

I reach out and give it a little nudge. It wobbles.

"Jack, honey?" I call. "Can you come down here for a sec, please? Alone?"

He does—and appears grateful to be summoned away from Grandma until he sees what I'm looking at.

"What's with the couch, sweetie?" I ask, not wanting to jump to conclusions.

"Mitch and I fixed it. See? No more broken leg."

"I see, but…why does it seem so…close to the ground?"

"We had to smooth off the top of the leg the movers cut because it was on a slant. Then it was shorter than the other legs, so we had to cut them to even things up."

I bend over and take a peek at the four wooden stumps, no longer than my pinkie finger.

Then I rise and look at Jack.

"What? You wanted me to fix it. So I did."

"Thanks," I say, clenching my jaw, not sure whether I'm trying to keep from yelling, or laughing, or crying.

"Tracey?"

We look up to see Kate, standing in the archway and holding a wad of sodden tissues.

"Yeah?"

"Do you have any bourbon? I think I need a drink."

Jack and I look at each other.

"No bourbon," Jack says, "and it's a Sunday night, or I'd run out and buy some for you. How about a Bud? Mitch and I bought a case and there's some left."

Kate looks blankly at me.

"It's beer," I tell her. To Jack, I say, "She doesn't drink beer."

"Hay-ell, Tracey, right now Ah'd drink mouthwash," is her anguished reply.

That night, late, Jack and I lie on a layer of blankets on the hardwood floor of our new living room.

It's warm and muggy now that the rain has passed, and all the windows are open. Through the screens we can hear crickets chirping and the porch gutter dripping. It's been a long time since I've lain awake listening to night sounds.

"Do you miss having central air?" I ask Jack in a whisper, lying with my head cradled on his upper arm.

"No. Do you?"

"No. I might, when it's August. But it's kind of nice to have the windows open."

"Yeah. It would be even nicer if we were in our own bed upstairs."

"I know. I'm sorry."

Grandma and Kate are in our bed. Stefania's on the duct-tape-patched air bed down the hall, with Katie beside her in a porta-crib Kate had the presence of mind to bring.

"Kate does know that Stefania isn't an au pair, right?" Jack asked when he found out where everyone was sleeping.

"Of course she knows. But Stefania's the only one who can make Katie stop crying and anyway, you've got to admit, Stefania didn't seem to mind much. I actually think, of the three roommate choices, she's got the best deal."

Kate drank herself into a beer haze of grief and finally collapsed into bed—ours—sometime after midnight, and Grandma—well, she was Grandma. She had plenty of advice for everyone—marital counsel, decorating tips, toddler-parenting guidance, even job-hunting hints for me. I took her with a grain of salt, as always. Thank God Kate was too piss drunk to absorb much of anything other than more alcohol, because Grandma basically told her to go back home to her philandering husband and look the other way.

"So how long is everyone staying?" Jack asks, grunting as he changes position, forcing me to move my head onto my pillow, which is old and thin and springy.

"Grandma and Stefania fly out on Saturday morning. Kate and Katie...who knows?"

"So it'll be almost a week before we get our bed back?"

"At least. Sorry."

Jack sighs in the dark.

Then he says, "Oh! I almost forgot to tell you. Raphael called earlier. He said he'd tried to call you on your cell a few times but it kept going into voice mail."

"I had to turn it off while I was driving." I decide not to tell him that was because his mother was driving me crazy with her phone. And in general.

"Did you tell Raphael I was out of town?" I ask Jack.

"Yeah. He seemed upset that you hadn't told him. I said it was a last-minute trip because your mother had been sick. He was upset you hadn't told him that, either."

"He's so self-centered."

"He's Raphael."

I sigh. To be fair, there really was a time when Raphael would have known my every move. We used to check in with each other by phone every time anything out of the ordinary happened during the day. But I realize now that I didn't call him when I needed help with the couch, or when I found out my mother was in the E.R., or when I was fired.

Why not? Isn't that what friends are for? Don't they vow to be there for each other in good times and in bad?

No. That's a spouse.

You don't take a solemn, official, legal vow with your friends. They're allowed to leave, without so much as a separation agreement.

Friends come and go. It hurts, but it's a fact of life.

I guess I always thought my friends were the exception, but maybe I was wrong. Maybe Raphael and I really are growing apart, and there's nothing I can do about it.

"Tell me about the new job," I say, to take my mind off the depressing stuff.

"It's a lot more responsibility. And a lot more travel. Are you okay with that?"

"Do I have any choice?" I shoot back, then add a hasty "Sorry. I didn't mean it to come out so cranky. I'm just tired from the drive."

"Well, you can sleep in tomorrow morning."

I wish I could see his face, because I can't tell if he means that as a dig.

"I'd gladly get on the train with you and go to work if I hadn't been fired."

"The train is no picnic. Mitch and I had to stand all the way to White Plains Friday night."

"Mitch. Right." How could I forget he was here this weekend? "How did he like the house?" I ask Jack, who hesitates.

"He…liked it."

"No, he didn't."

"He just said it needs a lot of work. Which it does."

"What else did he say?"

"Nothing much. He was mostly pretty bummed about the couch."

"Yeah, well, he would be, considering that he practically lived on it from the day we bought it. Let me guess—did he say I shouldn't have let the movers chop off the leg?"

"As a matter of fact, he did."

Of course he did.

I open my mouth to retort, but then something occurs to me.

Maybe Mitch was right.

Maybe I *shouldn't* have let them chop the leg off the couch.

Why, oh why, did I let them ruin our beautiful couch?

Because they couldn't get it through the door, remember?

Yes, but what goes in must come out. Right?

I should have stopped to think things through.

Not just the couch.

"I'm so sorry," I tell Jack around a gi-normous lump in my throat.

"For what?"

"For making us move."

That isn't what I meant to say. I meant to apologize for the couch leg, but—

"Tracey—"

"I ruined our lives!"

"Shh! No, you didn't." He gives me a *there-there* pat.

"Yes, I did."

"How?"

"I feel like if we hadn't moved, we'd still have friends, and money, and time together, and jobs—"

"I have a job—a better job—and you didn't lose yours because we moved."

"I know, but our little apartment was so cozy, Jack. It was comfortable. We had a bed."

"We still have—"

"We're on the floor." The ache that's been in my throat for a week now suddenly gives way to a sob. Sobs. Huge, heaving sobs, and I'm blubbering all over Jack.

"It'll be okay. It just takes a while to get settled."

"When we moved into our apartment, we were settled right away, remember?" I cry. "Remember all the time we had together? And we didn't have the stupid budget, or the car—I hate driving, Jack! I hate it! And we didn't have room for all these freaking houseguests…and we could order takeout for delivery whenever we wanted it? Remember how happy we were back then? Remember how easy it was?"

"That's because we didn't move to a new town, and we were younger, and we were just renting, so if it didn't work out…"

"What if this doesn't work out?"

"It will. It's where we wanted to be, remember?"

"I don't have any friends here. No one likes me."

"Now you're being ridiculous."

I wipe my nose on a blanket. "I can't help it. I just feel like it's all so depressing, and the next thing you know, I'm going to be a sick, middle-aged woman in the emergency room calling the doctor a *mamaluke.*"

Jack laughs.

I cry harder.

"Oh, come on, Trace. Things will look better in the morning. They always do."

"In the morning I have to lead a group tour in Manhattan. And that's not even in the budget!" I wail.

"It's all right. Do what you have to do and we'll figure something out later. Okay?"

"Okay."

"Good."

I sniffle. "Thank you."

Jack pretty much falls asleep right away.

I don't think I ever will, but eventually, I can feel myself growing drowsy.

My last conscious thought is that Kate once mentioned the Screaming Jesus wakes up pretty early.

As in predawn early.

15

The Screaming Jesus wakes the entire household at 5:00 a.m.

By seven, Jack has left for the train and I'm left to hold down the fort with Grandma, who has now monopolized the upstairs bathroom for two hours "getting ready." Stefania actually does seem to think she's an au pair because she's done nothing but tend to Kate's daughter, maybe because Kate is sick and hungover in addition to being generally devastated.

"I think I'm going to fly home to Mobile for a few weeks," she tells me, gingerly sipping a cup of black coffee. Did I mention we finally bought new filters? "It's not that I don't appreciate your offer to let me and Katie stay here. But there are reminders of Billy everywhere I look."

"It's a new place. Billy's never even been here," I point out.

"No, not like that. I mean you and Jack. I can't stand seeing the two of you so happy together. It's awful."

Here's the thing about Kate and me: we've been friends long enough that I can understand just what she means by that comment and not be insulted or take it personally.

"It's not like Jack and I don't have our problems," I tell her. "Everyone does."

"Jack would never leave you, Tracey."

No. She's right. He wouldn't.

Thank God I married Jack and not Billy. Thank God I have my life and not Kate's.

After I hug her and Katie goodbye, I call Jack.

He picks up his cell phone for a change. "Hi...how's it going at the Candell B and B?"

"Two of the guests have checked out."

"Which two?"

"Does it matter?"

He considers that, then chuckles. "No," he says. "I guess it doesn't. Either way we don't get our bed back till the weekend, right?"

"Right. Kate's going down to stay with her parents for a while in Mobile."

"That's probably a good idea. She seems to need someone to take care of her and Katie. She did bring Katie with her, didn't she?"

"No," I say, "she brought Stefania. Katie and Grandma are staying on with us."

At his horrified silence, I burst out laughing.

"Please tell me you were just kidding," he says.

"I was just kidding."

"You are one funny, funny gal. Listen, I talked to my mother a little while ago and she said she had a wonderful time with you and your family."

"She *did?*"

Then again, of course she did. What else is she going to say? Wilma is a true lady.

"Yes. She also said to remind you that the girls have some kind of talent show on Saturday afternoon and we're supposed to go."

"Saturday afternoon?" I echo. "Oh, no."

"Oh, no, what? Don't tell me you made other plans?"

"Yes," I say quickly, seizing the out. "I told Raphael I'd meet him for lunch in Manhattan. Bummer."

You might think I'm lying to my husband.

I guess I am…but it's for his own good, because there's no telling what I might do—and in public—if I have to sit through the devilmint twins in a talent show on my first free afternoon after Grandma and Stefania fly away.

"You can't reschedule?"

"Are you kidding? After the way Raphael has carried on about my abandoning him?"

"I guess you can't," he says. "It's okay. I'll go to the show with my mother. So what's on the tour schedule for today?"

"They want to see the Statue of Liberty."

"Take the Staten Island ferry. It's free and you get a great view from there."

"Good idea." Free is definitely in the budget.

After we hang up, I quickly call Raphael.

It goes into voice mail after several rings. I happen to know that Raphael always checks caller ID, no matter where he is—in a meeting, at a photo shoot, on the toilet—so I'm well aware he's screening my call.

"I'm taking you to lunch on Saturday in Manhattan, you choose the restaurant, no excuses." No, it's not on the budget. But sometimes, a girl's gotta do what a girl's gotta do. I hesitate, about to hang up, then add, "You know I love you. Still. Always. No matter what. Or where. Okay? See you Saturday."

Grandma—who wore a homemade gown fashioned out of a shower curtain to my wedding—dresses for the day in a romper that appears to be made from a bath towel.

"Is that terry cloth?" I ask her when she first appears in it.

"Yes. You said to wear something comfortable."

"I was thinking sneakers."

She, of course, has on strappy high heels, the better to show off her "gorgeous gams" (the quote is from her). Referring, of course, to her own gams. Which I'll admit are still decent, especially for a woman in her eighties, but shouldn't a woman in her eighties keep them—and other body parts—under wraps?

A few people on the train to the city give Grandma a wary once-over, and I find myself wishing we'd gone at rush hour so there wouldn't be an available triple seat and we could have all sat separately. I make sure Stefania sits in the middle and I pretend to be engrossed in my gardening magazine so that no one will think we're together.

Especially when Grandma announces, loudly and within earshot of everyone including the short, friendly and pock-marked conductor: "The conductor has a terrible skin problem, poor little fellow."

"What are you reading, Tracey?" Grandma wants to know, leaning across Stefania's lap, and I show her the cover.

"You're going to plant a garden?"

"Yes, just as soon as I get a chance."

"What kind of garden?"

"You know…like my mother has. And you, too. Herbs, flowers, vegetables…"

Grandma looks pleased. "That's so nice!"

Stefania is also pleased. "How nice!"

"Yeah. I already bought all the seeds."

"Seeds? It's already June. Too late to start a vegetable garden from seed!"

I frown. "Too late? Really?"

"Oh, yeah." She gives a dismissive wave of her hand, shaking her head. "You need to start seeds indoors in the winter, in little pots."

"My mother never did that!"

"That's because she gets her plants at the nursery. Most people do."

"They do? My mother does?"

"Yes," Grandma confirms.

"Yes," Stefania also confirms cluelessly.

Really. Who knew? I guess I never paid much attention to how—or when—the plants got there. All I ever noticed was the end result. The August tomatoes, warm from the sun.

"Oh, sure," Grandma says. "You have to get the plants in right at the start of the growing season. Go to a nursery. It might not be too late."

"I want to grow them from seed," I say stubbornly.

"You can't," she replies just as stubbornly.

"No." That's Stefania, also stubborn. She's getting on my nerves again. I should have put her on the aisle.

"What would happen if I planted the seeds now? They wouldn't grow?"

"No, they would," Grandma tells me, "and then next fall, the killing frost will come along before your tomatoes have a chance to ripen or your flowers have a chance to bloom."

Jesus, that's depressing.

"If you want to plant seeds, wait until next year," Grandma says with a firm nod.

"Next year," Stefania agrees with a firm nod.

Next year? I wanted to do it *this* year. I wanted to plant seeds and watch them sprout and pluck ripe tomatoes and peppers from their vines by my back door in August, the way my mother and grandmother have always done.

Why didn't anyone ever tell me they were getting their plants from the nursery?

Why is it that nothing ever works out the way I have planned?

And why is this damn garden so important to me?

I have no idea. It just is.

You mean was.

Whatever. It's over.

"I guess I'll save the seeds for next year," I tell Grandma with a sigh.

"Oh, you can't save seeds. You have to buy fresh ones."

I'm annoyed all over again. What a waste! I can't squander the seed budget like that.

Not that there was a seed budget in the first place.

Who knew there were so many rules in gardening?

Who knew I'd fail so miserably before I even started?

I put the magazine aside and spend the rest of the trip staring glumly out the window.

At last we arrive at Grand Central Terminal. I herd Grandma and Stefania up into the main concourse to *ooh* and *aah* over the lustrous sky-blue ceiling with its constellations, then hustle them back downstairs and onto the subway.

It's slightly strange being back in Manhattan after almost a week away. The territory is familiar, and my every move is second nature, yet I'm no longer a part of the city. Maybe that's why its hassles seem to have miraculously diminished. The crowds, the cost, the homeless, the noise…none of it's getting to me today. I feel emotionally insulated. Or maybe just emotionally isolated.

When the express train runs local all the way downtown, I shrug it off. Same thing when I emerge on Canal Street to a passing cab splashing me with a warm, stagnant puddle from last night's rain.

It's a muggy gray day, and the old-world air down here is thick with the smell of exotic cuisine and the East River and foreign strangers who stand too close.

For Stefania's benefit, we lunch on kielbasa and pierogi at a Polish diner on the Lower East Side. For Grandma's benefit, we have dessert and espresso at an Italian Pastry Shop a few blocks away on Mulberry Street.

Then it's on to Battery Park and the ferry, from which we can glimpse the Statue of Liberty.

It's funny. In all those years of living in Manhattan, I've only seen it a couple of times. I mean, it's not as though I cruise the New York harbor on a daily basis.

"I cannot believe I am here!"

I turn to see Stefania standing beside me, her hair streaming back in the wind, with tears running down her cheeks.

Grandma looks at her, then at me. I'm shocked to see that

there are tears in her eyes, too. "This is what my mother saw when she came over from Italy," she says, wiping at them and shaking her head. "She was just a kid."

"How old, Grandma?" I ask as Stefania moves on down the railing with her camera, snapping picture after picture from different angles.

"Fifteen, and a newlywed. My father was already here—he came for a year, then sent for her. And it was an arranged marriage back in the Old Country, so they barely knew each other as it was. How about that?"

"I never knew any of that," I tell my grandmother in awe.

"Well, you should. It's your history."

I nod solemnly, gazing at the Statue and at Ellis Island in the distance.

"She never saw her parents or her sisters and brothers again, you know," Grandma tells me. "Once in a while she used to cry for them when I was a little girl. And they wrote back and forth for years, until they all died back in Italy one by one and she was the only one left."

All I remember of my great-grandmother is a wizened old lady in a housedress and cardigan, baggy stockings and thick-soled shoes. She spoke no English, and pinched our cheeks, and gave us Root Beer Barrels. She died when I was little. I confess I never gave her much thought, before or after that.

Now I try to imagine her standing on the deck of a ship in this very harbor, embarking on a new life in a strange land, far from a homeland and family she would never see again.

"What was her name?" I ask Grandma. "Your mother."

"It was Carlotta. That means 'strong one' in Italian. And she was." My grandmother shrugs. "We all are. Especially you."

Surprised, I ask, "Me? Why?"

She laughs. "You're the only one who left home, followed a dream, the way she did. The rest of us…we all stick around. Stick together. It's easier that way. More comfortable. We play it safe."

I never thought of it that way. I never thought the rest of them admired me. I thought they just resented me. I've always felt like the outcast. Maybe I'm not.

As the boat glides past the Statue of Liberty, Grandma puts her arm around me and holds me close, stroking my hair the way grandmothers do.

I think about my old life, and my new life.

I think about Carlotta, building a new life alone in a new country, and how if she hadn't done what she did, I wouldn't be here.

Not here, as in Glenhaven Park. I mean here, in the world, at all.

She was strong.

Yeah, I've got quite a few years and a whole lot more life experience on Carlotta when she married and came to America, and my husband isn't a stranger. Still…

Maybe I'm strong, too. Stronger than I thought.

★ ★ ★

That night, before I go to bed, I open a drawer looking for my dental floss, and stumble across all those packets of seeds I stashed there last week.

Useless, according to Grandma.

I carry them over to the garbage can, step on the pedal and hold them poised to dump in.

It seems like such a waste.

What would happen if I planted them now anyway?

What if this were the one year without a killing frost?

It's a long shot, I know…but anything's possible, right? Global warming, and all.

I slip outside in my pajamas and sneakers, carrying a trowel and the packets of seeds.

It's a warm night. Crickets, and in the distance, the sound of a late train rumbling toward the city.

In the moonlight, I dig into the moist, crumbly ground beside the back door, creating a garden patch.

As I dig, a rich, earthy scent fills the air. It makes me think of spring nights when I was a kid, just before school got out, when my brother Joey and I would hunt for night crawlers for my father to take fishing. My mother would have to call us in repeatedly. I remember her voice, frustrated, then worried, echoing through the dark neighborhood. She'd make us take a bath before bed, and the water would be dingy, leaving a ring around the tub that she'd sigh about and scrub after we went to bed. And when my father came home the next day with freshly caught fish from the waters of Lake Erie, she'd fry it all up for dinner.

Lake Erie. For all I know, the fish was glowing green, but we never worried about stuff like that back then.

I sigh, remembering home.

Then I carefully tear open each seed packet and dump them all into the soil. After covering the whole thing with another layer of dirt, I stomp it down, and step back to look at it.

I have no idea what I just did, or why I did it.

All I know is that somehow, it makes me feel good.

16

"I don't know...I just feel like it's all over, Tracey," Raphael says mournfully across the table on Saturday afternoon.

We're having lunch in the Flatiron district at Raphael's favorite tapas restaurant. He's wearing a black bolero and a white blouse with a jabot in honor of the cuisine. On anyone other than a toreador or Raphael, the outfit would look ridiculous.

He, however, wears it with flair. That's one of the things I love about him.

One of the many things.

He, however, is convinced that I no longer appreciate him.

"What's over, Raphael?" I ask with a sigh. "Our friendship?"

"Isn't that what we've been talking about, Tracey?"

"No. We've actually been talking about whether the ghost of Anna Nicole is haunting you." Yeah. I'm serious. We have been.

"Well, that's not up for discussion. She is. Case closed." Raphael nibbles at a bacon-wrapped stuffed date.

"But why would she haunt you? Why wouldn't she go haunt Howard K. Stern or someone?"

"I told you," he says with exaggerated patience, "she didn't like me."

"I thought you only met her once, at that shoot, and I thought she liked you fine until you insulted her."

"I did not insult her! She kept tipping over and I made the stylists prop her against the chair."

"With rope?"

"Tracey! Not rope. Light twine."

"I see."

"But this isn't about the ghost of Anna Nicole. It's about you and me and our friendship."

Maybe, but it takes me a second to get past the image of a livid and strung-out Anna Nicole lightly twined to a chair.

"Raphael, how can you say it's over just because I'm living in the suburbs?"

"Because that's how I feel."

"But that's ridiculous."

"Tracey! It isn't ridiculous. Please don't invalidate my feelings."

"I'm sorry, I didn't mean to—"

"My therapist says I have abandonment issues, Tracey. She's helping me work through them and she said it's good for me to verbalize them."

"I thought your therapist was a he and that he said you have existential issues."

"That's my psychiatrist, Dr. Dre."

"The rapper?"

"No, the doctor. His name is Andre. Dre for short. But I was talking about my therapist, Soosan. With two o's."

Of course. Leave it to Raphael to entrust his mental well-being to a gangsta shrink and a u-less Soosan.

"So you basically have two therapists now?"

He hesitates.

"Wait, you have more?"

"Only three, if you count Jamboree."

"What—who?—is Jamboree?"

"She's the alternative cognitive therapist who's been helping me work through my adult-onset hippophobia."

I probably shouldn't ask.

I *know* I shouldn't ask.

I know that if I ask, I'll only lead him off on some ridiculous Raphael tangent.

But then, anything is better than discussing the fact that I no longer live or work in Manhattan.

"Hippophobia, Raphael? What is that—an acute fear of hippos?"

"No! Tracey, please! Why would I be afraid of hippos?"

He rolls his eyes as if he's never heard of anything so ridiculous in his life.

"No, I'm sure you wouldn't. I'm sorry. So what is it?"

"It's an acute fear of *horses.*"

"Aha." I nod and take a big long sip of my white sangria, telling myself to drop the subject. Now. Before I alienate him even further.

I bite into a toast point bearing a fried quail egg with Spanish sausage, which should do wonders for my complexion. I woke up with a volcanic pimple on my chin, which Raphael naturally noticed the second he saw me, and offered his tongue-clucking condolences.

"So you're getting cognitive therapy for an acute fear of horses," I find myself saying.

"Yes."

"But this is Manhattan. I mean, it's not like you live on a farm in Kentucky."

"There are horses in Manhattan, Tracey," he says indignantly. "There are mounted police, and those carriages in the park, and—"

"Raphael, are you serious? You're that afraid of horses?"

"Yes, and Tracey, please don't ridicule me for something I can't help. See? This is exactly what I'm talking about."

"What are we talking about?"

"Things are different now. I feel like you don't even know me now that you've moved on."

"Of course I know you. I've known you for years. And I haven't moved *on*. I've just moved."

"People constantly evolve, Tracey. I feel like you don't know who I've become."

"Sure, I do." *This week, anyway. You're being haunted by Anna Nicole and you have three therapists and an acute fear of horses.*

I reach across the table and take his hand, sensing that this isn't the time to joke around with him. "Raphael, I will always know you and love you and be your friend."

"You abandoned me."

"I'm here today, aren't I?"

"That's because you felt obligated. You didn't really want to come."

"Sure I did."

Okay, not really. I just didn't want to go to the twins' talent show.

But now that I'm here with him, I'm glad. I do love him. I just don't think he's being fair. He's a needy friend, and I'm feeling too drained these days for needy friends.

"I guarantee that you won't be coming in and out of the city on weekends for long, Tracey. Next thing I know, you'll be a stay-at-home mom. That's what happens with all the women I work with. They just fade away, one by one, into the suburbs."

God. He makes it sound so gloomy.

"Well, I'm not even a mom," I point out, "so don't worry about it."

"But you will be someday, Tracey. Right?"

I pause. I know where he's going with this. What can I say other than, "Right."

"That's what I mean. You'll settle in up there, have your babies, and I'll never see you again."

Somewhere in the back of my mind, I feel a twinge of bittersweet awareness. He might be right.

Of course he's right. Look at Brenda. Look at every friend I've ever had who has a baby and moves out of Manhattan.

Yet I feel compelled to assure Raphael, "That's not going to happen."

"No, and I don't suppose Lilly Pulitzer will design something in pink and green for the spring line, either."

"Huh?"

"This never would have happened if you didn't decide to move."

I sigh. "Raphael, please try to understand that Jack and I just needed more space."

"I gave you plenty of space, Tracey. Didn't I agree to give up Suds 'n Suds when you got married?"

Suds 'n Suds. I can't help but smile. Raphael and I used have a standing weekly date at the Laundromat, where we'd share a six-pack while watching the washers and dryers spin our clothes.

"That's not the kind of space we needed, Raphael. I'm talking about literal space. We outgrew our apartment. We wanted a house."

"There are houses right here in the city."

"Sure, carriage houses that cost twenty million. Speaking of which, don't you find it ironic that you want to live in a carriage house while you're suffering from horseophobia?"

"Hippophobia, and not at all ironic. It's all connected. That's what Soosan says. Getting back to you—"

"Let's not. Let's talk about something else."

He shrugs. "Fine. What?"

"Hey, how's Georgie?" I ask Raphael, settling on his all-time favorite subject aside from dissecting the last episode of *Project Runway,* which I would ordinarily love to dish about, only I was too busy to get into this season.

Raphael smiles. "Georgie's great, Tracey! I love that child. All I want to do is fill him with joy. You'll see someday when you're a mother."

Uh-oh, dangerous territory again. Mother=stay-at-home-mom=our friendship is over.

"When is the adoption going to be finalized?" I ask Raphael.

"In August, and he wants to go to Walt Disney World to celebrate."

"That sounds like fun."

"Oh, it will be. Donatello and I have never been. Why don't you and Jack come with us?"

"Maybe we will," I say, before I remember the budget.

It doesn't include an August vacation…or any vacation. Ever again.

Nor, now that I'm unemployed, does it include anything not directly food-and-shelter related.

"Can I get you anything else?" the waitress asks me and Raphael.

He looks at me.

"I'm stuffed," I say.

"What, no flan?"

I love flan, but I'm pretty sure flan isn't in the budget, either. God, I hate the budget.

When the waitress drops the check on the table between us, Raphael makes a grab for it, as usual. I've been privy to many a fancy Raphael expense-account lunch and shopping spree over the years. I always offer to pay, but he never lets me.

Still, I pull out my wallet. "Raphael, I invited you today. Lunch is my treat."

"Put that away. I've got the corporate card. I'll write you off as a supermodel."

I look dubiously at my reflection in the mirror behind the table, then at the litter of empty plates on it. "You said the last supermodel you lunched with ordered tepid water and a cigarette, and I bet she didn't have a gi-normous zit on her chin."

"And nose," Raphael observes. "I can see one flaring up there, too."

I say, through a clenched and probably soon-to-be pimply jaw, "Seriously, let me get the bill."

I've never put up much of an argument before. I guess I'm feeling guilty about wanting to check the Metro-North schedule in my bag and jump on the first train back to suburbia. The talent show should be over by now, and it'll be the first time Jack and I have the house to ourselves since we moved in.

Grandma and Stefania left this morning. They were both grateful for all the sightseeing expeditions, and kept hugging me when I left them at the airport. In the end, I was actually as sorry to see them go as I was glad. Who knows if I'll ever see Stefania again?

Or, for that matter, Grandma?

Yes, she gets on my nerves.

Yes, she may be slightly senile.

But she's getting older.

The truth is, my children might never know her. Or they might only remember her as a wizened old lady whose first name they don't even think to ask.

I've been thinking a lot about Carlotta this week.

And about me.

Naturally, Raphael refuses to let me split the restaurant bill, which naturally makes me feel as if I should at least hang out with him awhile longer.

"What now?" he asks as we emerge onto Broadway on an overcast windy afternoon that feels more like March than June, requiring lamps on indoors and hoods up outdoors.

"I don't know…want to walk down to the Strand?" I ask reluctantly.

"Sure. You're not in a rush to get home to suburbia?"

"No," I say.

"Don't you think Jack is lonely without you?"

"No, he went to a show with his family."

"Why didn't you go with them?"

"Because I already had a lunch date with you."

He looks so pleased I feel guiltier than ever, and determined to cling to what's left of our friendship.

"Why are we going to the Strand?" Raphael wants to know as we head downtown.

"Because you know I love bookstores as much as you love sample sales, and anyway, I need to research a couple of things."

Never mind that I'm pretty sure there was no category for books on the budget, and Jack has mentioned more than once that Glenhaven Park has a great little library. The Strand is a great place for bargain books, and I find myself wistfully wondering why I didn't visit it more often when I lived just a few dozen blocks instead of a few dozen miles away.

"What are you researching? How to survive Wisteria Lane?" Raphael asks, but there's a twinkle in his eye. Apparently he's moved past the resentment phase now that he knows I chose him over Westchester, at least for this afternoon.

"Maybe I do need some books on wisteria, actually. Not the lane. I'm going to do some landscaping."

"Tracey! You're so Martha! Oooh, you know what you should get? Denim overalls and a big straw hat. Oh, and plastic clogs would be just too, too much."

If it were anyone but Raphael, I'd think he was busting my chops, but Raphael takes his fashion very seriously.

Also, in Raphaelspeak, *just too, too much* translates into the *pièce de résistance.*

"That sounds great," I say, to humor him, thinking there is no way on God's green earth that I'd be caught dead in overalls, much less plastic clogs and a straw hat.

Not that my outfit today is a vast improvement.

I'm wearing my fat jeans—the unflattering baggy pair I keep around for PMS weekends—which this is—along with a nylon windbreaker because the breeze is chilly, and brown Aerosole loafers because they're comfortable to walk around in.

Raphael, who is wearing black boots with toes shaped like needlenose pliers and who isn't opposed to plastic clogs, deplores Aerosoles.

In the Strand, we go our separate ways: Raphael off to the parenting section, and I to horticulture.

There, perusing a row of books on landscaping, I find—of all the people in the entire world—Will McCraw.

Let's refresh our memories, shall we?

Back when I was young and single in the city, my narcissistic ex-boyfriend went off to summer stock and never came back. I mean, he came back to the city, but not to me.

Not that he was ever really *with* me to begin with, though I didn't realize that fact until he was long gone and I had finally learned what a "real" relationship entailed, with Jack.

I have to admit that Will—who was once dubbed hapless eye candy in a theatrical review (trust me, compared to the rest of what the reviewer said about him, that was a compliment)—is aging pretty well. Clean shaven and unwrinkled, he doesn't seem to have lost a single strand of his thick dark hair. He's wearing his ubiquitous black turtleneck and cologne, and has a black blazer slung over his arm.

Luckily, I see him before he sees me, which means I get to decide whether to greet or run.

What to do, what to do…

I stand rooted to the ground watching Will rub his chin and scan the bookshelf.

The last time we had any contact was on the phone almost three years ago. He had just returned from doing *La Cage aux Folles* in Transylvania, and was calling to see whether his invitation to my upcoming wedding had been lost in the mail.

It hadn't been.

I'll admit, I took some pleasure in informing him that he hadn't made the guest list.

Will was offended.

Which made us even at long last, because I was—belatedly—offended by just about everything he'd ever done to me in the course of our nonrelationship.

When I said goodbye to him that day and hung up the phone, I knew he was out of my life for good. It was a long time coming and I have to say, I haven't given him a whole lot of thought since.

Now, watching him, smelling him, I'm stirred by a couple of long-forgotten memories.

I remember inhaling that same cologne when it lingered in the sweatshirt he'd left at my place after we broke up. I used to bury my face in it and wish he were in it, though if we were in it he'd probably tell me not to slobber on him. He never could abide slobbering.

I remember that Will always had plants, even back in college. Not pot plants, or lame cactuses, but real, honest-to-goodness plants, the kind that needed special lighting and fertilizer and loving care. I remember feeling jealous that he was capable of loving care when it came to plants, but not humans. At least, not me.

I remember that I used to love to run my fingertips along that cleft in his chin, just the way he's doing now and probably just as lovingly.

Bottom line: there's only one person who was ever as crazily obsessive about Will McCraw as I was, and that's Will McCraw.

Even now, he's so wrapped up in himself—or maybe, to be fair, in the plant books as well—that he has yet to notice me. If I slink away now, he'll never see me here in my fat jeans and Aerosoles.

Then again, do I really care if he does see me? Am I still, after all these years, concerned about what he thinks of me?

Of course not.

That doesn't mean it's such a bad idea to dart into the ladies' room to slick on some lip gloss and run a comb through my wind-disheveled hair.

Or—since lip gloss and a comb can't possibly conceal the angry Vesuvius on my chin—it might not be a bad idea to just slink off to children's books, where I know he'll never set foot.

Will hates children.

I know, sounds like a great guy, doesn't he?

What can I say? I was young and overweight and incredibly insecure.

"Tracey?"

Too late. His gray eyes have landed on me and widened in surprise.

"Oh my God! Is that really you?" He grabs me and hugs me before I can answer no, it's not really me. Which is tempting, since he had to ask in the first place, insinuating that I've changed.

Of course, people do change for the better—and I actually have—but I'm not exactly showcasing my finer physical attributes today.

Still, Will says, "Wow, you look great!"

Oh, please. I don't, and we both know it.

"So do you, Will!"

We both know that, too.

Why can't he be puffy with graying facial hair and a bad combover?

"So, it looks like married life agrees with you," Will tells the pimple on my chin.

He never was one to overlook a blemish.

"Yeah, things are good. Jack and I just bought a house in Westchester," I say, like he cares.

"No kidding!" He shifts his gaze from my pimple to my pupils at last. Maybe he does care. "So did we!"

We?

Whoa!

Not only did Will—who has always had great disdain for suburbia—buy a house in Westchester, but Will is a *We!*

Incredible. Will is married?

But when I ask him—"so you're married?"—he shakes his head quickly and distastefully.

Oh, right. He never did believe in "contracts," as he liked to say.

"I'm living with someone," he says. "Can you believe it? Me, the raging commitmentphobe."

"No, I really can't believe it," I say, wondering if he got that phrase from me—because I really thought I only called him that behind his back. Among other things I doubt he'd call himself.

"Go figure. I guess the key is just to find the Right Person."

"Absolutely," I agree, the Wrong Person—for Will, anyway.

But that's okay, because the wrongness is mutual. What on earth did I ever see in this guy? Is it me, or did he change? Because he seems so very…

"Jerry and I met last year doing *HMS Pinafore*."

…very gay, for one thing.

He goes on, "We just clicked, from the moment we first met."

"You and Jerry," I say, just to make sure I heard him right.

"Yes. One look at Jerry, and it was as if my whole life just fell into place."

So they were right all along. And I didn't believe them. For all those years, I did my best to ignore my brothers and my work friends and Kate, all of whom were absolutely convinced that Will was gayer than Dumbledore.

As far as I know, they based their assumption on a series of clichés: his impeccable appearance, his affinity for show tunes and his appreciation for imported cheese and designer linens.

I had actually slept with the man on those designer linens, which I liked to bring up as evidence that Will was a straight arrow.

Looking back, though, I have to wonder if the passion might have been as one-sided as the rest of the relationship proved to be. I mean, Will was my first. What did I have to compare him to? Who's to say he wasn't phoning it in while fantasizing about George Clooney?

I guess I really was an unwitting beard for all those years.

Speaking of beards…

"Will, look, I found it," a male voice says.

Well, well, well, isn't this refreshing?

We've just been joined by a man I can only assume is Jerry. Whom Will curiously neglected to mention happens to be an Amish Warlock.

Yes, I'm serious. The guy has a big, bushy chest-grazing beard and he's dressed all in black, including black suspenders over a black turtleneck exactly like Will's, and a big, broad-brimmed black hat with a rounded—as opposed to pointy—crown. He's holding a cookbook, most likely chock-full of shoofly-pie recipes.

Needless to say, he isn't at all what I'd expected from Will. I'd have expected him to be drawn more to the buff, boyish actor type, much like himself.

"Tracey, this is my friend Jacob," Will says.

Jacob? I guess he must have said Jacob and I somehow heard it as Jerry, earlier when he was talking about his live-in love.

And it's funny because back when we were dating, he always used to introduce me as his "friend," too.

Here but for the grace of God go I, I think as I shake the Amish Warlock's hand and Will introduces me as his "old friend Tracey."

Old friend, new friend, girlfriend, boyfriend.

I'll admit, as little as I care about Will, I can't help but find some kind of profound satisfaction at this belated revelation about Will's true sexual orientation.

At least this explains why he was so immune to my feminine wiles and charms for all those years.

Then again…it doesn't explain Esme, or the many other women he slept with while he was supposed to be in a relationship with yours truly.

"Hi, how's it going?" Jacob flicks a disinterested gaze over me, apparently decides I'm not a viable threat, and turns back to Will.

"You have to get this for Jerry," he says, putting the cookbook into Will's professionally manicured hands. "It has the spelt-bread recipe she wanted."

Wait—Jacob isn't Jerry?

Wait—Jerry is a *she?*

Is she Jerry Hall?

Or Gerry?

"Great, she'll love it," Will tells Jacob, oblivious to my profound Noun (both Pro- and Proper) confusion. Turning to me, he says, "Jerry's a vegan."

A vegan with a vagina. And here I thought—

"She's turned me into one, too."

"A vegan?" *Sans* vagina, I presume.

Will nods. "She says she wants us to live to a ripe old age together."

"My sister-in-law Rachel is a vegan," is my lame response.

Will clearly doesn't care. Jacob doesn't care, either.

Even I don't care.

Awkward moment of silence. Which I, of course, feel obligated to fill. See, I like to make everyone comfortable. Even Will. It's one of my most annoying faults.

"So how's your career?" I make the mistake of asking Will, thus changing the subject to his all-time favorite.

"It's terrific."

Of course it is.

He is now going to reveal that he's starring in some obscure revival and manage to make it sound like a Tony nod is imminent. When I was young and insecure and infatuated, I was as convinced as Will was that he'd be the next Michael Crawford.

"Where in Westchester did you say you bought your house?" Will asks.

"Glenhaven Park," I say, wondering why he wants to know and what that has to do with his latest starring role.

"Ours is in Scarsdale," he tells me offhandedly, "and the nursery is in Larchmont."

This is how well I know Will: my first reaction is that he and Jerry Hall obviously have a kid, whom they keep in a separate town because apparently, she hates children as much as Will does.

"You should stop by sometime," Will goes on. "It's called Tigerlily."

I probably shouldn't be surprised that he refers to his own child as an *it,* but I am. Even Bunhead came around, and she was merely talking about a doll in the first place.

"How old is she?" I ask Will, emphasis on the *she.*

"How old is whom?" asks Will, emphasis on the *whom.*

"Tigerlily."

There's a pause.

Then he laughs. Hard.

Will reaches out and fondly ruffles my hair as one might do to a lovable half-wit.

Turning to Jacob, he says, "She thinks Tigerlily is a person."

"She's not?"

"No! Tracey, you're such a dope," he says with considerably more affection than he's ever had for me in the past.

Before I can respond with appropriate indignation, he goes on, very patiently, "I told you, it's a nursery."

Nursery, nursery…

Oh! Nursery!

As in landscaping and flowers.

Not as in baby.

I am a dope.

Then again…

"You have a nursery?" I ask Will.

"Of course."

Of course?

Since when does Will of course have a nursery?

"It's a nice little business," he goes on, and adds, gesturing at his friend, "Jacob works with me."

Yes, I'm sure the Amish Warlock is a tremendous help with things like harvesting grain and conjuring herbal potions.

"What happened to the acting?" I ask Will, who dismisses the question with a wave of his hand.

"I outgrew it," he says, as if we're talking about Tonka trucks.

Outgrew it? Ha. It's far more likely that one too many bad reviews sent the nonlegendary Will McCraw slinking past the footlights into obscurity.

"Maybe you can do some community theater someday," I can't resist saying. "I'm sure there must be one in Scarsdale."

Will squirms visibly.

Jacob checks his watch. "Wow, look at the time."

Are we late for a coven meeting? Or a barn raising over at the Stoltzfus place?

"Well, listen, Will, it was great seeing you," I say, "and Jack and I will definitely send our landscaper down to check out your nursery."

No, we don't have a landscaper.

But I love letting Will think we do.

I try to figure out a way to work a personal chef into the tail end of the conversation. Or a butler. Will has always wanted a butler.

Too late. "Great seeing you, too," Will says, giving me a brief, affectionless hug and an air kiss.

Smiling to myself, I watch him disappear into the stacks with his gaunt friend.

In a perfect world, Will would be a raging homosexual with a live-in male Mennonite lover, and I would be fully made up and wearing skinny jeans, with good hair.

Still, there's nothing quite like seeing Will McCraw again, even after all these years, to remind me that while my world isn't perfect, it turned out much, much better than I ever imagined during that slightly single summer so long ago.

17

It's official.

I, Tracey Spadolini Candell, am a suburban housewife.

I don't have to go back to work—not yet, maybe not ever, if I don't want to.

After all that wrangling, Jack's stepmother gave up and his inheritance came through in July. There are a few more details to work out before we actually get a check, but it will be more—much, much more—than we ever imagined. Enough to pay off the mortgage completely, if we want to.

We're not sure yet if we're going to do that, or invest it. We're going to talk to some financial advisers and figure it out.

It's October now, and I've been busy with the house. I got all the wallpaper stripped off and Jack painted on the weekends. Even the old icky brown cupboards. They're white now. They look a lot better.

We want to have the floors refinished, too, but we can't. I'm afraid of the fumes.

I haven't seen Raphael since he and Donatello got back from their Disney trip a few weeks ago. I haven't seen Latisha in over a month, or Buckley—who's holed up now in Beverly Hills, writing his screenplay—in three.

Mitch, we've seen. A lot. He was taking the train up here to visit us just about every other weekend over the summer. But not as much since he started dating this girl, Jen, around Labor Day. Jack's met her. He predicts an engagement.

I haven't seen Kate since the day she left my house to fly to Mobile. She's still there, and I have a feeling she's never coming back. She says her parents help her with little Katie, and anyway, Billy doesn't seem to care that his daughter and wife—soon to be ex—are over a thousand miles away.

I miss Kate.

I miss them all.

My mother has a little kit the doctor gave her. Every morning, she's supposed to prick her finger with it to check the sugar levels in her blood. I asked her if she does it. She said she does. I asked my sister. She said she doubts it.

But I hear Ma walks to mass every morning, though. It's only a few blocks, but my sister said she's lost a few pounds and looks good.

Jack and I are driving up to Brookside for Columbus Day weekend so I can see for myself. He's taking off Friday so we can beat the traffic. He hasn't had a vacation day all summer, but he likes his new job.

My niece Hayley turned three. Jack and I sent her a bunch of Polly Pocket dolls that were no taller than my thumb, made of plastic and on sale at the Toys "R" Us a few miles away. She loves them.

I haven't been back to Bug in a Rug since we moved in. My friend Kim, who told me about the Toys "R" Us, said she refuses to shop there for her son, Aidan.

Oh—right. I actually made a friend here. Remember the blue *It's a Boy* balloons on the mailbox down the street? That was Kim's house. I met her one day when she was pushing her stroller and I was out on our porch, rocking in my new rocking chair.

She used to be a vice president at IBM. Now she's a stay-at-home mom.

I didn't think we'd have much in common, especially since Kim has a baby, but it turns out we do. A lot more than I have in common with Cornelia Gates Fairchild and her circle of Yoga Moms. I met them for coffee once and knew instantly they weren't my type.

Kim is, though. And like I said, we have a lot in common. She has a fixer-upper, too. And an Italian family. And a commuting husband who works in publishing—Jack likes him a lot. We've been trying to get together with them for dinner, but one time their sitter flaked out, and the next, the baby got sick.

Oh, remember those seeds I planted by the back door?

A bunch of plants came up there. I couldn't tell what was what, and the deer chomped away at most of it before I could figure it out.

The guy at the nursery—no, not Will's—told me that if you soak cotton balls in coyote urine (which you buy at the local hardware store) and hang them in the garden, the deer stay away. I've been doing that religiously, and it really does work.

The nights are getting colder. The weather forecast says there will be a hard frost before the week is over. I haven't gotten any flowers yet, but there are buds on some of the plants. No tomatoes either, but there are hard green ones on the vine, which I bought at the nursery. Not Will's.

I check them every day. This morning, I found one that was just barely turning orange, so I picked it. I put it on the kitchen windowsill to ripen. If I get one tomato, I'll be happy.

And next spring, I'll start earlier. If I can.

I may not be able to, though, because the thing is, I'm due in March. Right on Saint Joseph's Day.

Of course Ma said if it's a boy, and he's born on the nineteenth, we need to name him Joseph.

We'll see.

Maybe I'll be early.

Or late.

It really is all about the timing.